The Devil and the Deep Blue Sea

CHERYL MILDENHALL

Black Lace novels are sexual fantasies.
In real life, make sure you practise safe sex.

First published in 1995 by
Black Lace
332 Ladbroke Grove
London
W10 5AH

Copyright © Cheryl Mildenhall 1995

Typeset by CentraCet Limited, Cambridge
Printed and bound in Great Britain by
BPC Paperbacks Ltd
A member of The British Printing Company Ltd
ISBN 0 352 33024 4

Chapter One

*T*here was no doubt about it, Hillary felt distinctly uncomfortable at being part of such an intimate gathering dressed in such a scant amount of clothing. Desperate not to draw attention to herself she carefully shifted in her chair, intent only on easing the uncomfortable sensation of warm, worn vinyl against the back of her bare thighs . . . Mind you, her quest for anonymity was fruitless. No sooner had she executed the surreptitious movement than a pair of blue-bottles landed on the school table directly in front of her, their rapturous buzzing drawing the irritated attention of other teachers in the overheated staff-room, including Michael.

Ignoring the copulating insects, Michael cast a sweeping glance over her body then caught her eye and winked. Blushing furiously she managed a tentative smile in return. The lightly tanned Australian ex-athlete was easily the most attractive member of staff and Hillary had made no secret of her desire to get to know him better, yet for the past three months he had hardly acknowledged her existence even though they were in the same department. The flies disengaged and departed and the small assembly hastily returned their attention to Mr Gleeson, the principal. By the sound of it he was approaching the end of his discourse.

'I think you'll agree we've all enjoyed a most rewarding term and I honestly believe the exam results will bear this out.'

Smiling weakly at the people gathered around him he removed his glasses and, using the corner of his knitted waistcoat, began polishing them furiously. It was a contrived action intended to signal the end of the meeting and after a few moments one or two people began to grope around on the floor beside them for books, papers, or handbags; a few of the braver ones actually rose from their chairs, being the first to help themselves from a tray of plastic cups half filled with warm sparkling wine.

Ignoring this feeble attempt at largess, Hillary moved quickly to the open window, thankful for the slight breeze that intermittently broke through the monotonous heat of the afternoon. She found herself wondering absently what sort of person Mr Gleeson must be to wear a knitted garment on such a stiflingly hot day. As far as she was concerned it was a red letter day, the last day of her first term as a fully fledged physical education teacher; 'games mistress' as James her last serious boyfriend had dubbed her. James. Now there was a disaster area. At twenty-six she was a relative latecomer to the teaching profession and when she'd first joined the staff of the large comprehensive at Easter, the forthcoming term had appeared endless and fraught with obstacles and professional pitfalls. Now here she was, the term suddenly over facing six whole weeks of summer with nothing to do.

It was strange but now that it was nearly time to leave she felt wistful and a little afraid. The kids and staff had become her family during the past few months, and she had enjoyed the structure of a timetabled day. Since that last bust up with James, she had needed some structure to her life. Whilst the prospect of a long, empty summer might be the idea of bliss for some it filled her with dread. She grinned at her own over-dramatisation. Perhaps dread was too strong a word for the way she was feeling but she couldn't say she was particularly looking forward to the summer break. Being the sort of person who needed to keep busy, perhaps she should look around for a temporary summer job.

Gathering the full length of her silky, chestnut hair in one hand and holding it on top of her head, Hillary leaned out of the window as far as she could, revelling in the sensation of a warm breeze against the back of her neck as it dried the beads of perspiration that nestled there amongst the fine, downy hairs. Despite the impracticalities of wearing her hair long she couldn't bring herself to have it cut short.

At that moment she felt a hand lightly brush against the back of her skirt and whirled around to find herself gazing into Michael's deep brown eyes.

He grinned cheekily and held out a plastic cup. 'You haven't drunk your wine.'

She didn't really want it but accepted the cup anyway and took a tentative sip. The tepid alcohol tasted every bit as disgusting as she'd expected it would. All this time Michael hadn't taken his eyes off her and under the thin cotton of her T-shirt she felt her breasts swell and her nipples harden. Without thinking she glanced down at them, blushing as Michael's eyes automatically followed her gaze and rested on the outline of her breasts with undisguised interest.

'I thought it was only cold weather that caused that reaction,' he said, laughing at her and enjoying her obvious discomfort.

For a few moments she was speechless, rooted to the spot in embarrassment until from deep inside herself she found the boldness to retaliate. 'Don't flatter yourself, Michael, I was just thinking about my boyfriend actually.'

She expected him to leave her then, to go off duly rebuffed and seek pastures new. To her surprise and pleasure he did no such thing but stayed at her side, his bare thigh casually brushing against hers. For a

3

while neither of them spoke, each apparently lost in their own thoughts, although Hillary found her senses totally occupied by his proximity and the responses this conjured within her own body.

It wasn't only his physical presence that excited her, not when her nostrils were filled with the musky, entirely masculine scent emanating from his body and her eyes were fixed on the smooth musculature of his upper arm as it rested on the window ledge next to hers. Even his breathing was a delight to her senses: rapid and uncontrolled it hinted at a barely restrained virile force lurking just below the surface of his apparently cool exterior.

As such thoughts filled her mind she found her body had started to tremble. Tentatively she glanced sideways at his profile and, with some surprise, she noticed that he looked younger at such closer quarters.

Still staring resolutely ahead he spoke to her. 'I think we should be going, don't you?'

She felt a small quiver of excitement at his words then, remembering something, she sighed reluctantly. 'I can't leave just yet. I still have to finish my half of the equipment inventory.'

He shrugged. 'That's okay. I'll give you a hand then it won't take any time at all.'

Filled with gratitude and anticipation, Hillary merely smiled and nodded. She looked around for her tote bag, then remembered that she'd left it in the changing room at the gym. Michael meanwhile made his way over to the group of staff still gathered around the drinks tray. Someone had produced a bottle of whisky and refilled the cups with the infinitely more palatable amber liquid. Her stomach clenched tightly with barely controlled longing, Hillary watched Michael as he spoke briefly to Mr Gleeson who nodded and raised his cup to her in a cheery farewell. By the time they were both in the corridor her heart was pounding heavily in her chest and the small sparks of desire in the pit of her belly were flickering into tiny flames.

4

A few kids still remained as she and Michael crossed the familiar expanse of the large communal playground although thankfully the playing field and gym were totally deserted. It was only to be expected that few of the pupils would choose to hang around the school premises any longer than absolutely necessary.

The communal equipment room was large, linking the boys' and girls' gymnasiums. On the boys' side the large roller-shutter door was closed and bolted. Pausing only to collect the inventory sheet from her office, Hillary started checking off the equipment straight away. Anxious to complete her task as quickly as possible, she rapidly filled the sheet with her small, precise handwriting. Dutifully she added to her list as Michael called out to her, his voice becoming more and more muffled as he investigated the deeper recesses of the storage room. It was hot and airless in there and she quickly began to feel exhausted. Never mind, at least the job was now finished. Glancing down she saw that her previously immaculate white skirt and T-shirt were creased and grubby.

'Take them off if you like, I don't mind.'

Startled she whirled around, surprised to find Michael standing behind her when she thought he was in one of the far corners of the room. His nearness was now indisputably arousing and it took every ounce of her willpower to resist moving the final couple of inches toward him and into his arms. Instead she rubbed her forearm across her brow.

'It's so hot and sticky in here,' she said, not complaining but merely stating a fact.

Michael raised a finger. 'Wait here, I have just the thing in my office.'

In less than a minute he had returned bearing a large electric fan which he proceeded to plug in, setting it firmly on top of a stack of boxes next to a pile of thick rubber gym mats. As it whirred into action he pulled down the shutter door until it was almost completely closed, blocking out all but a few rays of sunlight.

Hillary was amazed at the transformation as suddenly the storeroom felt cool and comfortable. Without waiting for her to respond, he hitched himself up onto the pile of mats and reached out with one strong arm to pull a startled Hillary up beside him.

For a few moments she allowed her body to bounce gently on the rubber, trying to quell the excitement building rapidly within her, the small flames of desire now grown to almost forest fire proportions. She glanced down: in such a position her short tennis skirt barely covered the tops of her thighs, a fact that hadn't gone unnoticed by Michael. Before she could stop him he put out his hand and, undoing the one button that held the skirt in place, pulled it from her body. Immediately, she felt the cool breeze from the fan waft over her feverish skin. Thank God she was wearing decent knickers, she thought to herself, cringing in embarrassment under his frank appraisal of her lower body. White like the rest of her outfit the thin, almost transparent triangle of her knickers moulded itself damply around her pubis, barely concealing the tangle of velvety curls beneath. Nor could the scant material contain the rush of her own juices as it soaked quickly into the delicate fabric, the pulsing of her sex gathering momentum in proportion to her rapidly mounting desire.

Groaning at the sight of her obvious arousal, Michael kissed her hard on the lips forcing her teeth apart and snaking his tongue around her mouth in a journey of exploration. Relaxing into the exquisite sensation of unfamiliar lips on hers, Hillary wrapped her arms around his neck and allowed herself to sink gently backward. She felt her eyelids becoming heavier as she gave herself up to the consummate harmony of their movements, her eyes gradually closing completely during the long blissful moments of their mutual caress.

Somehow, without interrupting their sensuous rhythm, he had managed to shed his clothing and she moaned as he pulled off her T-shirt and pressed his naked chest against her intoxicated body. In response, she allowed her finger tips to travel the ridges of his spine, kneading and massaging the muscles at the nape of his neck and shoulders. Eventually she dared to slide her hands slowly down the sides of his body and over his hips, pausing for just a fraction of a second to boost her courage before cupping the flesh of his well-defined buttocks in both her hands. As an expert in such matters, she appreciated the tautness of his gluteus muscles as they quivered tantalisingly under her gentle grip.

Squeezing them a little harder she eased them apart slightly with her fingertips, her long nails tormenting the sensitive flesh of his anus. For a moment his whole body went rigid and she wondered briefly if she had gone too far but he soon relaxed under her practised touch. Teasingly, tantalisingly, he began to mirror her actions, probing between her soft cheeks until she felt she would scream aloud from the delicious torment.

With urgent hands she reached between their bodies. Struggling slightly under the weight of him, she pulled her knickers down as far as she could before kicking them off into oblivion. As though this were his cue, Michael thrust himself deep inside her causing her to gasp with surprise and pleasure, his rhythmic pounding soon resulting in a mutual climax of mind-blowing intensity.

Instead of allowing herself to relax in the hazy after-glow, Hillary felt regret building within her. It had all happened too soon, was all over too quickly. Rebounding like a rag doll against the rubber mats she tried to pull away from him but he held firmly on to her wrists with one strong hand, using the other to caress her breasts which despite her mental resistance responded instantly to his touch. She bit her lip, trying hard to quell the fire already sizzling within her once again. Amazed at her own passion, she groaned as her nipples grew and hardened, her clitoris swelling and throbbing unbearably as she yearned for the release of his touch. Apparently reading her mind once again, Michael bent his head and sucked each nipple in turn before gazing deep into her troubled eyes.

'You're really hot, babe,' he murmured, his voice as thick and huskily-sweet as molasses.

She had dreamed, no, fantasised about this moment often enough during the past twelve weeks. An afternoon on the playing field was always sweet torture. Trying desperately to coerce the interest of a group of lazy Lolitas when their attention was clearly directed toward the boys' sports area was no easy task. How could she possibly hope to compete with classes that were, at the upper end at least, little more than a grunting, heaving mass of muscle and sinew permanently seething with sexual curiosity and unrequited lust.

Out on the playing field the girls would stand and pose, pouting and giggling, knowing the effect they were having on their target audience and sometimes Michael himself would look across and wink at one of them, running his eyes blatantly over her developing curves.

After the first two weeks she gave in and accepted that despite her best efforts nature would take its course. Eventually the kids she strove so hard to keep apart would come together anyway. Year after year the names and faces would change but their basic instincts never would.

What she couldn't bear was the thought that one day Michael might forget his responsibilities and give in to temptation. This noble concern wasn't the whole truth. What she really couldn't bear to imagine was his lithe, muscular body entwined with the willing, nubile flesh that surrounded him every working day; not when she wanted him for herself.

Now, here they were, her fears put on hold while she relished the time they had together. With the whole summer stretching out tantalisingly before them, she hoped this was simply their first time. From under

8

heavy lids she looked at him, her insatiable body melting all over again under his blatant scrutiny.

Leisurely he surveyed her, allowing his gaze to linger on her heaving breasts, her quivering stomach and the hot, moist place where their bodies were still joined. It was divine torment to watch him look at her in that way. Shocked by her own lack of inhibition, she couldn't help wriggling under him, moving her legs even further apart and using her strong vaginal muscles to draw his still hard cock deeper inside her. Arching her back she churned rhythmically beneath him, rubbing the swollen heat of her sex against his pubic bone, massaging him with her clitoris until she reached the point of no return and he could no longer hold out against her artfully contrived manoeuvres.

Taking over control he slowly pushed himself deeper inside her then withdrew almost completely, sliding his penis from her with agonising deliberation before plunging even deeper than before. Hillary spread her legs wider, trying to stretch herself open to accommodate more of him. She soon realised she couldn't force him to alter his pace. His powers of self restraint were too well honed. Instead she slipped both her hands into the secret furrow between her legs, using one set of fingers to skilfully rub her desperate clitoris and the other to probe inside the vessel of her vagina, not to usurp Michael's cock but to add to it and enhance her own enjoyment.

Far from resenting her interference, her action seemed to push Michael over the edge. This time the immediate force of their first orgasm was tempered by one of slow intensity, the waves building in a crescendo that she felt would never end. Now, at last, she felt replete. She sighed happily and stretched. A quick glance at the luminous dial of her watch warned her that the caretaker would soon be making his rounds and she mentioned this to Michael.

Lying on her side, her head resting on one arm, she watched him as he gathered up his clothes and her

9

own, throwing the scanty items at her with a cheeky grin. In no hurry to dress herself she continued to admire his body, allowing herself the often missed luxury of watching a man dress. It was strange but sometimes this simple act seemed almost more erotic than watching the same person remove their clothes. Perhaps it was because by this point she usually felt sated and therefore not in a desperate hurry to get to the next stage of the proceedings.

'Can I drop you somewhere?' Michael was jangling a set of car keys in front of her, bringing her back to reality with a jolt. She felt a little let down, having hoped that they could go on somewhere, perhaps to the pub, followed by a meal, and then – who knows?

'It's okay I'm in my own car.' She hesitated for a moment then took the bull by the horns. 'Do you have anything special planned, I thought we might go to the pub for an end of term drink?'

To her dismay he shook his head regretfully. 'I'm going home to pack, then I'm out of the country on the next available flight. My, er, fiancée and I are planning to do Europe this summer.'

The shock of his casual statement hit her squarely in the solar plexus. So, he had a fiancée tucked away at home, the bastard! She wasn't surprised that a gorgeous guy like him should have a 'significant other' but she did think he could have at least mentioned the fact a little earlier. Not that it would have made any difference to the outcome, Hillary thought to herself ruefully. She had wanted him badly enough and at last she'd managed to have him, at least for a little while. With feigned stoicism she sat up, reached for her T-shirt and smiled.

'Well, I hope you have a good time,' she said, looking around. 'By the way, have you seen my knickers anywhere?'

He looked about vaguely and shrugged. Hillary jumped down from the pile of mats and after a few seconds hunting found the missing underwear hanging from a netball hoop. Michael, reaching up for them, pressed the flimsy garment to his face and inhaled deeply before handing them to her.

'Just a little something to remember you by until next term,' he said, grinning but actually sounding quite wistful, Hillary thought.

She pulled them on then reached for her skirt. Glancing toward the still oscillating fan she said, 'We won't be needing that any more if you want to take it back.'

As if to underline her statement she unplugged it and, gathering up the flex, handed it to him. Still he seemed strangely reluctant to leave and hovered by the doorway until she made it clear that she had no intention of staying there any longer. After making sure the whole building was secure, they made their way across the playground together toward their car park, each pausing beside their respective cars waiting for the other to say something.

'Well, bye then!' Michael gave her a feeble wave over the roof of his brightly painted Volkswagen Beetle.

Hillary waved back more cheerily than she felt.

'See you in six weeks,' she called softly but she could see that in his mind he had already left her and was no doubt on a plane headed for exotic climes.

She shrugged. There was nothing left to be said. Michael folded his tall frame neatly into the tight confines of his car and in no time at all he was gone, leaving her to stare after him as he shot away in a cloud of dust. Riding off into the sunset on his wild stallion – she laughed to herself, her overactive imagination was getting the better of her as usual.

All she could do now was get in her car, go home and concentrate on getting the most out of the summer break. Just today she had achieved two major goals: completing her first term as a teacher and seducing Michael, something she had wanted to do for weeks. Now it was time to look forward, to move onwards and upwards to the next exciting phase of her life and enjoy whatever delights that might bring.

* * *

As luck would have it, fate intervened less than two hours in the form of a telephone call from her older sister, Alicia.

'Hi Hilly, it's me, Alix.' Alicia liked to shorten everyone's name if possible.

Hillary tucked her legs under her, making herself more comfortable in preparation for one of her sister's marathon calls which usually comprised the latest gossip on everyone Hillary knew, and even some people she didn't, plus all Alicia's personal news. Bearing in mind that she hadn't spoken to her sister for a few weeks there was every possibility that this conversation could go on into the small hours, perhaps she should make herself a snack to keep herself going?

'Alix, lovely to hear from you!' Hillary sucked in her breath before asking the sixty four thousand dollar question. 'How are things?'

'Wonderful, but I can't talk for long. I'm really calling to find out what you plan to do for a holiday this summer.'

Hillary was taken aback, Alicia didn't usually concern herself with other people's plans. 'I haven't really given it much thought, to be honest,' she admitted. 'There's not much in my piggy bank but if I'm lucky funds might stretch to a cheapo standby deal from the local travel agent.'

Alicia's tone was firm. 'Don't bother with all that and don't worry about money, just pack a bag and get yourself down to the station. Chloe and I have rented ourselves a wonderful old house for the summer. It's in Norfolk, almost next door to Sandringham.'

Hillary could just imagine Alicia smirking at her end of the line. Although entirely likeable, her sister was nevertheless an inveterate snob and would love nothing better than to be able to rub shoulders with the royal family. Quickly she returned her attention to the voice on the other end of the telephone.

'Anyway, darling, put quite simply the place is mega. Chloe and I are just rattling around here like a couple

12

of dice in a wellington boot. She's asked another friend of hers to join us and I immediately thought of you to make up a foursome. What do you think? Can you come?'

Hillary pondered the invitation for a moment. Alicia and her friend Chloe were okay in small doses but she wondered if sharing a house with them might be more like purgatory than a holiday. Also they had husbands, the last thing she felt like doing with her holiday was to play gooseberry.

'What about Clive and Gus?' she asked.

Alicia was quick to answer. 'My dear hubby and Gus only come here at weekends, they're still in the city all week, poor loves. They hardly interfere with our fun at all, do they Chlo' darling?'

Obviously Chloe had just entered the room because Hillary could hear the sound of a creaking door being closed loudly in the background. She jumped back as Chloe's strident tones ricocheted against her eardrum.

'Oh! Do come, Hilly, it's a positive mansion, we've got heaps of room and the weather's gorgeous.'

Under such a barrage of entreaties Hillary didn't feel she could refuse. Excitedly she noted down the address and telephone number, then checked the train times before calling Alicia back to confirm her estimated time of arrival.

The journey was uneventful, broken only by a handful of new faces joining her half empty carriage. She had bought a magazine to read but, as often happened to her on such journeys, she found herself unable to concentrate long enough to read a complete article. From time to time snippets of information caught her eye as she flicked aimlessly through the pages: an easy-to-make facepack recipe using summer fruits, how each subsequent generation of women conform to a larger average dress size, and how to lose half a stone in a week. Finally she came across an intriguing article, *'Fifty ways to please your lover'*.

This last item sparked her interest the most. Hillary

prided herself on being sexually adept but perhaps it would contain some handy sexual hints and tips, a few things even she didn't know about. She was out of luck. As she cast her eyes down the pages she discovered the content was disappointingly bland, only offering up such pearls of wisdom as, 'massage his feet as he watches his favourite TV programme,' and 'act out one of your favourite fantasies together.'

Sighing with a mixture of boredom and disgust she threw the magazine on to the empty seat next to her and stared out of the window. It was still light outside and from her vantage point she could see family after family barbecuing in their back gardens. Dads, proudly sporting chefs hats and striped aprons, wielded what looked like instruments of torture from a bygone era, whilst harassed-looking mums ferried trays of food and drinks from the kitchen to the patio, or chased their children, presumably to wash their hands and faces before they ate. If one-parent families were becoming the norm it certainly wasn't in this part of the world, she mused.

She checked her watch and sighed again as there was still over an hour to go before she reached her destination. All of a sudden she wondered if she would regret accepting Alicia's invitation. There couldn't be much to do in such a place, no nightclubs worth mentioning and although the house her sister had rented sounded grand it might turn out to be a draughty old mausoleum stranded in the middle of nowhere.

With yet another sigh she went back to staring out of the window. Whatever the outcome it was too late to turn back. Idly she found herself wondering where Michael might be by now, certainly on a plane if not already ensconced in a hotel in one of Europe's cultural centres. No, on second thoughts, culture was not really Michael's style, probably he had headed straight for the Mediterranean. Sun, sea and sex, three words that just about summed up the handsome Australian. She felt her stomach contract at the thought of him, their encounter would certainly fuel her dreams and fantasies for a few weeks to come unless she found someone else to take his place. Again she pondered her chances of meeting even one fabulous man in the wilds of Norfolk, an endeavour that was possible but not probable.

She allowed her freewheeling mind to take flight, perhaps she would bump into a real prince while out walking in the grounds and they would make mad passionate love under the shade of an oak tree where Queen Victoria sat. Of course, they would never be able to expect anything more from their relationship than fabulous, mind-blowing sex. Sometimes he might even keep his naval uniform on, she giggled to herself.

She must have laughed out loud without realising it because a voice spoke from directly behind her. 'Excuse me, are you okay?'

She turned around to find herself staring into a pair of soft hazel eyes. They belonged to a young man, probably a student, she thought to herself, judging from the way he was dressed and the fact that there was a plastic carrier bag full of text books on the seat next to him.

She smiled. 'I'm fine, I was just daydreaming that's all and I made myself laugh.'

He grinned. 'I do that all the time, and talk to myself,' he added.

She stared at him for a few seconds, taking in the long, straggly brown hair and the few days' growth on his chin. She obviously embarrassed him because he blushed and rubbed his face in a nervous gesture. 'I thought I might go back to university in the autumn sporting a beard.'

So she was right about him being a student. 'What are you studying? Art?' Hillary didn't know why she said this, although to her he did look slightly arty but then most students did.

He laughed. 'No, geography. Why did you say art? Do I look like Van Gogh or something?'

15

'No, of course not, besides you've still got both your ears.'

They both laughed and then and pretty soon fell into an easy camaraderie, their conversation taking them all the way into King's Lynn station, and making the hour seem to pass in a matter of minutes.

As she alighted from the train alone Hillary looked around, the platform was deserted although Alicia had promised that someone would come and collect her. Slinging her bulging bag over her shoulder, she stooped to pick up her cases. She never had managed the knack of packing light and besides, she didn't know how long she was likely to stay. Despite the fact that it was late evening the air was still warm and she soon began to perspire under the weight of her cases. Stopping to remove her jacket, she stared around her once again – this time she noticed the tall, dark figure of a man standing at the entrance to the station. He was obviously watching her but made no move in her direction.

As she approached him he stepped forward. 'Miss Hillary Fordham, I presume?'

Her breath caught in her throat; he was devastatingly good-looking with thick, dark, almost raven-black hair, quite short and glossy. His face was strong, tanned and slightly weathered as though he spent a lot of time in the open air, his deep brown eyes framed by perfectly shaped eyebrows and long, lustrous lashes. He extended a perfectly manicured hand toward her and she grasped it, holding on to it as she nodded fervently in reply to his question, not trusting herself to speak. He cleared his throat.

'Pleasant though it is to stand here holding hands like long-lost lovers, I was actually reaching for your suit-case.' His voice was steady and deep, as dark as his appearance and tinged with sarcasm.

Blushing furiously she dropped his hand and stared at her feet. 'I, I thought . . .' When she looked up she

16

saw that he was smiling, although the smile didn't quite reach his eyes.

'It doesn't matter. Shall we go? he said.

Without waiting for her answer he picked up her cases and, turning smartly on his heel, strode out of the station. Hillary had no option but to follow him outside and into the car park. Now, as day died slowly into late evening, the air temperature was cooling rapidly. He stopped at the rear of a dark green Range Rover and deposited her cases on the ground before unlocking the tail-gate. Hillary dropped her tote bag next to the cases and pulled on her jacket once more.

'It's become quite cool now hasn't it?' she said.

It was a throwaway question but she was determined to regain some semblance of control over the situation. She had been momentarily stunned by him but had now regained her composure. After all, she reasoned, he was only the hired help, probably a groundsman or something, there was no reason on earth why she should let him make her feel inferior. She turned to look at him again, her active imagination equipping him with a gun under one arm and a golden retriever at his side, striding across open fields in search of rabbits and pheasants and whatever else country folk might choose to shoot at. Being a city girl born and bred, she wasn't overly familiar with the finer details of such matters but definitely felt overcome by shades of Lady Chatterley's Lover.

Having stowed her cases away in the back of the Range Rover and unlocked the passenger door, he turned to face her once again. 'I do apologise, I haven't introduced myself. My name is Darius Harwood. I own Harwood Hall where you will be staying.'

Bang went her theory of him being the hired help. Nevertheless, she was determined that from now on she would keep her cool. In carefully measured tones she spoke. 'I'm pleased to meet you.' Then she added, 'Do we have far to go?'

His voice was low as he replied. 'Oh yes, I think

there's every possibility of that.' He paused as his eyes swept her body insolently. 'But for now we'll just take it one step at a time.'

She didn't understand what he meant by that reply and was going to make a comment when she found he was just staring at her, his expression inscrutable. Despite her exhaustion she felt herself growing warm under his gaze and, intending to stare back boldly, she was surprised to find her eyes were the first to look away. Suddenly she pictured him as the Lord of the Manor and she the innocent country virgin.

Despite the tension in the air she laughed wryly to herself, she, Hillary Fordham an innocent virgin – now that was taking fantasy a bit too far!

Chapter Two

*F*rom Alicia's description, Hillary had already formu-
lated an impression of Harwood Hall in her mind
but nothing could have prepared her for the reality. The
sight that met her eyes was that of a sprawling mansion
of grey-white stone, approached by a mile-long private
road lined with trees and shrubs of all descriptions.
Bounded on all sides by lush green lawns, the Hall
seemed more like a small palace with its ornate porti-
coed entrance reached by a wide flight of stone steps.

As her eyes feasted on its beauty, Hillary let out her
breath in a rush. 'Oh, it's beautiful!'

Darius's face softened into a genuine smile as he
replied. 'I'm pleased you think so, I couldn't imagine
living anywhere else.' He caught her surprised
expression and added quickly. 'I don't live in either of
the wings, they've been converted for paying guests.
My quarters are in the main part of the Hall. Most of
the time it's out of bounds but sometimes I open it up
to visitors, or for charity functions.'

Suddenly Alicia and Chloe appeared, not from the
entrance but from around the left-hand corner of the
house. They were both dressed, totally inappropriately
Hillary thought, in tight little satin and velvet cocktail
dresses.

Alicia waved a champagne bottle. 'Yoo hoo, Hilly darling, did you have a good journey?'

Without waiting for an answer she tottered around the Range Rover and contrived to bump into Darius as he lifted Hillary's suitcases from the rear of the vehicle. He put out a hand to steady her. 'Whoa there, Mrs Carruthers,' he said.

Hillary couldn't help wondering why he spoke to Alicia as though she were a horse.

'I had a very good journey actually, Alicia. Alicia!'

Her sister obviously had no interest in hearing her reply, draped as she now was around Darius in an overly familiar fashion. Patiently he removed Alicia's arms from around his neck, speaking to her slowly and carefully as though she were a young child.

'I think perhaps your sister would like to go inside and freshen up. She also looks as though she could do with a drink.' The words, 'and you look as though you've had enough,' hung in the air unspoken.

Hillary glanced down at herself, embarrassed to realise that she must look like a crumpled wreck to him. Damn – that certainly wasn't the sort of impression she hoped she was making. In her imagination she was cool and mysterious, uncharted territory so to speak.

Totally ignoring Hillary's luggage, Alicia took her by one arm and Chloe took the other. 'Of course, come on Hills we've got heaps to tell you,' Alicia said.

As Hillary found herself being propelled toward the house she turned around, hoping that Darius would be close behind. Disappointed, she saw he was already climbing back into the Range Rover and, in a few seconds, had turned it around and was heading up the driveway toward the main gates without even a backward glance.

Swallowing her disappointment she entered the house and found herself equally pleasantly surprised by the interior of Harwood Hall. Having expected that it would turn out to be dusty and draughty and sparsely equipped with ancient, lumpy furniture she was pleased to find the whole of the interior had been tastefully modernised and was very comfortable indeed. Naturally, they didn't occupy the whole wing, it was much too large. According to her sister, Darius's conversion meant that the east and west wings were now divided into half a dozen separate living quarters, although their share was by far the largest with four en-suite bedrooms.

Nestled comfortably in an armchair, nursing a large glass of vodka and tonic, she looked happily around the cosy sitting room.

Alicia misread her thoughts. 'Darius Harwood employs a live-in housekeeper to keep it all clean, a young Scots girl called Fearn.'

Hillary opened her mouth to reply, then closed it and simply smiled at her well-intentioned sister, eventually she said. 'Thank you for inviting me, Alix.'

Alicia dismissed Hillary's gratitude with a careless toss of her bobbed, blonde hair. 'I couldn't have you spending the summer in the city of all places, much too dirty and sticky. Besides you'll be light relief from Chloe.'

Hillary couldn't help smiling anew at this. Alicia often complained about her best friend Chloe, groaning at her cynicism and shallowness and how all she ever talked about were clothes, money and men. In reality the two women were as alike as two peas in a pod, the only difference being that Chloe was as dark as Alicia was fair.

At that moment they were interrupted by the arrival of a young woman whom Hillary had never set eyes on before. Immediately Alicia jumped up and grasped her by the hand, pulling her into the room. 'Hilly, you remember I said Chloe had invited a friend? Well here she is. Odile. Isn't she gorgeous?'

Hillary had to admit the young woman standing in front of her was very attractive. Tall and slim, with endless legs, her crowning glory was a head of lustrous deep auburn hair that fell in soft, thick waves to the small of her back.

21

Hillary smiled and extended a hand. 'Odile, that's a French name isn't it?'

The girl smiled back, squeezing Hillary's hand in response. 'Yes. I am half French on my mother's side but my father is English and I've lived here all my life,' she replied – her voice with its soft, melodic tones suited her admirably.

Just then Chloe sashayed into the room. Divested of the red suede stiletto heels she had been wearing earlier, she padded across the thick-pile carpet in stockinged feet.

'Oh, I see you've already met Odile.' She pouted, then asked, 'Where's that darling man Darius? Has he gone already?'

Alicia nodded her head. 'He didn't even bother to come in, I think Hillary must have said something to him to frighten him off.'

Thinking her sister was serious, Hillary started to protest. 'No, really, we hardly talked at all.'

Chloe patted her hand. 'It's okay, Hillary poppet, your darling sis was just having her little joke, the truth is,' she added, dropping her voice although there was no one around to overhear their conversation, 'we all think he's just a teensy bit fabulous, don't we, girls?'

Her smile took in Alicia and Odile who both nodded fervently. With a small sigh, Hillary realised that if she was going to make a play for the delectable Darius this summer she would have to join the back of a very long queue.

Their little party broke up soon after this exchange and Hillary was grateful for the sanctuary of her bedroom, her weary body longing to sink into the cool comfort of her bed. Her earlier session with Michael had overtaxed some of her less-used muscles and they were now starting to make their presence felt. Nevertheless she felt too tired to take a bath.

Slowly she removed her clothes, dropping each crumpled garment to the floor. Just like the rest of the rooms, her bedroom was spacious yet cosy with soft carpeting in a deep midnight blue and the walls and ceiling marbled in egg-shell blue. Fancying she could hear the sound of the tide, Hillary imagined herself to be immersed in a deep, warm sea. As she turned she caught sight of her naked body in the large mirror that graced one wall. Surrounded by an ornate gilt frame the square mirror took up almost half the wall and reflected the entire scope of the room behind her including the comfortable, oversized double bed.

Despite her weariness she contemplated her reflection for a few minutes, turning this way and that in unselfconscious appreciation of her own body until her attention was suddenly stolen by the hoot of an owl outside the window. Automatically she glanced away from the mirror, diverting her attention for a moment to the large picture window. Of course she could see nothing – owls are elusive creatures and the window was shielded from the outside world by thick velvet drapes. With a shrug she turned her head back to resume her study of herself and as she did so felt an inexplicable chill run down her spine, for a split second she could have sworn that someone was watching her.

In a flash she was across the room and, without stopping to wonder if she was being foolish, jumped into bed and covered herself with the sheet. Gripping it until her knuckles turned white, she glanced around fearfully to see if anyone, real or ghostly, was lurking in a shadowy corner. It wasn't entirely beyond the realms of possibility, she reasoned, for such an old building to be haunted.

Eventually the rapid beating of her heart slowed and her breathing and thoughts returned to normal but, despite the bright light of her reading lamp she couldn't relax enough for sleep. With a tired sigh she reached for her magazine and flicked through the pages; it almost had bored her to sleep on the train perhaps it would do the same for her now.

* * *

23

In another part of the house Darius Harwood was seated comfortably in a large black leather chair, smoking a cigar with deliberate enjoyment. Relaxed and mellow after a good meal and warm bath, he now reclined against the warm hide, his damp body shrouded by a thick towelling robe. In his hand he held an outsize brandy balloon from which he took a sip every now and then, licking his lips with satisfaction after each coating of cognac. It was his favourite part of the day, the time when most of his guests were safely tucked up in their beds. He leaned forward a fraction and at the mere touch of a button the bank of TV monitors in front of him flickered into life.

The closed circuit cameras had been installed on the advice of his local crime prevention officer but against the better judgement of a good friend of his who ranked high in the local constabulary. In a property like Harwood Hall, where priceless antiques sat incongruously alongside the cheap seaside tat invariably purchased by his guests, security was a must. Cameras were highly visible all around the perimeter of the building and in every room in the main house. Darius was, however, warned against installing them in the converted guest quarters.

'People won't take too kindly to being watched twenty-four hours a day and under all sorts of circumstances, I mean the bathroom and bed and so forth,' the police officer had warned him, his already florid face deepening in colour to an embarrassed crimson.

To this Darius had nodded, said he understood and thus reassured his friend without actually saying that he wouldn't go ahead and do such a thing. As soon as the closed-circuit TV contractors had done their job and left, Darius ordered his own man to fit a second set of minute cameras, one in every bedroom and sitting room, each concealed behind a large ornate mirror positioned so that he was afforded the widest possible view.

For good measure, he had tiny microphones installed

in the rooms as well. He didn't expect to be found out, the devices really were well hidden and he paid his man too well for him ever to reveal their existence.

One screen caught his attention instantly. The new guest, what was her name? Oh, yes, Hillary Fordham. She had just entered her bedroom looking happy but fit to drop. He leaned forward to watch more closely as she moved around the room, unbuttoning her clothes, stepping out of them, leaving them littered untidily about the bedroom floor. Darius tutted to himself, he hated clutter. With a wry laugh, he reminded himself that he was not interested in her as a prospective housekeeper, her other abilities and attributes were what intrigued him. As she walked toward the mirror he instinctively reeled back in his chair, the picture was so clear it was as though she was walking toward him.

He drew in his breath sharply, letting it out slowly as a low groan. God, but she was beautiful! Perhaps not in the conventional way but her body was superb. Like an athlete's body it was slim, well-toned and sinewy with high, firm breasts and a narrow waist. Despite the fact that the summer had only just begun in earnest she was already well tanned, he noticed, although her breasts were paler and, in stark contrast to the rest of her lower body, her pubis displayed a triangle of white skin.

Reluctantly he dragged his eyes away from her sex, moving up over her pink tipped breasts, lingering there only for a moment before continuing their ascent. Her heart-shaped face was not exactly classically beautiful or handsome but, well – pretty he supposed, with wide almond shaped green eyes, pink dimpled cheeks and pouting lips. Instantly he imagined those lips wrapped around his penis and he felt himself stiffen beneath the bathrobe. All in good time, he promised himself.

She posed for a long time in front of the mirror, admiring her own body. He appreciated narcissism in a woman as it hinted at hidden sensual depths. Again he found his imagination taking over and fancied himself kneeling in front of her in person, parting the delicate flesh of her labia and covering her with his tongue, lapping against her sensitive bud until she gripped his hair and begged for him to stop. But he wouldn't, he would do more, exploring her with his fingers as well as his tongue until she pleaded with him, not to stop, but to fuck her.

He couldn't ignore his own arousal now. Couldn't resist touching himself, lightly at first then with harder strokes. Encircling his shaft with both hands, he squeezed himself hard then slid his trembling fingers up and down with greater and greater agitation, rubbing and rubbing until the hot, sticky tribute spurted forth like a geyser. In his relief he smiled as the viscous fluid completely covered the TV screen in front of him where seconds before Hillary had just leaned forward to peer at herself more closely, her pinks lips forming a perfect O.

Darius slumped back, staring at her semen spattered face. He laughed weakly at the irony, that was precisely how he planned to see her in real life – in the flesh. He shuddered and let out his breath in a long slow stream, his eyelids drooping with fatigue. Just a few more minutes and then he would switch off for the night he told himself firmly.

Suddenly the spell was broken by the hooting of an owl. She looked away, looked back and – he almost cringed – there was a flicker of something in her eyes. Recognition perhaps? Whatever it was he could swear blind that she saw him watching her. But of course, that was impossible.

Impossible or not something had unnerved her. She bounded into bed, pulled the sheet up and looked around nervously. He held his breath, watching her changing expression as the panic subsided. For a while she just sat there, immobile, clutching the sheet to her chin with both hands. She was obviously debating what to do next, he thought. He could hardly stand the suspense, she must realise that whatever she thought she saw was in her imagination. Slowly she relaxed her arms, allowing the sheet to drop a little.

Darius leaned forward again his heart hammering with anticipation. Now she might seek a little self gratification, a tension releasing orgasm to lull her to sleep perhaps? His penis began to stir again. He found himself wishing he had the power simply to will her to do his bidding – what an interesting faculty that would be. He stared hard at the screen, using every ounce of concentration.

'Drop the sheet,' he urged, his voice a hoarse whisper in the stillness of the big old house. 'Lay back and spread your legs. Pleasure yourself so that we may both enjoy your body.'

For a moment it looked as though she was actually going to comply. Her hands let go of the sheet and it fell to her waist but instead of reaching for herself she stretched across the bed to the small oak cupboard that stood beside it and picked up a magazine. With a sigh he watched her turn the pages, no doubt she would now read until she fell asleep.

What a cruel irony, he thought. She was wakeful and needed comfort and he would be only too happy to give it. What a shame they weren't already better acquainted. He tapped his lips with his index finger thoughtfully, debating whether to zoom the cameras in on either the girl's sister, or one of the others: all three were currently delighting in their own bodies he noticed, glancing at the flickering monitors.

But he had tired of watching them during the past weeks and anyway, apart from the redhead the other two held no interest for him. They were too hard, too embittered about life and men and sex. And they chased him. He didn't like that sort of behaviour. By tradition, the Harwoods were the hunters not the hunted. No, he had had enough for now. Tonight he would go to bed early and wake refreshed, with enough vigour to rise to any challenges the coming day would bring.

* * *

Despite Hillary's conviction that she wouldn't sleep a wink all night, she actually fell asleep quite quickly and throughout those dark mysterious hours she dreamed of both Michael and Darius, their faces and personalities becoming transposed so that in the end it was not Michael she was making love to but the mysterious Lord Harwood. Despite their unreality, the images invoked were extremely powerful and although the next morning her mind could not remember the dreams of the previous night her body certainly could. Consequently, she awoke early the next morning feeling distinctly aroused, her breasts and sex heavy and tingling with excitement.

Not wishing to waste a minute of her first day she showered and dressed, choosing her outfit with care. As she didn't know everyone else's plans for the day she decided to play safe, selecting a pair of brief white denim shorts, a strappy turquoise T-shirt and underneath a plain white bikini.

The rest of the house was still silent, not surprisingly as neither Alicia nor Chloe were renowned for being early risers, so she decided to unpack before going in search of breakfast. Just as she was hanging up the last of her clothes in the capacious oak wardrobe there was a tentative knock on her door, followed by the smiling face of Odile.

'I'm glad you're awake. I was planning to go for a walk to the village. Would you like to come?'

Hillary nodded delightedly. 'Knowing Alicia I don't suppose there's any food in the place?'

Laughing, Odile shook her head. 'Not unless you count truffles, caviar and artichoke hearts.'

Hillary grabbed her bag. 'No, they're not exactly my idea of breakfast.' She smiled openly. 'Let's go in search of real food.'

If they had walked up the private road it would have taken them quite a while to reach the nearest village but Odile produced a roughly sketched map which depicted a short-cut across the grounds. In less than ten minutes they were on the main road and in another five had reached the outskirts of the village of Harwood which boasted around twenty houses, two pubs, a church and a general store.

The shop was surprisingly well stocked and they had difficulty deciding what to buy. In the end they chose a plentiful supply of basic groceries, with a few carefully chosen additions including smoked salmon, cream cheese and several French baguettes. The grocer offered to deliver the groceries but they took one of the loaves, the cheese and the salmon with them and walked on through the village and down the road for another mile or so until they arrived at a busy harbour. It was breathtakingly picturesque and they immediately decided to stay and enjoy an impromptu picnic breakfast, seated side by side on the harbour wall.

For a while neither of them spoke, each lost in their own thoughts as they watched the fishing boats come and go. Presently Odile jumped to her feet.

'I must get back to the house, I promised my boyfriend I would call him this morning. He's coming over to England to stay for the weekend,' she explained.

'Over?' queried Hillary, looking confused.

'From France,' said Odile, looking at her watch. 'He's a genuine French Negro – big, black and beautiful. In fact, he claims he's a descendant of Josephine Baker the infamous dancer of the 1920s.'

Being particularly fond of that era, Hillary had heard of Josephine Baker and the way she had scandalised Paris with her risqué costumes and dances. If his heritage was as he said she was looking forward to meeting Odile's boyfriend very much.

'I'll stay here for a while, if you don't mind, but you go,' Hillary added, noting how Odile seemed to waver uncertainly.

She stared after the retreating figure until the young woman rounded the corner, then quickly found her attention stolen by a group of children who were fishing for crabs using a single line baited by a small piece of bacon. Time after time they found a crab on the end of their line and hauled upward excitedly only to see their hopes dashed as the squirming creature broke free and fell back into the water with a loud plop. Sometimes the crab even managed to get away with the piece of bacon, yet this didn't daunt the children who simply returned to their task with renewed determination.

After a while she found herself becoming restless. The children had filled one bucket with crustacea of all sizes and were now intent on filling a second. Swivelling around on the clammy stone wall, she watched the car park filling up with holiday-makers. It was at that moment that she noticed the chandlery for the first time, or to be more precise, the chandler.

In common with all the shops that bounded the quay, the chandlery was built of local stone. Outside were stacked large coils of rope of varying colours and thicknesses, along with wooden crates and tubs of different sizes containing brass hooks and rings and all manner of things that Hillary didn't even recognise. On the other side of the doorway was a brightly coloured array of more commercial items: rubber dinghies, floats, fishing rods and nets, boxes of beachwear, sandals, hats, and a rack of T-shirts and swimwear. Idly she fingered the garments, wondering why a whiff of ozone suddenly gave people the urge to buy such tawdry items. It seemed to her a typically English phenomenon.

She had glimpsed a large, fair haired man as she sat on the harbour wall and now through the plate glass window she saw him enter the shop from a rear door. The sight of him made her catch her breath. He was, without doubt, the most amazing specimen of manhood she had ever seen. Pretending to be interested in a rack of swimwear, she studied him covertly, watching through the window as he bent his large frame over the counter to examine a ledger of some kind.

He was tall, well over six feet, and very muscular, although not with the exaggerated development of a body-builder. His superb physique was shown off to best advantage by a pair of well-cut blue denims which he wore with a plain white T-shirt. His whole ensemble was topped off by the most handsome face she had ever seen on a blond haired man. As a rule she was attracted mainly to those with dark hair and a swarthy complexion but for this man she was prepared to make an exception. She smiled to herself, amused at her own arrogance, perhaps she was not his type.

As if in answer to her thoughts he looked up and caught her watching him. Quickly she turned her attention to the garment she was holding and to her discomfort noticed it was a brief pair of men's bikini trunks. Doubly embarrassed, she let go of the offending item and pretended to study a selection of children's toy windmills instead. On impulse she picked one out and turned to go inside the shop to pay but he was already by her side.

'You would like to buy this?' he said.

She didn't need a degree in modern languages to recognise that he wasn't English. 'Yes, please. It's for my nephew,' she lied, wondering why she was bothering to explain herself to him. 'How much?' She fumbled in her bag for her purse and extracted a pound coin.

Reaching out with one strong arm he enfolded her hand, coin and all in a vice-like grip. With the other hand he relieved her of the windmill. 'I will wrap it and get you some change. Just a minute, please.'

His voice had a singsong quality which she recognised as being Scandinavian, although she couldn't tell which country he came from. By the time he returned she had unearthed a vestige of boldness and found herself staring deep into his twinkling emerald green eyes.

'Where do you come from? Is it Sweden?'

He smiled, displaying perfectly even, strong, white teeth. 'No, Norway. My father he was Norwegian, a sailor. I am Haldane.'

His tone of voice was proud, indicating to her that he was obviously pleased with his name and his heritage.

Smiling back, Hillary accepted the windmill from him and her change. Placing her purchase carefully in her bag and the coins in her pocket, she looked up at him, feeling dwarfed by his massive frame. 'I expect it was your father who taught you all about boats and things?' She gestured around the harbour, her sweeping glance taking in the fishing boats and the chandlery items outside his own shop.

Haldane's eyes followed hers but his expression had clouded over. 'No, I never actually met him. He went on a sailing trip before I was born and never came back.'

Regretfully Hillary realised that she had said the wrong thing and frantically searched her mind for something less controversial to say. She turned back to Haldane but he had already left her, retreating to the dark interior of his shop. Feeling guilty for upsetting him, Hillary gave a feeble wave through the window. Then she hovered on the pavement outside for a minute or two before turning on her heel and making her way back towards Harwood Hall. She walked away unaware that he stared after her retreating figure until she was well out of sight, a thoughtful expression on his golden face.

By the time she arrived back at the house, Alicia and Chloe were up and about and Odile was seated on the window seat in the sitting room, her face wreathed in smiles.

'I take it you got through to your boyfriend okay?' Hillary said, dropping wearily into the nearest armchair. The walk back had seemed much longer and more arduous than the one going.

'Yes, he is definitely coming this weekend. I'm so happy,' Odile replied.

'What's his name, how long have you known him?'

Odile leaned forward, a dreamy expression on her face. 'Well, his name is Theo,' she pronounced it Tay-oh, 'and we've been seeing each other for five months, one week and four days.'

32

Hillary laughed and added, 'But who's counting?'

She reached for her bag and took out the paper bag containing the windmill then holding the simple toy in front of her face she blew out a steady stream of warm breath, gazing thoughtfully as the bright colours whirled and merged into a gaudy blur. A moment later she caught Odile watching her and gave an embarrassed laugh. 'I bought it on impulse, she explained.

Alicia walked into the room, raised her eyebrows when she saw Hillary holding the windmill but didn't comment. She had grown used to her sister's odd behaviour over the years.

Hillary looked up. 'Oh, I'm glad it's you, Alix. I was wondering if you'd mind taking me for a proper guided tour? Darius mentiond that some parts of the house are out of bounds so I'd be grateful if you could show me where we can and cannot go.'

Of course, we'll do it now if you like.' Alicia smiled easily, then glanced at Odile, 'Would you like to come?'

The younger woman shook her head. 'No thanks, I just want to sit here and daydream for a while.'

Alicia understood but she couldn't resist asking her if she minded being in the house alone.

'Of course not, why should I?' Odile chuckled, looking more than a little confused at Alicia's strange remark.

Alicia shrugged. 'I just wondered that's all.'

As soon as they were out of earshot, Hillary repeated Odile's question. Trying to look nonchalant, Alicia replied, 'Oh, no reason really. It's just that – ' she hesitated.

'Go on,' urged Hillary.

'Well,' Alicia continued, concentrating hard on picking a minute speck of lint from her sleeve, 'it's just that for the past few days I've been getting the distinct impression that we're being watched.' She laughed, her embarrassment only too visible. 'Chloe thinks I'm going mad from spending so much time in seclusion. Perhaps she's right.'

Hillary glanced sideways at her sister. Like herself, Alicia had always been prone to flights of fancy. Even as a child her imagination had often got the better of her. Yet this time, Hillary thought, it went deeper than that. For once Alicia seemed genuinely disturbed.

'I can't say I've noticed anything untoward but then I've only been here a short while, less than twenty four hours in fact.' Even as Hillary spoke the words she realised they were not strictly true. But, she reasoned, the night before she had been tired and a little disorientated. What she had imagined was probably no more than the product of a need for sleep, it wasn't worth mentioning to Alicia or the others.

Her sister nodded and paused to push open a large pair of oak doors that separated their wing from the main house. They had barely walked more than a few paces along the corridor when a young girl appeared. Thin and waif-like she stood pigeon-toed and stared shyly at the two women, a questioning look on her wan face.

'Hillary, this is Fearn, Darius's housekeeper.' Alicia introduced her with an imperious wave of one perfectly manicured hand.

Hillary looked at the young girl, surprised that she should be charged with taking care of such a huge place. She smiled and extended a hand but the girl simply smiled weakly in return and wiped the palms of her hands on her skirt before carrying on silently past them and into a room on the left.

As soon as the girl was out of earshot Hillary turned to Alicia. 'How on earth does she cope as the housekeeper here? She hardly looks strong enough to lift a feather duster.'

With a typical lack of concern, her sister shrugged. 'Who knows? I think a couple of the estate workers' wives come in to help her.'

Hillary pursed her lips, for some inexplicable reason she couldn't help feeling concerned for the young girl's welfare. 'Does she live here alone as well?'

Alicia was beginning to feel a little irritated. She couldn't care less about the hired help. Nevertheless, she knew her sister wouldn't be satisfied until all her questions had been answered. 'Don't forget that Darius lives in this part of the Hall too.'

Hillary hadn't forgotten. In fact, although she hated to admit it, that was one of the things that concerned her the most.

'Do you think he and . . .?' She started, but Alicia interrupted her.

'No, I don't. She's definitely not his type, far too young and unsophisticated for him. And besides,' she added firmly in a voice that brooked no further questions, 'Fearn's brother normally lives with her and before you ask I haven't met him yet because he's been spending a few weeks in Scotland with their family apparently.'

Hillary laughed. 'Okay, I'm satisfied. Now let's get on with the tour.'

They had come to the end of the corridor and were now standing at the top of a wide mahogany staircase that curved down to a vast entrance hall. Hillary leaned over the banister. It was a very long way down she noted, with a quiver of trepidation, and the black and white marble floor tiles way beneath her looked hard and unforgiving. In her wild imagination she immediately conceived the full horror of falling from the spot where she stood. She shivered and straightened up. 'Can we explore downstairs?' she asked.

Alicia shook her head. 'Not really. At least, not without Darius's permission first. Apparently everywhere is heavily alarmed and one false move can set the whole lot off. You could ask him though,' she added, her attention suddenly stolen by the reappearance of Fearn.

'Your friend says could you come back right now as she's got a panic on?' The young girl didn't say which friend but both Alicia and Hillary immediately understood that she meant Chloe. Odile wasn't the sort of person to panic.

35

Alicia nodded her thanks to the young girl and turned to Hillary. 'I won't be a minute. She's probably got fluff in her nail varnish or some other unspeakable calamity,' she said, grinning.

Hillary smiled. 'I'll be okay.'

As soon as Alicia had left, she turned to study a large painting on the wall behind her. It was of a thorough-bred racehorse, its dark glossy coat tinged with creamy froth as though it had just that second finished running a race. Peering closer she found herself unable to recognise the names of either the artist or the horse.

The sound of the swing doors opening and closing told her that Alicia had reached their own quarters. For a few minutes she stood and waited, shifting from one foot to the other, glancing at the racehorse painting from time to time and then finally at her watch. Alicia had been gone for only a few minutes and she was already feeling restless. She looked over the banister again, tempted to walk down the staircase just to see what the ground floor was like. But she daren't, not if she risked setting off the alarm.

However, she reasoned, after a few more minutes of solitude, Alicia hadn't warned against continuing to explore the floor that she was on. She considered this for a second, then crossed the landing and continued along the corridor in front of her. Again, the thickly carpeted corridor was lined with doors on either side. Some of them stood wide open affording a good view of the rooms that lay behind. To her surprise, Hillary noticed that most of them were empty or almost empty.

She carried on, trying the handles of some of the closed doors. Some were locked, others opened into comfortably furnished bedrooms similar to those of her own quarters, or small reading rooms, lined with book-cases that sagged under the weight of an interesting mix of old hardbacks and new, dog-eared paperbacks.

As a lover of all kinds of books, she couldn't resist the temptation to peruse the shelves in one such room. She had just taken down an Agatha Christie first edition when she was startled by the sound of a creaking floorboard directly behind her. Whirling around she found herself confronted by the imposing figure of Darius Harwood himelf. Judging by his expression he was not pleased to see her there.

Chapter Three

*D*espite the heat of the mid-summer's day, Hillary suddenly felt very cold.

'I believe I mentioned that the main Hall was out of bounds?' His voice was polite but firm and she found herself quaking under his piercing stare.

'I . . . I . . . um . . . Alicia . . .,' she tried desperately to explain but couldn't find her voice. Her knees trembled and, without considering that it might anger him further, she sank onto the nearest chair. It was a mistake, she realised, now he looked even more imposing and she felt all the more disadvantaged.

Darius stared down at her, conscious that had she explored much further she might have stumbled upon his secret rooms. He took a step forward, placed a finger under her chin and tilted her face upward to look at him. His breath caught because her expression told him she wasn't frightened of him, she was too strong a woman for that. Nevertheless she did look distinctly unnerved.

Hillary tried to stare at him boldly but knew she was failing miserably. Her heart hammered in her chest and she wished she could simply melt away, anything to avoid his arrogant presence in front of her. As he took a step forward she fought an overwhelming urge to shrink away from him into the deeper recesses of the overstuffed, antique arm-chair. She didn't believe he would do anything to harm her yet she felt distinctly threatened. Adrenaline coursed through her veins, knotting her stomach and quickening her pulse. And, when he touched her beneath her chin, she felt as though she had been hit by a bolt of lightening.

Unwillingly she looked up at him, conscious of the fact that his crotch was a few inches away from her face and the intriguing bulge beneath the light cotton of his trousers exuded a faint musky scent that aroused her most primitive instincts. Fight or flight – faint or fuck. She still had a choice. Using every ounce of self control she rose to her feet, standing ramrod straight so close to him that she could feel the heat from their bodies interact. Her mouth felt dry and she licked her lips, not taking her eyes away from his for a second.

Somewhere in the house a clock ticked remorselessly, counting away the seconds as they stared at each other and fought a silent battle of wills in which neither one could be the victor.

He moved his hand and, sliding his fingers around her neck until his palm cupped the base of her skull, pulled her face toward his until their lips clashed. Stunned by the sudden violence of his action she stood stock still, on tiptoe, her arms straight by her sides as she allowed his tongue to plunder her mouth. She could feel the heat rising within her, suffusing her body with a force of passion she had never known before.

Suddenly, she felt as though she yearned to know this man in every sense of the word; and wanted him to discover her. Instinctively she felt that now she had allowed him entry into her mind there would be no turning back, events would take their course and sooner or later he would possess her completely. It was a scary thought.

She shivered, half of her wanting to pull away, to stop things in their tracks, the other half wanting to press herself against his hard unyielding torso, using her body to communicate the things she dare not speak aloud. Conscious of his body heat permeating her flesh and turning it to molten lava, her mind whirled. Should she stay or should she go?

The decision was taken away from her. In a single movement his free hand spanned her buttocks and pulled her toward him until she could feel his hardness pressing against her lower belly. He held her firmly, his lips and hands now both pinning her. For the first time in her life she felt helpless in the presence of a man, trapped like a rare butterfly. Her knees sagged and she felt her arms moving from her sides and encircling his body, her palms resting flat against the unyielding hardness of his back and shoulders.

Then, just as suddenly, from somewhere in the house a door opened and closed and voices could be heard – clipped female voices. It was Alicia and Chloe. Abruptly, he let go of her, releasing her mouth a mite more reluctantly as he took two steps backward. She continued to stare at him in silence, expecting him to say something. Eventually he did but it was not what she wanted to hear. 'That was a mistake. I apologise. Please forget it ever happened,' he said.

She almost laughed aloud. A mistake! Forget it! If only life were that simple. She could no more forget what had happened than walk on water. He must want me, she thought, we weren't play-acting just then. With a flash of inspiration she glanced down at his crotch, yes, he was still hard. She looked back up at him and smiled knowingly but he stared straight through her, looking over her shoulder at their reflections in the mirror that dominated the room.

At that moment, Alicia and Chloe poked their heads through the open doorway. 'Oh, there you are, Hillary. We've been looking high and low for you.' Alicia sounded genuinely relieved. She turned to Darius. 'I hope my sister hasn't been doing anything she shouldn't.'

Hillary would have been annoyed at such a patronising remark but given the circumstances she found it rather amusing.

Darius shook his head. 'Of course not, we were merely discussing literature.' He glanced at the book Hillary had dropped onto the chair. 'Agatha Christie, as a matter of fact.'

Alicia shrugged. 'I didn't know you were a fan of hers, Hills, you always complain when I want to watch it on TV. Oh, only at Christmas that is,' she hastened to add for Darius's benefit, or perhaps for Chloe's. Hillary smiled fondly, her sister was such a snob sometimes.

The four of them left the room, Darius shutting the door carefully behind them and following them as far as the staircase. Just to make sure they didn't decide to do any more exploring, he mused to himself.

Hillary followed Alicia and Chloe back down the corridor to their own part of the Hall, fighting the urge to look behind her to see if Darius was watching. Chloe chattered on for a few seconds about nothing in particular then turned to Alicia. 'Are we going to the beach darling, or what?'

Alicia nodded. 'You'll come too won't you, Hill? It's going to be a scorcher of an afternoon.' She didn't bother to wait for a reply.

When they went downstairs to the kitchen they found that Odile had prepared a light picnic, including a cool-bag containing a couple of bottles of white wine. Happy and laughing, they all piled into Alicia's Mercedes with its distinctive personalised number-plate. By car the journey to the beach took no time at all, although parking proved to be a bit more of a problem than they had anticipated. They were just turning around to drive up the coast road for the third time when Darius's familiar green Range Rover pulled up in front of them. The driver's door swung open and he jumped out, now dressed in khaki shorts and a matching cotton short-sleeved shirt instead of his usual smart trousers and jacket. He looked tanned and relaxed. Hillary realised she wasn't used to seeing him like that, it also made a pleasant change to see him smile.

Not only was he smiling but his tone was cheerful. 'Looking for somewhere to park, ladies? Follow me.'

He drove slowly down the road for about a quarter of a mile, then turned into a private road. As they drove on for about half a mile the road petered out into a track which ended abruptly at the edge of a heavily wooded area. Alicia parked next to him and they all climbed out, looking around in confusion.

Finally Chloe spoke. 'Where are we, Darius? Where's the beach?'

'You're back on Harwood land and the beach is on the other side of those trees. Although it's not a private beach, I think you'll find it's nicely secluded.' He pointed to a small sandy path that led off to the right.

Hillary followed his finger with her eyes, then noticing a similar path leading to the left, she asked, 'Where would that path take us? To the witch's cottage?' From the moment they arrived she had felt like a fairytale character lost in the forest, although one glance at Darius's baffled expression made her feel distinctly idiotic instead.

'That path leads to the local naturist beach,' he explained patiently.

'Oh, is it full of wild birds and things like that?' Chloe asked.

Hillary laughed and flashed an amused glance at her, automatically assuming that she was joking but her expression was completely serious. Hillary was relieved that Chloe's stupid remark easily outweighed her own.

Alicia was obviously used to her friend's naivete. 'He means it's a nudist beach, you idiot.'

Far from looking hurt at Alicia's remark, Chloe appeared fascinated. 'Really,' she gasped. 'We must check that out one day soon, Alix.'

Darius caught Hillary's expression and winked. Feeling extraordinarily pleased, she grinned at him then gestured toward their picnic basket. 'Are you busy? Would you like to join us?'

His sweeping glance took in the whole of her body, setting it instantly on fire once again and reminding her of their encounter less than an hour earlier. She had removed her T-shirt in the car and was now dressed only in her brief white bikini top and shorts. Under Darius's piercing gaze she may as well have been stark naked.

He shook his head regretfully. 'I would love nothing better than to spend the afternoon with four such gorgeous ladies but I have work to do, I'm afraid.'

Chloe giggled. 'There's no peace for the wicked, is there Darius?'

Looking genuinely sorry to leave them, he gave a little wave before turning the Range Rover around and heading back in the direction of the main road. As soon as he was out of sight Hillary, Alicia, Chloe and Odile collected their assorted bags and rolled-up towels and trudged, slightly dejectedly, down the sandy pathway to the beach.

From the moment they rounded the trees and surveyed the breathtaking view Hillary felt her spirit lifting. Mile upon mile of golden sand stretched out endlessly in front of them and to either side as far as the eye could see. In the distance something shimmered in the heat haze but Hillary couldn't be certain if it was the sea, or merely the horizon. For a split second she forgot she was in Norfolk, it was so easy to imagine that such a beach was somewhere more exotic.

Although it was a public beach, it was scarcely populated and they were spoilt for choice. Being the most practical of the four, Hillary suggested that they walk as little as possible and the others readily agreed with her. There really was no need to venture very far. After about ten minutes of unpacking and unrolling they found themselves reclining comfortably on their respective towels and deckchairs, dousing their burning bodies with liberal quantities of suntan lotion.

Hillary closed her eyes, her olfactory sense revelling in the unmistakable aroma of coconut milk on salty, perspiration drenched skin. She sighed contentedly, summer was definitely her favourite time of year. She loved the beach and worshipped the sun. There was no doubt about it, right at that moment she was in heaven.

Odile uncapped a bottle of cold Frascati and using her free hand she groped around in the picnic basket. 'Damn, I forgot to bring the plastic cups,' she said.

'Never mind, darling.' Chloe reached out with one perfectly manicured hand and took the bottle from her, raising it to her lips. 'We'll manage.' She took a long draught and offered it to Alicia who shook her head dejectedly.

'I can't, I'm driving remember.'

The other three tut tutted in sympathy, then Hillary produced a second bottle. 'I don't know if you packed this intentionally but it's a low alcohol wine, you could have a sip of this, Alicia.'

Alicia glanced at the label, then raised the bottle to her lips. 'Thanks, Hilly.'

For a while they lay back and soaked up the sun in silence until, fortified by alcohol no doubt, Chloe declared out of the blue that she intended to find at least one lover with whom to spend the summer.

To Hillary's dismay her sister agreed. 'I'll say, I can't lay around here for weeks on end wearing hardly any clothes and not have my many desires satisfied.' From under her lashes she studied Hillary's shocked expression. 'Don't look so horrified, little sister. It won't be the first time I've had a little flingy-wingy and let's face it,' she added, her voice taking on a slight edge, 'darling hubby's not exactly lily-white in that department.'

'Do you mean he's had an affair too?' asked Hillary, aghast.

Alicia laughed wryly. 'An affair. An affair!' She paused for effect then, speaking in a low voice, said, 'You may not be aware of this Hillary but Clive has screwed over half the women in his bank, he sees it as a perk of the job.'

Hillary took another gulp of wine, she wasn't sure that she wanted to know all the sordid details of her sister's marriage. But it was too late. By now, Alicia, bolstered by interjections from Chloe, was warming to her theme, the two of them denigrating their husbands totally, both in bed and out of it.

Only Odile, it appeared, was satisfied with her sex life. 'My Theo is a wonderful, sensuous lover.' Alicia eyed her jealously. 'Well, Odile, what exactly do you mean?' she asked. She stopped and glanced at the young woman's profile as she turned her face up to the sun.

'Mmm,' Odile responded. 'I don't want to go into details. Just take my word for it.'

'Come on, Odile.' Alicia took another sip of low alcohol wine obviously hoping it would have some kind of placebo effect. 'I *want* the details! You can't just say he's wonderful and leave it at that. What exactly do the two of you get up to?'

Odile threw back her head and laughed. 'All I can say is he's wonderful. In my limited experience anyway. Believe it or not Theo is only my second lover.'

Chloe looked at her askance. 'But I thought . . .?'

Odile smiled an easy smile and rolled onto her stomach. 'I'm so sorry I'll rephrase that. Theo is only my second male lover.'

The three women stared wordlessy at Odile's back. Alicia gave Chloe a questioning look but the dark haired woman shrugged and shook her head. Hillary stifled a giggle – for two such women of the world it didn't take much to shut them up. Nevertheless, she couldn't help stealing a glance at Odile herself, wondering what it would be like to be made love to by such a beautiful young girl. Feeling herself becoming embarrassingly warm, she stood up abruptly. 'I'm going to find the sea,' she said.

The others made no attempt to follow her as she

strode determinedly along the beach. After a few hundred yards she slowed her pace, allowing her mind to drift as she scanned the horizon. Although it had only been the day before that she'd had sex with Michael she was already feeling unbearably frustrated; her erotic senses had been stirred first by her meeting with Darius, then Haldane and now Darius again. If she was being honest, she too was longing for the start of a holiday romance of her own. The question was, with whom?

The rest of the day passed uneventfully. A brief swim was followed by a picnic, then sunbathing, more swimming and finally home to take-away pizza and an early night. Hillary thought she would never hear the last of it as Alicia, Chloe and even Odile ribbed her about being an old fuddy-duddy and a party-pooper. Even Hillary's protestations that at least she had been swimming and walking on the beach while they had not moved from their towels cut no ice with them.

'Come on Hillary,' Alicia urged. 'We're only going to the village local for a drink, that won't kill you.'

Hillary shook her head, laughing. 'It's no good, I'm whacked and I just want an early night. Besides,' she added, 'I'm not much of a drinker.'

She knew Alicia was likely to take her remark as a criticism of her own drinking habits and was proved right. 'Nor am I.' The older woman pouted. 'And remember who had to stay sober this afternoon because she was driving.'

Her voice rose a little at the end and Hillary tried to placate her. 'It's okay, I'm not saying you shouldn't go. Just don't hassle me simply because I don't always want to follow in your footsteps.'

They were tiptoeing onto dangerous ground now. An oft-trod, sisters-only battle zone. Odile was quick to intervene. 'Leave Hillary alone for God's sake, Alicia, and let's just go before they call last orders.'

Hillary waited until they had gone then wandered into the sitting room. She switched on the television and stared blankly at the screen. Given that she had no other diversions a half hour or so of mindless situation comedy was her best option, at least until tiredness overtook her completely.

From the seclusion of his own rooms, Darius watched the women return, eat their pizza and argue about going to the pub. In a way he was disappointed that Hillary had declined to accompany them. If Hillary had agreed to go he would have contrived a casual meeting with her there and possibly even detached her from her sister and friends. Now there was no possibility of meeting up with her tonight, unless she decided to go exploring again, of course. His sex organs stirred at the thought, remembering the way she had felt that morning and the way she had looked the night before, naked before the mirror. If she trespassed into his domain tonight she would not escape lightly, he would make sure of that.

Observing her as she watched the television soon began to bore him but his ennui was relieved by the ringing of the telephone. Not taking his eyes from the screen he picked up the receiver and held it to his ear; the voice at the other end was familiarly soft and sexy with a husky Scottish burr.

'Ilona!' He said, genuinely pleased to hear from her.

'Darius, I have been thinking about you. Torran is almost ready to return and I wondered if you would like to see me too for a few days.'

'I always want to see you, you know that.' Darius's tone held genuine affection. 'I'll send Farboys up for you and Torran tomorrow, if that's not too soon.'

'Really, Darius,' the woman admonished, 'there's no need to fly us down. The boy and I can always travel by train.'

Darius was firm. 'I don't want any arguments. Unless you hear from me to the contrary the 'copter will be waiting for you at the brewery landing pad at four tomorrow.'

The woman acquiesced and they spoke for a few more minutes, catching up on a little gossip even though they would be seeing each other in person the following day. Then she rang off and Darius returned to watching Hillary.

Damn! She had fallen asleep on the sofa. By the look of her she would be out like a light until her friends returned home. He flicked around the other TV screens then switched them off completely. Reclining in the familiar embrace of his dark leather chair, he contemplated the imminent arrival of Ilona.

Darius was right in his assumption that Hillary would not waken until disturbed. Oblivious to his secret observation, or the flickering television screen, she slept on until the peace of the house was shattered by a cacophony of laughter and drunken giggles. Alicia, Chloe and Odile had returned from the pub more than a little worse the wear for drink.

Chloe struggled with the front door key. 'I can't get it in, I can't get it in,' she wailed over and over again.

Alicia snorted. 'You sound like my Clive.' She put on a whining voice intended to emulate her husband, 'I can't get it in, Alicia! My dick is so small, I can't get it in!'

The three women screamed with laughter all over again.

Odile wiped her streaming eyes. 'My God, Alicia, you are so cruel.'

The older woman wagged a finger at her and tutted. 'Not cruel, Odile darling, just honest. Anyway,' she added, after a moment's consideration, 'you don't appreciate what it's like. Your boyfriend is some kind of superstud, remember?'

Odile looked at her, embarrassed. 'I didn't say he was a superstud, Alicia. And for goodness sake don't let on to Theo that we've been discussing him in that way.' She blushed coyly, then glanced at Chloe who was still struggling with the front door.

Alicia put out her hand. 'For goodness sake, Chlo',

give me that fucking key before we wake up the whole place.'

Odile watched amused as Chloe handed over the key meekly. She couldn't help grinning at Alicia's words. Hearing her cultured tones say 'fucking' was similar in shock value to hearing the Queen fart. Not that she ever had, of course. The thought made her chuckle out loud.

Chloe looked at her friend askance. 'Come on, share the joke.'

Odile shook her head and tried to keep a straight face. At that moment Alicia managed to wrestle the door open and they stumbled into the darkened hallway. The light shining from the sitting room and the muted sounds of the TV told them that Hillary was still up. Immediately they all turned to each other, put their fingers to their lips and hissed, 'Shh,' very loudly.

Hillary woke up with a start and for a split second wondered where she was. Then Chloe, Odile and finally Alicia staggered into the room, all looking equally dishevelled.

'I take it you had a good time,' Hillary said, drily stating the obvious.

The three women nodded in unison, then collapsed in giggles. Hillary sighed, it could turn out to be a long night. As it happened, a few minutes later Chloe suddenly decided that she felt sick and bolted for her bathroom and Alicia sank down on the sofa and promptly passed out. Hillary glanced at Odile a questioning look in her eyes, Odile nodded silently.

With a bit of a struggle the two women managed to get Alicia up the stairs and into her own room, with a final heave they threw her on the bed.

Odile glanced down at her crumpled form. 'Should we undress her, do you think?'

Hillary felt guilty. Normally she would have agreed immediately but, bearing in mind Odile's disclosures on the beach about sleeping with women, she decided Alicia probably wouldn't thank her for it.

'No, that's okay, let the silly bitch sort herself out in the morning.' She knew she sounded unnecessarily harsh but she didn't want to be forced to explain her reasons for not wanting to undress her sister in front of Odile.

Although she looked a little taken aback, the young woman nodded and started to leave the room. Hillary followed her and bade her goodnight before opening the door to her own room. Despite the fact that she had slept for a good few hours already that evening, she felt as though she hardly had the strength to undress herself. Deciding it must be the sea air that was tiring her out she stripped off her clothes and jumped into bed, falling back into a deep sleep as soon as her head hit the pillow.

The next day dawned just as hot and as humid as its predecessors. The sun's warming rays were already permeating the thick, stone walls and forming an invisible blanket of heat over the fresh, early morning atmosphere. Hillary lay back against the pile of soft, downy pillows too relaxed to move as a magpie alighting on the window ledge commanded all her attention. As though initiating a conversation with her, the magpie opened its beak and emitted a strange cry that she knew she would never forget and broke the silence of a place that otherwise still slept.

A few moments more peace ensued, then she heard the customary first thing in the morning symphony begin: footsteps and banging doors, the hiss of a shower and the clanking deluge of a cistern emptying, whispered voices and giggles. Another half hour and her second full day at Harwood Hall would begin.

She felt the slight feeling of anticipation bubbling up within her that she had often felt as a child, the expectation of the unexpected. And, although she truly felt a valued and accepted member of their little group, the prospect of the coming day thrilled her for more than just intellectual reasons. Her sensual self, which already revelled in the relaxed heat of a summer's day

50

and the scent of salty skin, was on red-alert to the possibilities of a lascivious encounter with not one but two very different, very delectable men.

Feeling as though she was operating in slow motion, Hillary peeled back the sheet and thus exposed her naked body to the morning air. Swinging her legs gracefully over the side of the bed, she rose to her feet and stretched luxuriously, noticing with pleasure how her stomach flattened and her pink-tipped breasts rose high on her ribcage. She pulled her arms back, as though working an invisible chest expander, glancing downward to see how her breasts now jutted forward proudly. Relaxing her shoulders she cupped one brown orb in each hand, rolling the nipple gently between thumb and forefinger for a brief moment before releasing them and running the palms of her hands firmly down her sides, following the curve of her waist and hips.

She felt tempted to climb back onto the bed and explore herself further but the early morning sounds were fast becoming a cacophony, urging her to start the day voluntarily before someone knocked at her door and forced her into it. With a slight shrug Hillary bowed to the inevitable and padded into her bathroom, pausing only to check in the mirror that her face was as relaxed and smiling as it felt before stepping into the shower.

Basking for a few seconds in the steam cloud she began to slowly rotate her body, her face turned up to the invigorating spray as she soaped and rinsed her slick bronzed skin over and over again. Her hair rapidly gathered moisture and parted into thick silky cords. As she turned completely round for the second time she noticed, with a slight feeling of surprise, that her view from the window was not obscured by opaque glass as was usually the custom with bathrooms. Admittedly, she was some thirty feet above ground level and the Hall was hardly what one could describe as overlooked, but nevertheless she felt a shiver of unease, remembering that Alicia had thought someone was watching her. Now she too felt vulnerable and exposed to someone's eye.

Feeling slightly foolish, Hillary rinsed her body for the last time and quickly wrapped herself in one of the thick, white, towelling robes thoughtfully provided by their temporary landlord as a home comfort. Each of the luxurious robes sported a breast pocket hand-embroidered with the Harwood Hall 'HH' logo in a different colour. She glanced down – hers was embroidered in navy blue. She wrapped one of the matching bath towels around her hair turban style, then spent a few moments cleansing her face and brushing her teeth. By the time she had finished she felt fresh, alert and ready to meet the day head on.

Without bothering to dress, she made her way to the kitchen where she found Odile and Chloe munching on thin slices of unbuttered toast.

'I don't know how you can bear to eat it like that,' she muttered, taking a piece that had just popped up from the toaster and spreading it thickly with butter and marmalade. Ignoring Chloe's envious stare she bit into it, wincing as a little hot butter ran down her chin.

'I suppose, being sporty, you can eat what you like,' Chloe said, sounding as though she could cheerfully tear out Hillary's heart and roast it on a spit.

For a while they all ate in silence, then Odile piped up. 'I wonder what time the boys will arrive?'

Hillary was confused for a split second, then remembered that it was Friday and therefore the menfolk would be arriving later in the day. With a fleeting feeling of envy she wished someone was coming to spend the weekend with her. Her thoughts automatically returned to Darius and Haldane. She knew with certainty that it was only a matter of time before she won one of them over, the question was, which would it be?

Inexplicably, Chloe looked at her watch, then proceeded to answer Odile's question. 'Gus called last night and said he and Clive would be arriving sometime this afternoon. Probably after they've stopped for a pub lunch,' she added grimly.

'What about work?' Hillary asked, pouring herself a cup of coffee. She looked enquiringly at Chloe who snorted derisively.

'What about it?' She leaned back in her chair, clasping her hands behind her head. 'As far as Gus and Clive are concerned, work is just something they do when there's nothing better on offer. And to make pots of money of course,' she added, fingering her impressive diamond engagement ring and thick gold wedding band.

'Theo promised to be here by twelve,' said Odile, looking smug. 'I can't decide whether to take him out somewhere for lunch, or just take him to bed when he gets here.'

'You mean you seriously think there's a choice?' Chloe's voice was heavily tinged with envy. 'If I know Theo food will be the last thing he'll have on his mind.'

Odile blushed hard and giggled. 'Oh God, I hope so!'

Hillary smiled. She couldn't help thinking how pretty Odile looked and how relaxed and happy everyone seemed. Even Alicia, who had walked into the kitchen just at that moment, was smiling broadly. 'Did I miss something vital? Was it to do with sex?' She sat down next to Hillary and looked around expectantly.

'How did you guess?' Hillary drained the last of her coffee and stood up. She glanced at the other three women. 'I can't tell you how much I envy you all right now.'

Alicia tutted sympathetically. 'I could always ask Clive to bring along a friend for you. I'm sure I could still catch him if I 'phoned now.'

Hillary was horrified at her sister's well meant suggestion. 'Oh, no! I mean, it's a nice thought, Alix, but I think I'd rather find my own man, thanks all the same.'

Alicia looked doubtful. 'Well, if you're sure, Hills. Great men are a bit thin on the ground around here you know.'

'Oh, I wouldn't say that,' Hillary smirked.

'If you're thinking of Darius I'd steer clear of him if I were you.'

Sometimes, Hillary thought, Alicia sounded exactly as an older sister should. Although she couldn't help wondering if her man-mad sibling had set her own sights on Darius. 'I was under the impression you thought he was fabulous.'

Alicia had the grace to blush. 'Yes, well, I do. But not as a serious partner.'

Hillary sighed heavily, then grinned. 'I'm not looking for a husband, Alix, I just want a good fuck.' No sooner were the words out of her mouth than Hillary noticed Fearn hovering in the doorway. Blushing wildly she said, 'Alicia.'

Her sister followed the direction of her eyes and smiled at the young girl. 'You can start on the bathrooms if you like.'

Fearn nodded, turned briskly and walked out of the door. As soon as they were certain she was well out of earshot the four women collapsed in gales of hysterical laughter. As their laughter died, Hillary couldn't help wondering how much the girl had heard and if she would relay the conversation to her employer. In some ways she hoped she would, it might clear any doubts that Darius may have had about her reciprocating his advances. As it turned out, Fearn had heard everything but wouldn't dream of saying a word. Not that it mattered. From the seclusion of his monitoring room Darius had already overheard the whole conversation.

After a few more minutes the women's chatter subsided and one by one they made their excuses and left the room. Hillary went straight to her bedroom to change. She had decided to go to the beach alone taking the magazine that she'd been unable to concentrate on reading on the train and a light picnic lunch.

When she announced her intention Alicia tossed her the keys to her Mercedes. 'Don't wreck it, that's all,' she warned, sounding just like a big sister for the second time that morning.

54

Chapter Four

By car the journey to the beach took no time at all. Hillary parked carefully in the same place Darius had shown them the day before but instead of walking straight down to the main beach she headed in the direction of the sand dunes. After about ten minutes she stopped, stood on top of the tallest dune and surveyed her immediate surroundings.

As it was the end of the week the large beach was quite crowded and some of the lower sand dunes were dotted with small groups of people – mainly randy teenagers, she noticed with a smile. The girls were bravely sunbathing topless but laying firmly on their stomachs, refusing to turn over onto their backs despite endless pleas, inducements and trickery on the part of their male companions.

Hillary walked further on until she came to a relatively secluded area, in seconds she had unrolled her towel and stripped down to a pair of minuscule black G-string bikini bottoms. Despite the fact that there was no one in the immediate vicinity, she still felt strangely exposed and glanced around nervously once or twice before uncapping a bottle of suntan oil and anointing her whole body with it. Quickly she covered her limbs and shoulders, taking a little more care as she massaged her breasts and stomach with the slick liquid.

Tremulously she stroked her hands across her own body, enjoying the sensation of skin on skin, even if it was her own. Gradually she became self-conscious, aware that she was arousing herself and that she was no longer in the privacy of her bedroom. Although a swift glance around her showed she was still completely alone, she couldn't help feeling slightly embarrassed until finally she paused, her hands cupped around her naked breasts, a shiver coursing through her body despite the overpowering heat of the noonday sun. Someone was watching her, she was certain of it now and, far into the distance, she could see the sun glinting off something reflective – a pair of binoculars perhaps?

Quickly she replaced the lid on the bottle and lay down on her back, her arms held stiffly by her sides. She felt as though she was waiting for the unknown to happen to her, like a virgin on a sacrificial altar about to be given to a pagan god. Of course nothing did happen: no bolts of lightning, no sudden appearances by mad axe-men or sex maniacs, just the relentless rays of the sun beating down upon her trembling body.

The heat worked its soporific magic, gradually soothing her and gently easing her tensed muscles until her body relaxed completely into the sand. In the distance she could hear the faint cry of seagulls, the rhythmic ebb and flow of the tide telling her that she was nearer the shoreline than before, although quite safe in the shelter of the dunes. Safe – she was safe. Safe and happy. Safe, happy and hot – very hot.

Her body felt heavy, as though it didn't really belong to her at all, although parts of her felt super sensitive and alive to the slightest breeze or shift in the sand. Her breasts felt particularly heavy – large, brown, glistening orbs, the delicate skin covering them a mass of nerve endings. And the tips, oh! How they yearned to be stroked, or sucked – to be stimulated beyond the capability of her own imagination. She felt her nipples growing, becoming hard as she concentrated her mind on them.

She was floating somehwere between dreams and reality, or perhaps she was dreaming, dreaming that someone gently brushed their fingers over her breasts. Surely it was a breeze, or a small cloud of sand? She wanted to touch them herself, to discover what had caused the fine hairs to thrill but her arms were leaden, pinned to the sand by an invisible force. Her eyelids too were heavy, far too weighted down to flicker open even for a fraction of a second. It happened again, the faint brush of fingertips against her naked skin, this time across her belly – once, twice, backwards and forwards, featherlight stimulation that set her whole body on fire.

This was not a force of nature, this was man, exploratory man with a knowledgeable hand, teasing her body with barely perceptible touches. She was not dreaming, of that she was certain, but did it matter who was doing this to her? It was a confusing thought. Should it matter? Would it make a difference if the hands working their magic upon her desperate flesh belonged to someone not of her own age, if he – and she was certain they did belong to a he – was very old, or a teenager perhaps? But the touch was too practised, too skilled for a very young person and the hands were large, the skin on the palms slightly coarse, the arms where they brushed against her too hairy to belong to someone of tender years, or to a woman.

She found herself concentrating on the hands themselves almost as much as on what they were doing. Judging by the slight roughness of the palms, the owner must carry out a certain degree of manual work, although they were not the hands of a labourer. The fingers teased her nipples, rolling them, then twisting and pulling them gently. They were large fingers, large and wide. Occasionally she felt the slight scratch of a smooth-edged fingernail, so they were manicured nails, not bitten or broken but well cared for; that suggested the owner was either quite wealthy, or took inordinate care in his appearance, or both. She was desperate to look, to satisfy her curiosity once and for all, but the whole episode had a dreamlike quality that she was unwilling to shatter. She was certain that her mystery man would disappear the moment she opened her eyes.

Now the hands were roaming her body freely, gliding across her oiled skin like skaters on ice. Every now and then the hands dipped between her legs, stroking her inner thighs, stray fingers occasionally fluttering against her barely covered mound. At those times she felt as though she would explode from frustration and curiosity, her clitoris pulsating so hard that she was certain he must be fully aware of her desire. He did it again, his touch no more than a whisper against the desperately swollen hub of her arousal, as a reflex she clenched her buttocks, simultaneously allowing her legs to part slightly. Her eyelids flickered of their own accord and the caresses stopped.

She remained motionless, almost holding her breath in the urgent need to feel the hands once again upon her tormented body. The longed for touch never came, not as the long minutes ticked by and a cloud symbolically blotted out the sun. Relucantly she opened her eyes. As she expected she was alone, completely alone. Her mystery lover had gone whence he came and Hillary was left to spend the rest of the afternoon in a confused state of disappointment and extreme arousal.

By three o'clock she had endured all that she could. For hours she had lain motionless, eyes tightly closed, waiting expectantly for a renewed caress that never came. Now her skin was burning and her head aching. Slowly she sat up and fastened a bikini top around herself, clipping the halter neck too hastily so that she pinched the skin on the back of her neck. With tears of frustration in her eyes, she gathered her few possessions together and rammed them angrily into the backpack, pausing only to take a long draught of mineral water before rising to her feet and plodding dejectedly across the sand dunes back in the direction she had come.

By the time she reached the edge of the dunes she realised she had somehow veered off in the wrong direction; the Mercedes was nowhere to be seen, only a wide expanse of deserted beach to one side of her and a thick forest of trees to the other side. She knew she didn't want to go back onto the beach so her only option was to step into the cool, pine scented gloom of the forest. Tentatively she walked amongst the trees, occasionally stopping to stare upward, following their apparently topless trunks until her vision was blocked by a thick canopy of branches.

She felt a little like Red Riding Hood, having strayed off from the safety of the path despite her mother's warning – any minute she would fall into the clutches of the wolf. She giggled nervously to herself, not expecting to see a wolf exactly but half wondering what sort of wild animals inhabited English forests. Being a city girl her imagination was unrestrained by a knowledge of the countryside and its wildlife.

Suddenly she heard a sound behind her. Something was trailing her. When she stopped it stopped. Nervously she looked around her; she could see nothing yet it was close enough for her to hear it breathing. She ran forward then stopped abruptly. The footsteps stopped dead too but a twig cracked underfoot.

'Is someone there?' she called out tremulously, trying to sound braver than she felt.

There was no reply but the breathing was even closer. She could feel it against the back of her neck. She whirled around and found herself staring at a man's chest – it was Darius.

'Oh, it's you.' She giggled weakly, groping blindly with her right hand until it came into contact with a tree trunk. She leaned her weight against it gratefully.

'It's not safe to go wandering about in the forest alone.' The sentiment was one of concern but he looked anything but, his expression was a strange mixture of amusement and something else, something indefinable that caused a strange sensation in the pit of Hillary's stomach.

'I didn't mean to. I got lost.' She wondered why she felt so gauche. Beneath her halter top her nipples hardened. She cleared her throat. 'Can you tell me how to get back to the car? I parked in the same place as yesterday.'

Darius stepped back and leaned his tall frame against the trunk of a large fir tree. He regarded her in thoughtful silence for a few moments, his fingers playing with the barrel of a rifle held between his legs like a phallic symbol as he turned it around and around. Hillary was mesmerised and wondered why she hadn't noticed before that he had a gun. She shivered but tried valiantly to hold his gaze.

'No one but myself ever ventures into the forest.' Darius's voice was low and controlled.

Unsure of the message he was trying to convey, Hillary didn't know how to respond. The whole scenario seemed unreal.

He continued to finger the rifle. 'You're not very well protected, are you?'

She wasn't too sure what he meant by this either. Did he mean her clothing was inappropriate for trekking through forests, or what? She glanced down, her gaze following his as he flicked his eyes insolently over her body, which was barely covered by the halter top and tiny G-string. He was right, she wasn't very well covered at all, not for anything other than the beach. Hastily she reached into her backpack intending to take out her towel and wrap it around herself – she had bought no other clothes.

Darius put out a hand as if to stop her. 'No, don't cover yourself up. You're quite the most beautiful thing I've seen in a long time.'

Hillary wasn't sure that she liked being referred to as a thing but she smiled and nodded her acceptance of the intended compliment. Darius allowed a flicker of a smile to cross his own face, his eyes momentarily leaving her body to look straight at her. 'It's a shame you decided to cover your breasts.' He glanced at her halter top and she felt herself flush with embarrassment, immediately wondering if he was her mystery man, the one who caressed her with such finesse as she lay in the sand dunes. She opened her mouth to ask but he interrupted her, his voice still low and filled with emotion. 'Take if off, please.' His gaze told her he was referring to her top.

Her mind whirled. How dare he? He couldn't be serious – but at least he said please. What should she do?

He was still staring at her with an inscrutable expression on his face. She rose to the challenge and, reaching behind her, undid the halter top allowing it to fall to the ground. Surprisingly, his eyes didn't move from her face, not even a flicker of emotion clouded his expression. 'If this were another time I would make love to you right now; take you here amongst the pine needles, in the shade of the world's most majestic of trees.' His eyes swept around their immediate surroundings and she felt her pulse quicken. Did he mean to rape her? Of course not – the very word implied violation against her will and she wanted him as much as he apparently wanted her.

Still, she felt as though she should offer at least a suggestion of protest. 'We're quite near the beach, anyone could come.'

He smiled confidently and finally lowered his gaze to her naked breasts. 'Yes, anyone could.'

Shocked and excited she gasped at his words, feeling a trickle of her own juices gather in the thin material of her G-string. She tightened her buttocks and clenched her legs together simultaneously. Of course, that was what turned him on the most, the prospect of being discovered. They were a pair of naughty children playing with each other in the woods.

He stepped forward, bent down and plucked at a

length of succulent green ivy that snaked its way through the undergrowth. He broke off a length and stood again, winding the ends around his hands. She watched, fascinated, her stomach contracting with a mixture of fear and excitement. He looked as though he was about to strangle her. For a split second her face paled, surely he wouldn't harm her?

As though reading her mind he smiled, but his voice was serious as he said, 'I'm not going to hurt you.'

She hadn't realised that she was holding her breath but she let out a long sigh of relief. She looked at him. Despite his words he was still holding the ivy in that same strange manner – somehow she trusted him, although she didn't know what was about to happen.

As he stepped forward her mind cleared, she started to move away from the tree but it was too late. In a flash he blocked her escape with his body and lashed her to the tree, winding the length of ivy around her chest and torso, pinning her arms to her sides.

She looked around her wildly. The whole thing was preposterous – she was tied to a tree in the middle of a forest in broad daylight, when anyone might happen along. Except no-one ever did, unless they were tres-passers. She remembered the words of warning she had read on the trespass notice the day before – this was Harwood land, out of bounds to all except any living member of the Harwood family, or their guests. Anyone caught there could be dealt with according to the wishes of the prevailing Harwood landowner – in others words, Darius.

'You can't do this to me,' she protested, her words sounding feeble even to her own ears.

Darius merely laughed. 'You know that's not true.' He stepped forward and stroked a finger across her breasts. 'You know I can do anything I dammed well like.'

He brought his other hand to her breasts and fingered her nipples absently, considering them as though they were inanimate objects. Hillary fought to control her emotions. She was embarrassed that her body should betray her so shamelessly – under Darius's expert stimulation her nipples had swelled and hardened – but further down her clitoris throbbed and her tingling vagina let forth another gush of liquid.

Moaning, she parted her legs slightly, rubbing her buttocks against the rough bark of the tree trunk. Darius noticed her discomfort but forced himself not to oblige her just yet. He wanted to play with her, make her desire him so badly that she would let him do anything, anything at all.

With maddening slowness, Darius allowed his hands to drift down her body, reaching a certain point before returning to caress her breasts. She wanted him to take her there, as he had suggested, to plunge his cock into her time and time again, relentlessly filling her up and bringing her to an explosive orgasm. She could almost feel him within her and, for a moment, wondered if her wishes were about to be fulfilled – Darius had stepped back from her and was now unzipping his shorts, releasing a rock hard penis of ample proportions. She felt her legs turn to water at the sight of it and spread them even further.

With unashamed fascination she watched him stroke it fondly for a minute or two, then he stepped forward and rubbed it against her belly and cotton covered mound. She could feel its heat against her body and the power pulsating beneath the tightly stretched skin of his shaft. Groaning, she urged her pelvis upward, cursing the restrictive binding that held her torso firmly to the tree trunk. She tried to move her hands, wanting desperately to touch him.

'Why don't you untie me now, Darius,' she urged, hoping that he would at least loosen the binding.

At her words he stopped what he was doing and looked at her seeing how the verdant twine made small tracks in her flesh. Hooking a finger under a length of ivy which ran around the tops of her breasts and arms he surveyed the damage underneath – a bright white stripe now quickly turning red. Releasing the twine so that it snapped back into place he considered her dilemma for a moment, and his. If he released her completely it would ruin his enjoyment and probably hers too, on the other hand he found no enjoyment in causing actual harm.

After deliberating he stepped around the back of the tree trunk and loosened the knots a little. Immediately her knees sagged with relief and she sank a little; this gave him an idea.

Going back to the front of the tree he commanded her to kneel down, legs apart so that he could lash her ankles together. Instead of binding her whole body he simply brought her arms back and down and tied the wrists together, then he linked the wrists and ankles in such a way that any attempt to struggle would result in a tightening of the knots. He warned her of this, smiling at the force of human nature that compelled her to test the truth of his claim immediately. Of course it worked as he said it would.

Hillary was surprised by this new development, she had expected him to simply untie her and then screw her in the undergrowth, as it was she couldn't see any advantage to this position. Darius could.

He stood in front of her once again, his swollen cock swaying in front of her face like a metronome. For a moment or two Hillary watched it, mesmerised, her body aching to feel its length inside her.

He stared down at her, saw how she looked at him, wide-eyed not with fear but with an eagerness to find out what would happen next. Curving his lips into a slight smile he decided to show her. He put his hand down to steady his cock, then guided the tip toward her closed mouth, the tip following the outline of her full fleshy lips like a large red lipstick. She wouldn't open up. Of course, she was stubborn, stubborn to the last like a horse he had had once. To win the horse over he had used a careful blend of kindness and cruelty, perhaps that was what was needed now. 'Open your mouth, Hillary.'

She shook her head defiantly, either he could fuck her or forget it. 'No,' she hissed through clenched teeth.

'Don't be a silly girl, do as you're told.'

Hillary fumed at his words. How dare he? The arrogant bastard! She longed to tell him to screw himself but didn't dare open her mouth to speak.

'If you don't cooperate I'll simply have to make you.'

She snorted derisively – oh yes, make her – she'd like to see the day any man made her do something she didn't want to.'

She suddenly felt amused and mocked him with her eyes. So the Lord of the Manor wanted a blow job, did he? Well, he'd have to make it worth her while. Okay, she was tied up but that didn't mean he could have exactly what he wanted. Not straightaway, anyhow. She looked up and saw his disbelief as she kept her mouth firmly closed. Of course he could force her, but she had a feeling he wouldn't do that. He wouldn't want to seem so desperate.

His face was thunder as he looked down on this stubborn, gorgeous woman. No-one had refused Darius before. Not like this. If she refused because of coyness, it wouldn't be so bad. But this was sheer pig-headedness. Then he had an idea. Hillary saw it flash across his face and he smiled and took away his penis.

Darius crouched down towards her. He looked straight into her eyes and, with an expert hand, reached towards her crotch. His fingers hovered tantalisingly at the outer lips of her vagina. She gasped. He stopped, looked down, and said, 'We'll see what happens now shall we?' And with that his fingers delved inside her and started to explore her deepest place. She felt a certain orgasm rise as he fingered and played with her. Then he stopped.

She howled, 'You bastard! You can't do that!'

'As I said before, I can do anything,' he smirked.

Then just as quickly as he'd stopped, he started again, this time bringing her off spectacularly.

He let her recover for a couple of minutes, then stood up and held his penis once again to her lips. She greedily swallowed him, milking him with her mouth, loving it, feeling as though she was the one in control. Then, in a fit of sudden chivalry he withdrew and rested his aching, throbbing shaft against the soft flesh of her cheek, allowing the powerful jet of semen to soak her hair.

They remained silent and still for some time afterward. Hillary basked in the afterglow of her own orgasm which had erupted from her unexpectedly as he came against her face leaving her dimly aware of the slow trickle of viscous juice running down her neck and shoulder. He was stunned by the quick build up and the ferocity of his release. Only one woman had ever had that effect on him before and that was Ilona.

Suddenly, remembering his promise to Ilona the night before, he glanced at his watch. Damn, she would be waiting for him at the house already. With no time for apologies or regrets he wiped himself with a handful of leaves and zipped up his shorts.

Hillary stared at him. 'What are you doing?'

'I've got to go.' He offered nothing by way of explanation as he untied her from the tree.

Unsteadily, Hillary rose to her feet, rubbing her wrists then bending to do the same to her ankles. It was a mistake to bend forward so quickly but she realised too late. Suddenly she felt light headed, her mind was going blank and her legs had turned to water. She groped blindly at thin air for a few seconds, her lips silently mouthing a plea for help. Darius moved swiftly but it was too late. Overcome by a powerful cocktail of heat and emotion Hillary fell to the ground in a dead faint, cracking her head on a tree root as she fell.

When she came round she was laying on the back seat of Alicia's Mercedes. She turned her head cautiously to see Darius leaning against the side of the car nonchalantly polishing his rifle. Sensing her movement he turned around and smiled down at her. 'I'm glad to see you're alright, you must have had too much sun.'

Hillary struggled to sit up. She looked at her watch – it was half past five, over two hours since she had first bumped into Darius in the forest. It was obvious that he had carried her to the car but she couldn't quite remember how they had passed the time. Darius mistook her look of confusion. 'Do you feel okay to drive?' His voice brought her back to reality.

She nodded automatically which made her head feel as though it were about to split in two. She clasped it in both hands, the pain bringing tears to her eyes. 'I don't think so actually,' she muttered weakly.

Darius shut the car door, went around the back of the car and placed his rifle in the boot, then climbed into the driver's seat. 'Lay down and I'll drive you home.'

As they pulled up outside the house Odile came sauntering out to greet them. With a look of surprise she glanced at Darius and then rushed to the car as she saw him help Hillary to her feet. 'My God, what happened to you?' she said.

Before Hillary could reply Darius spoke, his tone gentle and reassuring. 'It's nothing to worry about, she just spent a little too long in the sun that's all. She fainted in the forest and hit her head, after a good rest she'll be as right as rain.'

Odile thanked Darius and then led Hillary inside the house and straight to her room. Hillary couldn't help noticing that everywhere seemed strangely quiet.

'Alicia and Chloe have gone for a picnic,' Odile explained. She looked embarrassed. 'In fact, Theo and I were just about to go for a walk but if you'd rather I stayed?'

Hillary went to shake her head and then thought better of it. 'No, really, I'll be fine. You go ahead and I'll meet Theo later. All I want to do now is sleep.'

Odile still looked doubtful. 'Are you sure that's wise? You could have concussion.'

'I'm sure, now go have a good time.' Hillary pushed her gently from the room, refusing to acknowledge any further protestations.

As soon as Odile had left she sank gratefully onto her bed and within minutes fell into a deep sleep broken only by dreams of being an innocent wench ravished alternately by the dark, mysterious Lord of the Manor and hoards of pillaging Vikings. When she awoke several hours later she had no real recollection of her dreams, or of that afternoon's encounter with Darius, only a vague feeling of restlessness and an overpowering desire for sexual satisfaction. By the time Odile returned, she was feeling more like her normal self and rushed to meet the renowned Theo. She wasn't disappointed.

Towering over both herself and Odile at well over six feet, Theo was the epitome of African splendour. Big, black and beautiful were the three words that summed him up most succinctly, Hillary decided. His looks were matched perfectly by an air of innate confidence, his movements almost choreographed in their fluidity and grace and his voice sent shivers down Hillary's spine – the carefully enunciated words dripped like treacle from his tongue and formed smooth, dark rivulets of conversation. Hillary fell instantly under his spell.

Far from feeling threatened by Hillary's obvious adoration, Odile was pleased her man was such a hit with her friends – Chloe and Alicia had been similarly impressed when they had first met him. She left him regaling Hillary with stories of Paris and his opinion of French fashion versus British and went to make some coffee. She returned with a tray to find Hillary sitting alone, staring out of the window.

Odile glanced around. 'Where is he?'

Hillary turned around. 'Oh, sorry. I was miles away. He's just gone to use the bathroom.' She nodded in the general direction of the door.

Odile set the tray of coffee down on a side table and began to pour it into three cups. 'You look pensive, is everything okay? Theo didn't say anything to upset you did he?'

'Of course not,' Hillary said, laughing, 'I was just daydreaming, that's all.'

Odile wasn't convinced by her friend's apparent nonchalance. 'Did Darius do something?'

To her acute embarrassment Hillary felt her cheeks redden. 'No, what makes you say that.' She glanced down at her hands as Odile handed her a cup of coffee. 'In fact if it wasn't for him I could still be laying unconscious in the forest.' It was obvious that Odile was intrigued but their conversation was cut short by the reappearance of Theo.

For a second he stood in the doorway, filling it completely; he even had to stoop a little. 'Is this one for me?' He walked over to the table and picked up the remaining coffee up as Odile and Hillary both nodded.

Just then the front door opened and the house was once again filled with a cacophony of voices. Theo looked alarmed.

'Don't panic!' Hillary said, laughing. 'It's only Chloe and Alicia.'

He rolled his eyes in mock alarm and, in one bound, crossed the room and grabbed Odile by the hand. 'Come, ma cherie, we will depart this, this mad-house for a little while.'

Odile laughed. 'We'll go to the pub for a while. Would you like to come Hillary?'

Normally Hillary would have tactfully refused but the sound of Alicia and Chloe screeching at each other was too much for her pounding head to bear. She nodded gratefully. 'I think a hasty retreat is just what *he doctor ordered,' she said, glancing at her watch, 'besides which Gus and Clive should be arriving any time now. They would probably appreciate a bit of time alone to get reacquainted.'

'If you say so.' Odile snorted derisively. 'You forget I've known Chloe and Gus for quite some time, unless he has the sense to bring her something horrendously expensive she'll be nagging him within an inch of his life before he's even had time to pour a drink.'

Hillary smiled ruefully. 'The same goes for Alicia, most of the time Clive can't do a thing right as far as she's concerned.'

The two women looked at each other for a moment and smiled conspiratorially; Hillary put their thoughts into words. 'Thank God we've the sense to stay single.'

Theo didn't comment on her remark but looked enquiringly at Odile who caught his expression and shrugged. He had seen her look at other women that way before and knew from past experience how events invariably unfolded. Nevertheless, he was positive that Hillary was a complete innocent regarding anything outside the realm of heterosexual sex. He felt his pulse quicken, perhaps this would prove to be a most interesting visit after all.

Chapter Five

To Hillary's profound disappointment Gus and Clive arrived just as she was leaving with Odile and Theo, their open-topped cars screeching to a halt either side of the trio.

Clive stood up on the driver's seat and gestured rudely to Gus. 'That's a tenner you owe me, you slow bastard!' He glanced down at Hillary. 'Hi, sis-in-law, where's the old millstone?'

'If you mean your wife, she's in the house.' Hillary nodded over her shoulder, her attitude deliberately off-hand. She knew Alicia had her faults but Clive always managed to rub her up the wrong way, invariably she would end up leaping to her sister's defence regardless of whether she needed it, or even deserved it. Gus wasn't much better but definitely the more bearable of the two – at least she wasn't related to him.

Alicia and Chloe had obviously heard the screech of brakes because they came tottering out, dressed once again as though they were about to attend a cocktail party. For a few minutes the air was filled with the sound of false gaiety. Hillary counted over twenty exclamations of 'darling' and watched amazed as both couples managed to kiss without actually touching.

Then Gus had her in a bear hug. 'Come on, Hilly, tell

us what our ever-loving other halves have been up to all week.' He urged her toward the house with Clive, Alicia and Chloe following close behind.

She looked pleadingly over her shoulder at Theo and Odile but they were laughing.

'We'll leave you to play happy families for a little while and catch up with you later,' Odile called out, winking at Hillary who looked suitably horrified at being abandoned.

Still, there was nothing she could do, her weak protests were drowned out by the loud chatter of the others. They all went inside the Hall and she made straight for the sitting room where she poured herself a stiff drink. Clive and Gus were suitably impressed by their surroundings.

'The chap who owns this must be absolutely rolling in it,' Gus said, rapping his knuckles on the wall as though he knew the difference between a building that was structurally sound and one built of twigs.

Hillary giggled to herself. Gus had filled out a little since the last time she met him and, with his stomach already visibly protruding over his waistband, he was well on his way to becoming porcine.

'What did you say this chap is called, Alix?' Gus asked.

'Darius Harwood.' Hillary interrupted, feeling a slight flutter in the pit of her stomach at the mere mention of his name.

After a couple of drinks she decided that it was quite pleasant having Gus and Clive there as well, particularly as she was unattached. It meant she could sit back and enjoy the floorshow without having to pander to someone else's whims herself. Despite being out all afternoon, Alicia and Chloe had managed to concoct a delicious supper. As she walked into the dining room and surveyed the table laden with fresh salads, cold cuts and a variety of seafood Hillary realised that she hadn't eaten all day and was now starving.

'We found this marvellous little deli just a few miles

from here and the seafood is fresh from the quay,' Alicia explained.

Breaking a crab claw with a decisive 'crack' Hillary immediately thought of Haldane. He was the only person who could take her mind off Darius, but even then she couldn't help wondering what both men were doing right at that moment. She glanced down the table at the two couples; thanks to a combination of good food and a few drinks they had mellowed considerably and were becoming distinctly amorous toward their respective partners. Alicia was sitting pertly on Clive's knee, dropping fresh prawns into his open mouth one by one, while Chloe was suggestively peeling a banana for her spellbound husband.

Since they had begun eating, Clive and Gus had done most of the talking. Apparently they had just invested in a racehorse, each taking a quarter share. Clive explained that a business contact of his had successfully bid for the yearling colt at auction. Then a few months later he found he couldn't really afford it – a couple of friends of his had already expressed an interest in part-ownership so he'd offered to sell the other half to anyone who was interested. After a quick conflab with Gus, Clive had jumped at the chance. 'At the moment he's at a training yard near Newmarket. We're hoping to go down there and take a look at him next week if we can,' Clive said.

'Well I hope we're invited,' said Alicia stiffly. 'I always like to see first hand whatever you've been wasting our money on.'

Clive looked genuinely hurt. 'It's a good investment, Alix, honest. And just think how proud you'll feel standing in the owner's enclosure.'

Hillary couldn't help smothering a smile. He certainly knew how to hit the right note with her sister – Alicia began to glow as the implications of his remark began to sink in.

'We could end up meeting the royal family!' She smirked. 'And we could make a packet. Oh! Clive, you are clever.' She kissed him long and hard, just to show her appreciation.

Chloe was similarly impressed, although less demonstrative than her friend. 'I'll need some new clothes, especially hats,' she warned Gus.

He laughed and patted her hand indulgently. 'That's okay by me, sweetheart, you get whatever you want.' He winked at Clive who smiled back.

Hillary sighed inwardly. Well there were four people who were going to enjoy the next couple of days at any rate; and the nights.

Deciding this was her cue to leave, Hillary pushed her chair back and stood up. 'I promised to meet Odile and Theo at the pub, I'm sure you don't need me around playing gooseberry.'

Gus looked up at her and leered. 'The more the merrier I always say. Ouch! What did you do that for?' Chloe had elbowed him hard in the ribs.

'Don't mind him,' she said to an embarrassed Hillary, a patently false smile fixed to her face, 'you go and enjoy yourself.'

Hillary walked out of the room, grabbed her short, tan, suede jacket from the coat stand in the hall and let herself out into the cool evening air. Under the porch light she glanced at her watch, already nine-thirty; if she didn't hurry the pub would be closing by the time she got there. Fortunately it was only a short walk to the village across the grounds surrounding the Hall, and for as long as it lasted she found herself relaxing in the luxury of solitude in such picturesque surroundings. As pleasant as her walk was, she was pleased to see the welcoming sight of the Baker's Arms pub, its uneven half timbered walls bulging outward over the narrow pavement.

She pushed open the heavy oak door, stooping automatically as she crossed the threshold. Her eyes immediately alighted on Odile, seated directly opposite the doorway. She glanced around and saw Theo standing at the bar, his closely cropped head grazing the low ceiling. He spotted Hillary and pointed to the row of bottles behind the bar. Not wishing to play charades or shout across the crowded room Hillary walked up to him and leaned her elbows on the bar, staring for a while at the rows of bottles.

'I think I'll just have half a lager, thanks.' She smiled up at Theo but her expression froze as she noticed a familiar figure seated alone in the farthest corner of the pub. 'Excuse me a moment, I've just seen someone I know.'

Trying to appear a good deal more casual than she felt, Hillary sauntered across the room. 'Hello, Haldane isn't it, from the chandlery at the quay?' Of course she knew full well who he was but she couldn't be sure if he would remember her. She needn't have worried.

'Oh yes, I remember.' Haldane said, 'You are Hillary?'

She nodded, excitement bubbling up within her.

He gestured to the chair opposite his own. 'Please, join me.'

She sat hesitantly, glancing at Theo who was still standing by the bar holding her glass.

Haldane followed her eyes with his own. 'Oh, I am sorry, you are with someone else. I didn't realise.'

'Yes, no, I mean – ' Hillary stumbled over her words, feeling as gauche as a teenager.

They were interrupted by Theo who placed her glass of lager in front of her. 'Odile and I are going after this drink but perhaps you would prefer to stay with your friend?'

Hillary nodded. 'Thanks, Theo, I'll catch up with you later.'

She raised the glass to Odile who was grinning from ear to ear. 'They are friends of mine,' she explained to Haldane, 'we're all staying at Harwood Hall.'

'Ah, yes, the great Hall. I am impressed.'

Hillary thought he looked anything but impressed, but let the remark pass. Now they were alone she found she had already run out of conversation. For a while they sipped their drinks in silence and before they knew it the bell was being rung for last orders.

'Would you like another?' Haldane gestured toward her empty glass.

Hillary shook her head. 'No thanks, I've already had a couple of drinks and some wine with supper.'

'And you don't trust yourself to have another?'

Hillary thought there was more than a hint of interest in his voice. 'Perhaps,' she said.

'In that case I'll get you a double.'

He stood up, his large frame dominating the small room. Before she could protest he had walked over to the bar and was ordering another round of drinks. He returned with two small glasses filled with colourless liquid. She looked enquiringly at him as he set them down on the table.

'It's Schnapps,' he explained, 'you drink it down in one go, like so.'

He threw his head back and tossed the liquid down his throat in one swift movement. For a second Hillary hesitated, then followed suit. The fiery liquid quickly burned its way down to the pit of her stomach. For a second her body felt weak and she gripped the edge of the table with one hand to steady herself. Haldane reached out and pulled her to her feet, prising her fingers from the table and enfolding them in one large hard. 'Come on, we'll go for a walk.'

It wasn't exactly an invitation, more a command. Hillary didn't feel she could refuse even if she wanted to, which she didn't. Hand in hand they set off in the direction of the coast road, their pace slow and steady, no more than a casual saunter. Every so often Haldane would stop abruptly and point out a particular star or constellation.

'See that star there, the really bright one?' Hillary followed the direction of his index finger, one star glowed much more brightly than the rest.

'Mmm, I see it.' Pretending to crane her neck, she

used the opportunity to lean a little closer into the side of his body. Haldane didn't back off.

'Well, that is the dog star – wherever they are in the world sailors can rely on that star to guide them.'

Hillary nodded sagely. 'Have you sailed much, to many different places, I mean?'

'No, not really.' She thought he looked wistful. 'I was a fisherman not a sailor. I haven't sailed outside the North Sea.'

'I get the feeling you're not very happy working on dry land?'

Without knowing it Hillary had touched upon a raw nerve and Haldane dropped her hand and began to walk off down the road, his head down. Panicking, she ran forward to catch up with him.

'I'm sorry, what did I say?'

He stopped and turned to look at her. 'I think maybe I will go back.'

Hillary wasn't sure what he meant. 'Go back? To being a fisherman, you mean?'

Haldane nodded. 'Yes, that too. But mostly I miss my home. I want to go back to Norway.'

She didn't know how to respond. It was typical really, no sooner did she meet a man she really liked than he wanted to leave the country. What was it about her? She reached out and took his hand again. 'Come on,' she said simply.

They seemed to have reached a mutual understanding. After they resumed their walk Haldane's pace quickened, becoming more deliberate. In no time at all they had reached the quay; it seemed very strange to be there at night, almost eerie. Haldane took a huge bunch of keys from the pocket in his jacket and unlocked the door to the boathouse behind the chandlery. Inside it was pitch black and Hillary groped around blindly for a few seconds until Haldane lit an old oil lamp.

'I have electric lights of course but this is more, more . . .'

'Romantic?' Hillary ventured.

Haldane snorted. 'If it is romance you want then you are with the wrong man, Hillary. I am just a coarse fishermen, remember.'

Hillary laughed at the unintentional pun. 'I think you're an exceptional man, Haldane. Quite wonderful in fact.'

He looked straight at her then, his expression displaying a mixture of emotions. In one swift movement he was standing in front of her and bending forward he kissed her tenderly on the lips. 'Thank you, Hillary.'

She reached upward and clasped her arms around his neck, returning the kiss with slightly more fervour. He tasted of cherry schnapps and smelled of the sea which was an irresistible combination. She could feel her heart pounding hard behind her ribs. She felt engulfed by this man, both body and mind. He held her gently but firmly, one hand in the small of her back, the other cradling her head, despite his size he was so tender, so thoughtful in his demeanour.

Even his tongue was temperate as it explored her open mouth, flickering lightly against her teeth and gums and then sliding gingerly across the inside of her upper lip. Hillary felt her stomach contract as he did this, amazed that he seemed to have discovered an erogenous zone that she never knew she possessed until that moment. She moved her body ever closer to his, clutching his hair in handfuls as her passion for him increased. Her nipples swelled and she could feel them straining to escape the confines of her thin cotton shirt; surely he could feel them too, digging into his chest like two hard little bullets.

Evidently he could. No sooner had the thought left her mind than he ran his hand up her back and around to cup her breast, teasing the nipple between his fingers and thumb. Hillary heard herself groan with pleasure. Tentatively she ran her hands over his shoulders, marvelling at the sheer breadth of the man, the tops of his arms were surely wider and more muscular than her thighs! She could feel the contours of his musculature beneath his thick chambray shirt – oh, God, she fancied she could come just through feeling his body beneath her hands. Now he was massaging both her breasts, although he hadn't attempted to unbutton her shirt. It was exquisite agony, her nipples sending small currents of desire directly to her clitoris. She could feel it swelling and throbbing with pent up desire.

Her legs suddenly felt weak and her body sagged a little, swiftly he caught her and held her until she regained her composure. As soon as he was sure she was okay, Haldane released her and turned to the boat behind him – a small cabin crusier he had recently started to repair. He climbed on board then held out his hand to her and in seconds they were down below in the cabin seated next to each other on a comfortable double bunk. Haldane pulled her to him once again and kissed her, harder this time, with more passion. With one hand he began to undo the buttons on her shirt. Anxious to reveal herself to him Hillary unfastened the last two buttons herself then shrugged the shirt from her shoulders. She sat before Haldane, naked from the waist up, enjoying the look of appreciation on his face as he feasted his eyes on her bronzed, naked breasts with the dark pink tips so hard and swollen.

He covered her breasts with his hands, kneading them with skilful fingers, then he bent his head and dropped a kiss on each nipple. Hillary moaned, she wanted him so badly yet she didn't want the moment to end. With trembling fingers she unbuttoned his shirt, placing her palms flat on his chest and just enjoying the sensation of his bare skin beneath her hands. Then she allowed herself to explore the upper part of his body, stroking and squeezing each new portion of flesh as she encountered it with her fingers.

The tension within her was mounting rapidly, her breathing was shallow, her mind devoid of any thought other than the tumultuous sensations Haldane's deft touch wreaked upon her rapturous body. He rubbed her through the thick denim of her jeans, his large hands pressing the seamed crotch mercilessly against her urgent flesh. Again she fought to release herself quickly from the strictures of her clothing but he stopped her, purposefully removing her trembling hands. There was no possibility of her rushing the moment toward its natural conclusion, Haldane was in control, he made that very clear and, in a strange way, this only served to add to her excitement.

Desperately she massaged his chest with her breasts, almost fainting at the initial sensation of skin against slick, perspiring skin. Still he held her firmly, one large capable hand spanning her naked back, the other grinding rhythmically against her crotch. She threw her head back, her mouth moving in a silent scream, she was going to come. Wordlessly he watched her, his face devoid of expression as hers portrayed a whole realm of emotion.

Gradually her orgasm subsided and she felt herself regain some vestige of composure. She glanced at him and he nodded as though to indicate his satisfaction at her gratification. Now he allowed her to remove her jeans, moving slightly to one side so that he could also remove his own.

For a few minutes they sat side by side, completely naked, not saying a word. Each eyed the other, their eyes feasting on every contour. Almost shyly Hillary allowed her eyes to drift down over his chest and stomach before coming to rest between his legs. She had almost expected his penis to seem small compared with the rest of his body but it was entirely in proportion, just like the rest of him it appeared large and solid and perfectly formed. She sucked in her breath, wondering how it would feel inside her.

He obviously wondered the same thing and had no intention of waiting another second to find out. With one swift movement he reached out and grabbed her, lifting her and turning her around so that she straddled him. The sudden change of pace took her by surprise and she cried out as he pulled her close to him and plunged into her. Wrapping her legs tightly around his waist, Hillary rocked her hips as she tried to in vain to maintain some vestige of control but she was no match for Haldane and after a few seconds she conceded, allowing him to raise and lower her as though she were a doll, a lifeless thing incapable of independent movement.

Liberated from the effort of having to think about her own performance, Hillary found herself carried along on the crest of a gigantic wave. Her whole being was consumed in the fire incited by the golden god whose manhood filled her to capacity. Her hands grappled weakly on his shoulders as he rammed into her, his thigh muscles quivering under her buttocks as he raised his pelvis to thrust ever deeper into her.

From somewhere she heard a sound that was only vaguely human, a deep moaning that could have been the wind if only it hadn't been such a still, balmy night outside. Her throat hurt and Hillary realised, with amazement, that she was the one making all the noise but she was past caring, past everything except drowning in the most monumental orgasm she had ever experienced.

Sensing her growing excitement, Haldane had moved his hands to grip her buttocks, rhythmically moulding them until she was delirious with ecstasy. She bucked wildly, unable to get enough of him yet hardly able to bear what she had, it was exquisite agony.

Mimicking her own response, Haldane gradually reduced the intensity of his caresses, easing Hillary gently into a state of satiated bliss. For over an hour she lay limply in his arms, allowing him to stroke her body gently but unable to reciprocate in any way other than to give a soft murmur of appreciation from time to time. Eventually she glanced at her watch and reluctantly eased herself into a sitting position.

'I should be getting back, Haldane,' she said, groping around for her knickers. 'I didn't actually say I would be out late and my sister tends to worry about me.'

Far from looking put out or disappointed, Haldane smiled and helped her on with her shirt. 'That's nice – to have a family who cares; you should be happy.'

'Oh I am, it's just that . . .,' Hillary glanced down at her hands, embarrassed despite their previous intimacy, then she looked up at his gentle face. 'I hate to leave you like this.'

'Like what?' Haldane gave a little laugh. 'I will walk you back to the Hall and then tomorrow we will go out on my boat.'

'Really?' Hillary's heart leaped. Thank goodness she wasn't just a one night stand as far as he was concerned. She was far from being a prude but she hated one-off sexual encounters as they always left her feeling a little sad and empty. This way, even if things between them didn't progress past the following day, she would at least feel as though they'd given it their best shot.

Walking hand in hand back up the coast road to Harwood Hall, Hillary was glad she had taken a jacket along with her. At that time of night the air was distinctly chilly but it gave her a good excuse to snuggle against Haldane for warmth. When they were within a few hundred yards of the Hall itself Haldane stopped.

'Will you be alright from here?' he asked.

Hillary glanced over her shoulder at the enormous white stone building then smiled up at him. 'Of course I will. Does it bother you that someone might see us together?'

He shook his golden head. 'Not really, but I'd rather not bump into your lovely sister if I can avoid it.'

Looking as surprised as she felt Hillary said, 'I didn't realise you knew Alicia.

'I don't, but that is not her fault, she has been putting in the most extreme effort.' He threw his head back and laughed loudly. 'She keeps coming into the chandlery for one reason or another and I think I know why.'

Hillary frowned. 'She could have a perfectly legitimate reason.'

82

'Yes, she could, but I think otherwise. Perhaps I am too sensitive.'

She almost laughed at that remark, bearing in mind his size and musculature, then instantly remembered his tenderness with her and realised she was being unfair. 'You're almost certainly right, Haldane. I know Alicia only too well and so far she's made no secret of her determination to have some extra-marital fun this summer.'

To her discomfort Haldane now looked interested but any fears she may have had about her sister becoming a rival were wiped out as he enfolded her in his arms, bent his head and kissed her for a long time.

Reluctantly he let her go. 'Meet me at the quay tomorrow morning, as early as you can manage but not later than midday or we'll miss the high tide.'

Hillary nodded happily. She had almost forgotten about going out on his boat. 'I'll be there.'

He kissed her briefly one last time before turning on his heel. She stared after him until his large frame became no more than a tiny speck in the distance, then made her way around the building. As she let herself into the hallway she found everything as silent as the grave apart from the occasional loud snore coming from Gus and Chloe's room. She checked her watch, almost three o'clock, no wonder!

Pausing only to use the bathroom, she stripped off her clothes and stood before the mirror, trying to see herself as Haldane had seen her. Gently she cupped her breasts, playing thoughtfully with the still swollen nipples, amazed that fresh tremors of desire automatically disturbed her recently satisfied body. With regret she wished she was back at the boathouse.

Moving to the bed she lay down and spread her legs, one hand reaching down to stroke the sensitive bud that throbbed with agonising intensity. As she massaged herself she tried to concentrate her mind on Haldane, imagining that her fingers were his, yet she was surprised to find Darius's image intruding on her fantasy. For some inexplicable reason she felt her desire increase with a vengeance and thrust her fingers desperately inside herself. Without withdrawing her hand she got to her knees on the bed, rocking her pelvis backwards and forward as she plundered her own body, rubbing and probing until she thought she would go mad from her desperate need for release.

As her knees dug into the mattress a flicker of memory crossed her mind – her nostrils filling with the scent of pine, she imagined she was being overpowered but loving it. Masculinity was very near and she never felt more feminine. Suddenly, she remembered it all – meeting Darius, being tied to the tree trunk, his hands on her breasts and her welcoming his cock in her mouth.

'Oh, God,' she moaned aloud, arching her back, stretching herself wider, jamming herself full with her own fingers until her body conceded defeat and exploded like a volcano in an orgasm of such ferocity that her thrashing body forced the heavy wooden bed away from the wall.

Gradually the waves subsided. Removing her fingers gently she wiped them on the sheet. Across the room her reflection was of a wild woman, flushed with exertion. Her whole body was throbbing and tingling and still desperate for more. If only Haldane had been there, or Darius. But she was alone.

Regretfully she slipped her naked, slightly stiffening body between the cool sheets. Gingerly she put her hand between her legs, the whole area was still tingling and a little sore. Imagining it was a man's hand that rested protectively upon her sex she drifted off into a deep, dreamless sleep.

In another part of the house, Darius was pouring glasses of champagne. The woman seated next to him smiled her thanks and sipped slowly.

'I see what you mean about her,' she said.

The woman inclined her head toward the TV monitor linked to Hillary's room. Having just watched the

84

young woman pleasure herself with such wild abandon, she felt an equal mixture of envy and arousal. Tentatively she stroked her own nipples through the thin gossamer of her gown.

Darius watched her, admiration on his face. 'I thought you were the past master at self-gratification.'

The woman smiled. 'Mistress, Darius. I am the past mistress. You are the master.' She turned her head and looked deep into his eyes, her expression speaking volumes. Deliberately, she parted the front of her gown, exposing her full, heavy breasts to his appreciative gaze. She reached out and brought his head down, until his lips brushed against her nipples, moaning softly as his mouth started upon a familiar journey.

Hillary came to slowly the next morning and lay for several minutes just staring blissfully out of the window, her mind devoid of all thought. Then suddenly she remembered her date with Haldane and glanced at her watch in panic. With relief she saw it was only eight-thirty, plenty of time to shower and make herself beautiful for him. A little later, as she stood thoughtfully in front of her wardrobe, she realised she had no idea what people wore to go sailing. In fact, she wasn't even sure if Haldane's boat was a sailing boat, or if it had an engine and all mod-cons like the one they had made love in the night before.

After some consideration she decided to wear her newest plain white bikini under a pair of navy cotton shorts and a white T-shirt. She glanced at her reflection in the mirror, pleased that she looked suitably nautical. After slipping her feet into a pair of matching navy and white canvas sneakers and stuffing her bag with a few essential items, she made her way to the kitchen which was surprisingly busy for that time of the morning. Gus and Clive were both seated at the table drinking black coffee, whilst Alicia and Chloe bustled around them in matching pink and white gingham aprons, both looking uncannily, not to mention uncharacteristically, like Doris Day. Hillary failed to stifle a smile.

Chloe looked up, her face flushed from the heat of the grill. 'Oh it's you. Well don't just stand there grinning, tell me how you know when sausages are cooked.' She held out a pair of kitchen tongs, obviously expecting Hillary to simply take over.

Hillary sighed inwardly, it was typical of Chloe to try and pass on the chores as soon as someone else more appropriate put in an appearance, although this time, Hillary decided, she could jolly well stew in her own bacon fat. 'I'm sorry, I'd love to join you for breakfast but I've arranged to meet someone and if I don't get a move on we'll miss the tide.'

She looked anything but contrite and Alicia didn't miss the overt reference to sailing. She stopped slicing mushrooms and stared hard at her. 'Who are you meeting exactly?' Alicia asked.

Hillary blushed, knowing that she'd deliberately goaded Alicia into asking the question, yet also aware that her sister was interested in Haldane herself. She didn't know if it was simply her imagination working overtime but everyone seemed to be staring hard at her, poised for her answer. She felt trapped, like a rabbit caught in the headlights of a car. Just then, to her intense relief, Odile and Theo came into the room, momentarily stealing everyone's attention. Within seconds she managed to make her excuses and flee.

She walked quickly without stopping, or pausing to glance behind her, until she reached the main road, then and only then she slackened her pace a little. She felt as though she had been awake for hours although it was barely a quarter to ten by the time she reached the quay. She glanced around. Haldane waved to her from the chandlery and gestured that he would be only a few minutes. Smiling and nodding she found a clean spot on the harbour wall and sat down to wait for him. As usual children were armed with string and bacon to fish for crabs, while fishing boats came in and out of the quay at regular intervals to unload their haul.

She studied a number of empty boats which were moored together to her right, wondering if one of them belonged to Haldane. She hoped not as they all looked pretty unseaworthy even, to her inexperienced eye.

'Don't worry. None of those belong to me.'

She started in surprise. Haldane had come to stand in front of her without her realising it.

He put out a hand, hauled her to her feet and led her around the quay to another group of boats. He stopped alongside a particularly nice looking cabin cruiser and pretended to pipe her aboard. Smiling broadly, she reached out with her left foot until it came into contact with the top step then, with a slightly unsteady wobble, she climbed down to the deck. She glanced around, surprised at what she saw – instead of the rough fishing boat that she'd expected him to own the cruiser was sleek and ultra modern. Sliding perspex doors protected the outside helm, which looked more like the cockpit of an aeroplane, and a similar door led to the lower deck, in addition, the perimeter of the upper deck was bounded by squashy white leather seating – all in all it was the last word in luxury. Gradually she realised she was feeling a little wobbly on her feet and sat down gingerly; despite her best intentions to prove herself a hardy sailor she was already feeling a little queasy from the gentle swell of the ebbing tide.

Haldane noticed her unsteadiness and her worried expression. 'Try not to think about being aboard a boat. Just concentrate on the fresh air and the scenery.'

At that moment all Hillary could think about was the overwhelming stench of fish which had not bothered her at all when she had been standing on dry land.

Haldane unlocked the door to the saloon. 'Perhaps you would prefer to go below and make us something to drink while I get us on our way?'

Hillary nodded gratefully and immediately felt much better on the lower deck which seemed more like a house than a boat. Just like the rest of the cabin cruiser, the accommodation was very comfortable and modern with a lounge, a dining area, a well equipped galley and a separate cabin which offered more luxury than her bedroom at the Hall. Just when she thought she couldn't be more impressed by her surroundings she opened what she assumed to be a wardrobe door only to find it concealed a fully equipped en-suite bathroom. Now she felt well and truly at home, and not at all seasick.

When she returned to the upper deck, a mug of steaming coffee in each hand, she was surprised to find that they were already well out to sea. With a slight feeling of trepidation she looked around her. 'I can't see any land, Haldane.'

He smiled down at her, accepting his mug of coffee gratefully and taking a huge gulp despite the fact that it was boiling hot. 'You will soon. I am taking us to a secluded little cove, there we can swim and sunbathe to our heart's content. No-one will disturb us.'

Hillary felt brazen. 'If there's no-one around to bother us I don't think we should waste our time sunbathing.' She slipped a hand down the front of his shorts and grasped his thick cock. Immediately it began to stiffen.

Now Haldane was looking unsteady. Without saying a word he released his grip on the wheel, placed his coffee mug on top of a white plastic tool box, then turned around and kissed her hard, his tongue snaking around her open mouth. With a grin of satisfaction he released her. 'I have a favourite English word that describes you exactly.' He smiled down at her as her mind whirled through all the possibilities but she gave up.

'What word, Haldane?'

He paused then ran his hands down her body, outlining the swell of her breasts and the curve of her hips. 'Luscious. You are luscious, Hillary, luscious, luscious, luscious.'

Each time he said the word he kissed a part of her:

her eyelids, her earlobes, her neck, until finally he bent his knees and ran his tongue slowly and lasciviously down her throat to her cleavage. She felt her nipples stiffening in response, arching her back she cradled his head against the soft pillow of her breasts feeling the first stirring of a familiar fire being kindled deep within her.

Although eventually he had to replace one hand on the wheel, they stayed locked together, like two pieces of a jigsaw, until land appeared on the horizon.

Chapter Six

*H*illary watched in fascination as Haldane moored the cruiser to a buoy and then dropped anchor just for good measure. She was surprised by the location as they were still quite a way from the beach.

He noticed her confused expression and laughed. 'From here we swim.' Then a thought struck him. 'You can swim, can't you?'

Hillary laughed and nodded. 'Yes, of course.'

'We can use a dinghy to get to shore if you prefer.'

He pointed toward a clear polythene pack which contained a deflated dinghy and a pair of oars but Hillary was already stripping off her shorts and T-shirt. Then she kicked off her shoes and stepped up onto the edge of the boat. Haldane watched her appreciatively, a sudden rush of lust almost overtaking him as she stretched and flexed her lithe, athlete's body, her deep suntan providing the perfect background for the tiny white G-string bikini she had chosen to wear. He reached out to her but her eyes were already staring into the distance at the deserted cove of golden sand spread out tantalisingly under the bright blue summer sky. The backdrop of dunes shimmered in the heat haze.

'I'll race you,' she said, laughing, and diving into the deep green water without a backward glance.

For a brief moment she regretted her action because the shock of hitting the cold water took her breath away and she almost panicked. Fixing her eyes determinedly on the shore she struck out in a fast crawl. After she had swum over halfway she dared to look behind her. The cruiser still bobbed gently on the tide but Haldane was nowhere to be seen. She flipped over onto her back so that she could catch her breath and also look around but every time she thought she could see Haldane's golden head rise above the waves it turned out to be a clump of seaweed, or a piece of driftwood. Her heart was pounding and not simply from the effort of her swim, she was becoming genuinely concerned.

In a split second she reached a decision. She flipped back onto her stomach and began swimming as fast as she could. As soon as she reached the shore she would find a telephone and call someone for help, get out a lifeboat or something to search for him. In all honesty she didn't know what one was supposed to do in these situations. Just then she felt something brush against her left leg, then the right. She kicked furiously, assuming that her legs were becoming tangled in a clump of seaweed – thank goodness she had almost reached the beach. Suddenly something grabbed her by the ankle, Hillary was horrified, were there sharks in these waters?

Her heart was hammering in her chest and felt fit to burst. She sensed that whatever had touched her was swimming directly below her thrashing body, just the sort of encouragment sharks liked best she seemed to recall. Despite her determination to survive she just couldn't swim any faster, or smoother. Suddenly, without warning, there was a huge surge of water directly in front of her and she stopped swimming, alarmed. This was it now, certain death. When she saw what had caused her panic she screamed aloud, but with anger not fright.

'Haldane, you, you – stupid bastard!' She trod water frantically, desperate to lash out at him and make him pay for scaring her half to death.

Looking far from remorseful, or hurt at her outburst, he trod water in front of her. 'I don't know what came over me, I just couldn't resist.' He tried hard to smother a grin. 'I'm sorry, Hillary.' He held out his arms to her and, despite her fury, she swam into them straight away.

'I could have drowned, Haldane.'

'No way. I was there to save you remember?'

'You were the cause, you, you . . .'

'Stupid bastard?'

'I'm sorry I called you that. You're not stupid.'

'Or a bastard,' he added, laughing.

'No. But you're a sod.'

With a sudden twist of her body, Hillary broke free from his grip and splashed him furiously a couple of times. Then she struck out for the shore, swimming as hard as she could for the few remaining yards until her feet touched the sea bed. As she glanced behind her Haldane was hot on her heels. The laughter caught in her throat as she desperately tried to put some distance between them but it was no good, with a tremendous lunge he caught her legs in a rugby-style tackle and brought her down into the surf, covering her body with his own, using his size to pin her down so that she couldn't even move let alone escape his clutches. Not that she particularly wanted to she decided instantly.

His lips met hers in a salty kiss, his hands holding her wrists as she squirmed uselessly beneath him. Her bikini top had risen up above her breasts during their struggle and now her naked orbs grazed his chest. As his hardened cock jabbed against her pubic mound she became acutely aware that he was becoming aroused by their tussle.

Pushing her heels into the sand she urged her pelvis upward, grinding herself against his obvious arousal, at the same time returning his kiss with renewed passion. Suddenly she stopped kissing him, a thought occurring to her.

'Haldane,' she mumbled. 'Perhaps we should swim back to the boat if we're going to carry on like this.'

'Why? There's no-one to see us.' He pushed himself away from her, allowing her to look around them at the deserted beach. As far as she could see there was absolutely no-one to disturb them.

'I've often dreamed of something like this,' she said. Then, recognising an opportunity to wriggle out from under him, she moved quickly, knelt up and took off her bikini, tossing it onto the beach well away from the water's edge. With a slight gasp of surprise she noticed Haldane was already naked. She looked him up and down boldly, her eyes feasting on his magnificent physique.

'I take it you've been here before?'

He nodded enthusiastically, perhaps a little too enthusiastically, she thought ruefully, desperately seeking to resist the urge to ask him for exact numbers. Although she believed in making the most of the here and now, she didn't like to imagine that she was just another summer conquest as far as he was concerned. Sensing her uncertainty Haldane stood up and took her in his arms, kissing her with a passion tempered by tenderness.

A little reluctant at first, she gave herself up to his kiss, standing on tiptoe in an attempt to even out the difference in their heights. By this time the sun was high in the sky and Hillary felt it beating down remorselessly against her naked back and buttocks, or at least on whatever portion of flesh Haldane's large roaming hands left uncovered. Her desire for him had returned with a vengeance and she gripped his gluteus muscles with both hands, feeling them quiver under her fingers as she stroked and kneaded.

Pressing against her gently, he forced her to bend her legs and gradually lay back down on the golden sand. Idly staring up into the deep blue, cloudless sky she sifted the scalding granules between her fingers, her tension mounting as Haldane parted her legs and began to explore her. With skillful fingers he stroked the most intimate parts of her body, gently spreading her labia so that he could tease her clitoris until it swelled and throbbed almost unbearably with pent up excitement. She felt uncomfortably hot, not just from the sun but burning inside with lust for the man who now thrust his fingers deep within her, pressing secret magic buttons to trigger her release.

Moaning with ecstasy she ground her buttocks further into the sand and urged her legs still wider apart. Every so often a slightly larger wave would creep up the sand and lap soothingly against her tender, pulsating flesh, cooling down the heat of her desire and washing way the juices that oozed from her each time Haldane probed and fondled.

The tide was obviously coming in, she thought absently, feeling the cool surf all around the lower part of her body and the sand shifting beneath her buttocks as each wave ebbed away. The sea seemed to mirror her own mounting passion, grouwing and swelling, engulfing her body as she thrashed and gasped with a mindless craving for the man who stimulated her to the brink of madness.

She couldn't take any more torment, she had to have him.

'Haldane.' Her voice was hoarse with passion.

Without disturbing his rhythmic rubbing and probing, the Norseman raised his head and looked straight into her lust-glazed eyes. She realised she had never seen him look more serious and began to tremble from a mixture of nervousness and pent up excitement. Reaching out with both arms she pulled him on top of her, urging her hips upward, rubbing her moist sex up and down the length of his rock hard shaft. For a few moments he gave himself up to the motion of her pelvis, his head thrown back in enjoyment of the sensations her manoeuvres created. Then, reluctantly he pulled away, groping about in the sand beside him until his fingers found their objective.

Turning her head slightly, Hillary saw that he was holding a sort of plastic money belt and trying desperately to undo the zip pocket using only one hand. She reached down his body, twisting slightly at the waist until she was able to cup his testicles in her hand, feeling the weight of them as they rested in her palm.

She started to squeeze slightly, compressing and releasing rhythmically until a low moan broke from his parted lips. Moving her fingers lightly up the shaft of his penis and over his glans, her fingertips came into contact with a small droplet of semen. Gently she circled the very tip of his swollen cock, using the viscous fluid to provide lubrication as she stimulated the most sensitive part of him.

Feeling the juices surging and gathering beneath her fingers she could tell that he was almost about to ejaculate. She stopped caressing his sex, moving her hand back up his body instead, gathering granules of sand between sticky fingers. Now they were both more than ready for each other. Despite her distracting caresses, Haldane had managed to extract a condom from his belt and offered it to her so that she could put it on him. Hillary smiled weakly, waggling her tacky, sand encrusted fingers in reply.

'I shall do the honours then,' he said, grinning.

With a deliberately ostentatious gesture he ripped open the packet, reached between their perspiration soaked bodies and a split second later plunged deep into her, making her gasp with surprise. At the same moment they were engulfed by a particularly large wave and she clung to him, wrapping her arms and legs around his naked body like a limpet. He thrust hard, pushing his hands underneath her buttocks and raising her pelvis to meet his. With a small grunt he pulled her over until she was on top of him, then over again until they were rolling madly in the surf, their waves of passion matched only by the incoming tide. It was like nothing she had ever experienced before. It wasn't just the location or the beautiful weather that made it different but their wild, abandoned style of coupling. It was as if no-one and nothing else in the world existed, just herself and Haldane lost in a single, endless moment of unrestrained desire.

When they came it was with a sudden overpowering violence that wracked their bodies, both of them calling out in unison, their voices carried away on the tide. For a while Hillary lay beneath him, happy that he was still inside her body, content with her own satisfied desire. To her surprise he didn't feel too heavy as he lay on top of her, his head touching hers, his palms beneath her buttocks. It seemed right that they should be there together. Somehow, despite his size, their bodies seemed to fit each other perfectly.

Hillary let out a small sigh of pleasure. 'This is heaven.'

'You can say that to me again,' Haldane mumbled, his accent sounding thickly.

As he spoke Hillary felt the vibration of the words through his body and then she sensed a growing, stiffening feeling inside the tight, wet chamber of her sex. His reaction came as no real surprise, already her desire for him was flickering and growing again. It seemed she just couldn't get enough of him, or he of her. Fortunately, they had no reason to do anything other than make love time after time, after time. Only a few times did they take a break from each other's bodies to swim. For the rest of the day they explored each other's bodies, or lay naked and spread-eagled on the golden beach, warm blue waves lapping gently around their ankles, their salty bodies drying quickly under the relentless rays of the summer sun.

For his part, Haldane couldn't look at her, or lay stretched out next to her like that, without wanting her as much as she wanted him. Slowly, deliberately, his hands would drift cross her willing flesh, stroking and caressing her until she either begged him to take her, or she straddled his glistening, muscular body and took control of the situation herself, riding him mercilessly until their cries of ecstasy echoed around the dunes.

For that day they were free spirits, a part of the earth

like sand and sea and cliffs, yet they were also a part of each other. Over and over again they aroused and satisfied an endless lust, feeling pleasanly satiated for only a short while until a new wave of passion encompassed them.

Like all good things it had to come to an end and by late afternoon Hillary became uncomfortably aware that once again she had fallen into the trap of underestimating the sun's power which now was making her feel a little dizzy. They hadn't eaten or drunk anything for hours and she couldn't help recalling the way she had felt the day before when she had fainted in the forest. Feeling as though the movement would use up all her strength she raised herself on one elbow and rested her chin in the palm of her hand. She stared at him as he lay next to her, one arm flung carelessly across his face to shield his eyes from the strong sun as he dozed contentedly.

'Haldane?'

He didn't look at her but grinned broadly. 'Surely you're not horny again?'

Hillary laughed. 'Yes, of course, but that's not what's bothering me at the moment.'

He moved his arm and squinted at her. 'What's up?'

'I think we should go back to the boat, the sun's beginning to get to me.'

Haldane was immediately contrite, he rolled over to face her and reached out with one large hand to push the hair back from her reddened face. 'You do look a bit hot. Are you feeing okay?'

She nodded but the movement made her head pound.

He saw her wince and looked at her with concern. 'Come on.' He stood up, then put out a hand to help her to her feet.

Bending down to pick up her discarded bikini he stuffed it in the empty pocket of his waterproof belt. It's entire contents, a generous number of condoms, were dead and buried in the sand. Despite her temporary discomfort Hillary laughed ruefully, hoping he had more supplies on board the boat or it would be a very chaste end to an entire day of blissful lovemaking.

Strapping the belt around his waist, he took Hillary's hand and they padded across the beach and then waded out into the sea until it reached Haldane's waist and Hillary's chest. In direct contrast with the heat of the day the chill water took their breath away. After a few seconds their bodies became accustomed to the change in temperature and they both struck out with strong, determined strokes for the cabin cruiser which bobbed enticingly on the high tide about a quarter of a mile from the shore.

Hillary felt invigorated by the cool waves and enjoyed her swim back to the boat, almost forgetting how ill she had been starting to feel. However, as soon as she was safely on board her legs buckled under her and she had to cling on to Haldane for support. In no time he had unlocked the door to the saloon and was guiding her through the living quarters to the comfortable aft cabin, as he called it. His deep green eyes swept over her wan face with a look of genuine concern and he told her to make herself comfortable, promising to return as quickly as possible with something to eat and drink.

Feeling grateful for such luxury, Hillary made the most of the en-suite bathroom, revelling in the powerful spray of the shower as it removed all traces of sand and sea-water from her skin and hair. A quick check in the medicine cabinet revealed a tube of after-sun lotion and she had just finished anointing her body with the soothing lotion when Haldane reappeared carrying a heavily laden tray and a couple of bottles.

'How are you feeling?'

'Oh, much better now, thank you.' She felt strangely shy all of a sudden and pulled the towel tighter round her body in a delayed attempt at modesty.

'Good, I am glad.'

Haldane masked a smile, thinking to himself that he would never understand women. He set his burden down on the small dressing table, unscrewed the caps of the bottles and poured them each a long glass of iced mineral water and a smaller glass of very cold white wine. Hillary downed her glass of mineral water in one long draught, thinking to herself that it was the most welcome drink she had ever been given. Then she accepted the glass of wine from him, turning the stem between her fingers as she eyed the tray of food greedily; after all those hours of swimming and making love she felt absolutely starving.

Once again Haldane had excelled himself. Not content with a rudimentary sandwich or a wilting salad, he had prepared a feast of grilled peppers, sardines and mackerel, crisp lettuce, cherry tomatoes, crusty bread and plump black and green olives.

At first they tucked in with gusto then, feeling replete but still very greedy they fed each other with titbits, allowing the olive oil and juice of the tomatoes to run down their chins, stopping every so often to lick each other's bodies clean, all lingering inhibitions thoroughly relinquished.

Hillary stretched luxuriously on the comfortable double bed, loving the way Haldane's eyes followed her every move with undisguised lust. He was certainly the most insatiable man she had ever met and his sexual appetite was contagious, making her feel more wanton and desirable than she had ever felt before. Opening her legs in invitation she moaned contentedly as he buried his golden head between her quivering thighs.

God, but he was good with his mouth! She closed her eyes and spread her thighs still further in blissful abandon as he flicked the tip of his tongue over the swollen bud of her clitoris. She felt his fingertips flutter over the sensitive flesh of her inner thighs, sending a bolt of white hot desire through her entire body. His breath caressed her swollen flesh, cool on the inner rim of her vagina as he spread her open as wide as possible. Seconds later his tongue was inside her, twisting and turning until she heard herself scream aloud from the delicious torment.

Now he spread her labia wide, pulling back the delicate membrane of skin that protected the very core of her desire. His tongue was upon her there, lapping her flesh, sliding over her demented sex until she clutched his hair and thrust herself against his mouth. Using only his fingers to stimulate her, he rose to his knees between her thighs and watched her face as she rode the waves of her climax.

By the time they returned to harbour it was quite dark; although Hillary was not wearing her watch she guessed that it was after ten. Haldane walked her back to the Hall but this time didn't hesitate to take her right up to the front door. They hovered on the doorstep like guilty teenagers until the porch light went on signaling the imminent appearance of one of her holiday companions. Poised to beat a hasty retreat, Haldane was stopped in his tracks by the sudden appearance of Gus and Clive in the driveway who were obviously returning from the pub.

'Well, well, well, if it isn't my sexy sis-in-law and her muscle-bound boyfriend.'

Hillary groaned inwardly but fixed a smile determinedly on her face. She looked up at Haldane who was still hovering on the point of flight. 'Take no notice of him, he's a self-confessed slob.' She flashed a pointed glance at Clive's waistband.

The front door opened behind them and both Alicia and Chloe jostled for the doorstep. Ignoring the return of her husband, Alicia looked straight at Haldane. 'Well, hello,' then she added, 'I didn't realise you knew this man, Hillary.'

Smothering a grin, Hillary put her arm around Haldane's waist in an almost protective gesture. 'Haldane, I'd like you to meet my sister, Alicia, her friend, Chloe and their husbands, Clive and Gus.'

Haldane flashed a white toothed smile that encompassed all of them. 'I am most pleased to meet you.'

Blushing prettily as though his words and smile were directed at her alone, Alicia stepped back, almost knocking Chloe off her stiletto-clad feet in the process. With an expansive wave of her arm she ushered him through the doorway. For a second he hesitated then, with a slight push from Hillary in the small of his back, stepped across the threshold, inadvertently brushing against Alicia as he did so. Hillary caught both their expressions and sighed inwardly, there was no possibility of keeping Haldane to herself now.

Odile and Theo were watching TV in the sitting room as they entered. Odile gave Hillary an enquiring glance then smiled up at Haldane. 'Hi, I'm Odile and this is my boyfriend, Theo.'

Haldane gave her a genuine smile in return and shook hands with Theo. In no time at all the two men were deep in conversation, Paris being Haldane's favourite European city. Hillary sat down next to Odile, the two girls exchanging a look of surprise. Neither would have expected their lovers to strike up such an instant rapport as they both seemed so different. In appearance alone they were complete opposites of each other.

Alicia seemed more than slightly miffed that Haldane was ignoring her presence and strove to gain his attention, pouring him a drink, deliberately bending forward in front of him to turn off the television so that her short skirt revealed her shapely legs and the enticing curve of her buttocks.

Nevertheless it was all to no avail. Theo revealed that he had recently discovered a passion for boats and consequently he and Haldane were now well and truly buried in discussing the merits of various styles of cabin cruiser. At one point Haldane invited Theo aboard his own cruiser and Hillary blushed at the memory of their last encounter there only a few hours previously.

Chloe was quick to pick up on Hillary's expression. 'So tell me Hillary, what have you and Haldane been up to all day? You weren't at the beach.'

Giving what she hoped was a convincing illusion of

physical exhaustion, Hillary explained that they had spent the day sailing and swimming.

'You certainly caught the sun,' Alicia observed, handing her sister a tumbler filled to the brim with iced gin and tonic.

Stifling a yawn with the back of her hand, Hillary stretched. 'Did you have a good day?'

'So, so,' Alicia mumbled. 'It's Fearn's weekend off so we decided to play happy families at the beach.'

'What's wrong with that? It sounds lovely.' Hillary had just received a surreptitious wink from Haldane and felt she could afford to be magnanimous.

Chloe and Alicia sighed in unison. 'It's Clive and Gus,' Alicia explained. 'They just don't seem to be able to grasp their roles.'

Chloe nodded vigorously. 'Would you believe Gus flatly refused to hire a speedboat?'

'And Clive kept complaining that the sun was too hot, or the sand too gritty, I mean really,' Alicia added, with more than a tinge of annoyance. 'All either of them really wanted to do was spend the day playing golf, or in the pub.'

They both flashed a similar look of pure contempt in their husbands' direction. Unable to help herself Hillary giggled aloud. Both women seemed to forget that these weekends were the sum total of their husbands' summer holidays.

'It's alright for you, floating around deserted coves with your hunky boyfriend but we've been having a really miserable time,' Alicia complained.

'Excuse me,' Gus interrupted. 'But we didn't have to come here this weekend at all. If we're so terrible we'll just go off and find something else to amuse us won't we, Clive?'

Hillary shifted uncomfortably and glanced at her sister. Realising that she had overstepped the mark Alicia sought to redress the situation. 'We've got a lovely day planned for tomorrow though, haven't we?'

She nodded at Chloe who quickly plastered a happy

smile on her face before turning to look at Gus and Clive. 'That's right, we're all going to the beach again but this time we're going to buy a dinghy.' She caught Haldane's eye. 'Perhaps we could get one at your shop, do you open on a Sunday?'

Haldane gave a small smile. 'I'm sure I could make the effort for two such lovely ladies.'

Suddenly overcome with protectiveness for their wives, Gus and Clive walked across the room and stood close to them.

'That's very decent of you.' Gus looked anything but grateful. He clearly didn't relish the prospect of leaving his wife alone during the week in such close proximity to Haldane. He glanced overtly at his watch. 'I think it's time for us to hit the sack if we want to get an early start in the morning.' He ran a finger tantalisingly across Chloe's bare shoulders and she shuddered although Hillary couldn't be sure if it was from desire or repulsion.

'Not just yet sweetie, I'd like another drinky-poo.' She held out her glass but Haldane had taken the hint and was already rising to his feet.

'I must be going now.' He said, turning to Theo. 'Come to my yard anytime and I'll show you that thing we were talking about.'

Hillary was intrigued but didn't get the opportunity to ask him what it was he had to show Theo. Haldane shook hands with everyone in turn and as he made for the door, he waved to her. 'Don't worry about seeing me out, Hillary. I will call you soon.'

She sat down again reluctantly and made do with blowing him a kiss. Even though they had made love countless times that day she still yearned to be close to him and to nestle in the safety and comfort of his arms. As soon as they heard the front door close, Gus and Clive stood up, making a great show of stretching and yawning. They looked expectantly in the direction of their wives, who both blatantly ignored them.

Odile and Theo stood up. 'Goodnight everyone.'

They left the room hand in hand, their body language speaking volumes.

Alicia sat next to Hillary on the sofa. 'By the way, you'll never guess who turned up here yesterday.'

Sensing that the women were about to indulge in a long bout of gossip, Clive and Gus reluctantly decided to go to bed alone. Hillary turned to look at Alicia whose face was lit up with excitement.

'Prince Andrew?' Hillary struggled to keep the sarcasm from her voice.

Alicia laughed. 'No, silly, of course not.

'I wish,' muttered Chloe.

Hillary grinned. 'Okay, if it's not a member of the royal family, I give up.'

'Fearn's brother and a woman, his mother I think, judging by her age,' Alicia added a mite bitchily.

'Oh, really, how interesting.' Hillary didn't know what else to say. She couldn't understand for the life of her why the appearance of Fearn's brother should be so earth shattering.

Chloe whispered conspiratorially. 'You don't understand, Hilly darling, he is gorgeous.'

'Oh, I see.' Now she got the picture. 'What's he like then? how come he's so gorgeous? Fearn's not that outstanding to look at.' Hillary instantly regretted her words, she didn't mean to sound cruel.

'No, I know she isn't.' Chloe smiled thinly. 'That's one of the reasons I like her. Anyway,' she continued, 'Fearn's brother is very good-looking, tallish, darkish and very Scottish.'

'Well, he would be,' Hillary commented dryly. 'How old is he?'

'Young,' Chloe asserted.

'Early twenties, if that,' Alicia interjected. 'Probably more your age, Hills,' she added gloomily.

'Hardly, Hillary said. 'Anyway I've got my hands full at the moment.'

Alicia allowed her head to drop back, she stared

silently at the ceiling for a minute or two. 'So I noticed, you lucky bitch! When did that happen?'

Feeling slightly embarrassed, Hillary looked into her half empty glass. 'I bought that toy windmill from his shop, remember?' She blushed.

'Was that all it took? I never realised he was such an easy target.' Alicia sounded almost bitter.

'No, not really, in fact I said something to upset him that day. We actually met properly yesterday evening in the pub.'

'No wonder you came home so late. Odile just said that you'd bumped into a friend and decided to stay on at the pub for another drink.'

'Is he that well built all over?' Chloe was more to the point.

Hillary blushed harder and nodded. 'What about Fearn's brother? We were talking about him, remember.' She was desperate to change the subject.

'Oh, we haven't seen him naked yet, have we, Alix? He only arrived this afternoon for God's sake.' Chloe sounded positively shocked.

'I didn't mean that.' Hillary laughed. 'Can't either of you get your minds above a man's waistband even for a second?'

Chloe and Alicia looked at each other, then they turned to Hillary genuinely dumbfounded. Alicia said, 'No, what's the point? Unless they keep their wallets higher up of course.' The two women broke out into gales of unrestrained laughter.

Hillary couldn't help but laugh along with them. Their mercenary attitude often shocked her but deep down they were harmless and both totally incorrigible. The ice well and truly broken between them, the three women relaxed into no-holds-barred girl-talk covering all aspects of their favourite subjects – men, sex and money. Consequently, it was well after two o'clock by the time they staggered, still laughing and more than a little worse the wear from alcohol, to their respective bedrooms.

Collapsing gratefully on her own bed, Hillary lay and stared at the ceiling for a long time. She had spent a wonderful day with Haldane yet ever since she had returned to Harwood Hall she hadn't been able to get the recurring image of Darius's dark, brooding good looks out of her mind. Talking about sex with Chloe and her sister had stirred up a maelstrom of emotions that she was hardly aware existed within her.

She thought back to the day before, when a mysterious, unseen person had caressed her breasts on the beach and then there was the still hazy memory of her strange encounter with Darius in the forest. It seemed incredible that those events had taken place less than thirty-six hours previously.

Desperately trying to blank out the unwelcome sensation of longing and desire for a man who obviously didn't have a conventional approach to sex and relationships, she stripped off her clothes and climbed between the cool sheets, eventually drifting off to a shallow, shadowy dreamland.

For once, Hillary was not the subject of Darius's regular nightly intrusion. Ilona had expressed an interest in one of her friends, the auburn-haired girl with the large, ebony skinned boyfriend. He glanced at the older woman who sat with rapt attention in front of the monitor, her fingers absently stroking her own sex as she followed the couple's movements.

'My God!' she exclaimed to Darius, not taking her eyes from the screen. 'Can you imagine what it must be like to have that beautiful man inside you?' She was referring of course to the Frenchman whose cock now rested upon Odile's quivering buttocks. At the moment it looked as though he was debating between one of two orifices.

Darius felt his own sex harden – he was certainly not averse to a little anal exploration of either sex.

'Look, Darius, look!' The woman urged him closer to the screen, her voice eager. 'See how beautifully their bodies contrast, she so delicate and pale, he so huge and black.' She sat back in her chair and smiled dreamily. 'Oh, I would love to paint them. Do you think they would pose for me, Darius?'

Darius shook his dark head, the blue of his irises so dark at that moment that they looked almost black. 'I honestly don't know. They are my guests remember, not simple village folk who will do anything I tell them.'

The woman pouted. 'I wish you wouldn't talk about your villagers that way, most of them are not simple by any means.'

Placing a placatory hand on her shoulder, Darius zoomed the camera in closer to the couple on the bed by means of a remote control panel. 'You know I didn't mean it like that.'

To Darius's slight disappointment, Theo had chosen to take his girlfriend in the conventional way, ramming his huge shaft into her vagina from behind, urging her forward so that she rested her forearms on the top of a wooden chest of drawers, the pale globes of her buttocks thrust high in the air to receive him.

The woman watched open mouthed, moaning slightly as she parted her own legs, stroking herself more forcefully. She looked up at Darius. 'Won't you help me out here?' She pleaded softly in her soft Scots burr.

Darius shook his head, his expression stony. 'I'm not in the mood, Ilona. Besides,' he added, glancing at her fingers as they slid fervently between her fleshy sex lips, 'I like watching you do it.'

She opened her mouth to speak, thought better of it, then decided to go ahead anyway. So what if she risked incurring his wrath, he wouldn't take her tonight anyway. 'Your father would have obliged. He was always in the mood.'

As she expected, Darius's expression darkened a little. 'My father was an old man, he had to take it when he could,' he said, cruelly.

The woman flinched at his words, removed her hand

and closed her legs primly, all desire extinguished in a flash. She searched her mind desperately, determined to hurt him in return. 'I expect Torran will soon be saying the same thing about you to some young girl.' By the look of hurt and anger on Darius's face she saw she had hit the target.

But he recovered quickly and delivered a scathing retort. 'You forget. Torran is not my son, he is yours. The bastard product of your relationship with my senile old father!'

She refused to allow him to hurt her in return. 'You forget so quickly, Darius.' She smiled triumphantly. 'Your father wasn't so senile that he forgot to add that all important codicil to his will, leaving the Caithness house and half his disposable income to myself, Torran and Fearn.' She stood up and glared down at him. 'Don't overstep the mark, Darius, or I may just take Fearn away from here and withdraw my support completely, then you'd be forced to sell your precious Harwood Hall.' With a toss of her elegant, dark head she left the room, leaving an uncharacteristically subdued Darius to ponder the seriousness of her threat.

Chapter Seven

*I*t seemed strangely quiet when Hillary awoke the next morning. No shuffling of slippered feet, no frantic flushing and tooth-brushing and, most noticeable of all, no shouts, whines, or streams of vicious invective from either Alicia or Chloe. For a second she wondered if she had woken up in the wrong house, or if they had all suddenly decamped in the night and left her there alone. Then she heard Clive's deep tones and lay back against her pillow with relief.

After a few moments of contemplation she threw back the sheet and pulled on her bathrobe. Walking down the stairs she noticed that the hallway looked as though World War Three had broken out. She eyed the overflowing bags, picnic baskets and numerous items of beach equipment, then looked enquiringly at Clive as he shuffled out of the kitchen, a mug of coffee in one hand and a cigarette in the other. Seeing Hillary there he glanced guiltily at the curl of smoke rising from his right hand.

'Christ, don't tell Alicia please, Hillary.'

'I wouldn't dream of it, Clive. You're a grown man and you can do as you please.' Hillary personally detested cigarettes but didn't feel she had the right to preach to others.

He looked relieved. 'I wish Alix was as tolerant as you, she won't allow them in the house.'

Hillary glanced around them. 'Where is she now – Alix I mean?'

'She's getting dressed and Gus just said Chloe's putting on some make-up so it could be quite some time before we actually go out.'

'I can imagine.' Hillary giggled. 'I can't quite envisage Chloe stepping foot outside the door without her full war paint, not even to go to the beach.'

Clive nodded his agreement, puffed on his cigarette and raised his mug of cofee. 'There's plenty in the pot if you're interested.'

'Mmm, yes please.'

Deciding that she liked Clive when her sister wasn't around to goad him, she followed him back to the kitchen, her nostrils twitching automatically at the aroma of fresh coffee. They sat down at the kitchen table. Clive lit a fresh cigarette and they sipped their coffee in companionable silence for a few minutes.

'Hillary?' He cleared his throat nervously.

'Yes, Clive?' She looked up, surprised to see him looking so serious all of a sudden.

'You – you would tell me, wouldn't you? I mean, if?' He seemed to be having great difficulty forming each word and his face was bright red with embarrassment.

Hillary patted his hand and she spoke gently. 'I would tell you what?'

He took a tentative sip of his coffee and several huge drags on his cigarette. 'If Alix was having an affair. You would tell me, wouldn't you? I mean you'd be honour bound to, being my sister-in-law and all that, wouldn't you Hilly?'

The words tumbled from his lips in a rush and he looked pleadingly at her, almost like a little boy. Hillary felt compassion toward him but she couldn't forget what Alicia had said about him screwing everyone at work either.

She sighed and raised her eyes to the ceiling hoping,

she supposed, for divine inspiration of some kind. 'I would, Clive.'

His face brightened and he took another, more controlled, sip of his coffee.

'But,' Hillary added quickly, 'it would really depend upon the circumstances.'

It was a lame reply and she knew it, although her brother-in-law appeared to be satisfied with her response.

'I suppose you'd have to be certain,' Clive said. 'I mean, you wouldn't want to risk destroying our marriage for no reason.'

She sighed again, more deeply this time. She recognised a no-win situation when she saw one and she knew full well that Clive and Alicia were doing a good enough job of destroying their own marriage without any help from her, or anyone else for that matter.

'That's right Clive, no need to worry.' She patted his hand again, then downed the last of her coffee and stood up. 'I'm going to get dressed myself now.'

He nodded absently, lighting yet another cigarette. Out in the hallway Hillary bumped into Odile, she too raised her eyes when she saw the clutter all around them.

'I take it they're all going out for the day?' She commented dryly, inclining her head toward the stairs.

Hillary giggled softly. 'Shh. Alicia and Chloe are already up and Clive's just in the kitchen.'

'Oh.' Odile put a finger to her lips and grinned. 'Are you going out with Haldane again today?'

'We haven't made any arrangements.' Hillary looked despondent for a moment. 'What are you and Theo planning to do with yourselves?'

Odile gave a little shiver of excitement. 'We're going for a trip in a hot air balloon.'

Hillary was immediately envious. 'You lucky things!'

'You can come with us if you want, I expect they can squeeze you in.' The young woman offered generously.

'It's a lovely thought.' Hillary did feel genuinely

tempted but the last thing she felt like doing was playing gooseberry to two such obvious lovebirds as Odile and Theo.

'You sound as if you're not going to accept.'

'I'm very grateful for the offer Odile, believe me, but . . .'

'But you want to hang around the house in case a beautiful, blond Norwegian comes knocking, I know.' Odile laughed, assuming she had all the answers.

Hillary didn't bother to correct her. 'You never know,' she said smiling. 'Anyway I fancy being really lazy today, just sunbathing out on the patio, all alone.'

'Whose going to be all alone?' The voice belonged to Alicia. She and Chloe were coming down the stairs, their arms filled with more things and the pair of them looking as though they were planning to take a second holiday.

'Do you really need to take all that stuff?' Hillary was incredulous.

Before either of them could answer, a male voice interrupted. 'My God, what's going on here?' Gus appeared looking around in amazement at the mayhem. In no time at all he had stacked the necessary equipment by the front door and made everyone, with the exception of Odile and Theo, assemble in the sitting room.

Hillary felt he ought to be given due credit for his organisational skills if nothing else and, thanks to Gus, she was soon waving them off in two cars as they embarked on their second family day at the beach. Peace at last, she mused gratefully.

For a while she mooched around the house in her bathrobe, idly flicking through a few magazines, trying out a couple of new hairstyles in front of her dressing table mirror and finally showering and dressing in yet another minuscule G-string bikini, this time in a bright electric blue.

She had toyed with the idea of going out after all. Perhaps to wander down to the village and stop at the pub for a drink, or even carry on down to the quay.

Although she hardly liked to admit it to herself, she was anxious to bump into Haldane again and she felt more than a little nervous about spending the day at Harwood Hall alone. Giving herself a mental shake she wandered into the kitchen and fixed a jug of heavily-iced Pimms, taking care to slice the fruit into even, manageable slices.

She carried the jug, a glass, her sunglasses and a few magazines out to the patio and set them down on a small wooden side table next to a comfortable sun lounger. Shielding her eyes from the glare of the sun she looked up at the sky, sighing with pleasure at the unbroken expanse of clear, deep blue. Remembering her suntan oil she stepped back inside the house. To her surprise when she returned there was someone else seated on her sun lounger. At the sound of her footsteps he jumped up guiltily but Hillary had already spotted him and she guessed he must be Fearn's mysterious brother.

'Hello.' She gave him what she hoped was an open, friendly smile.

His voice was soft and lilting as he spoke. 'I thought everyone had gone out.'

'Not everyone.'

For some inexplicable reason Hillary didn't want him to assume that she was completely alone at the Hall. She eased herself down on the sun lounger and looked around for a second seat. His eyes followed hers and they both homed in on a small, folding chair propped up against the wall to the kitchen garden. He crossed the patio in a couple of strides, picked up the chair and shook it open.

Sitting down some distance from her, he surveyed his surroundings in silence. Hillary groped around unsuccessfully for something else to say and when nothing came, gave up and uncapped her suntan oil instead. For several minutes she concentrated on oiling her arms and legs then she turned to him, surprised to see that he was staring at her, a blank expresion on his face.

'What part of Scotland do you and Fearn come from, er, er . . .?' She realised she hadn't asked him the most basic question, his name.

'Torran.'

'Oh, Torran, that's very unusual.' She couldn't help wondering why such a young man should make her feel so gauche. As Chloe had estimated, he only appeared to be in his very early twenties.

'It's a traditional Caithness name, so's Fearn for that matter. That's where my sister and I are from you see, Caithness – in Scotland,' he added.

Hillary smiled. 'They're lovely names, both of them.' Then she added, 'Are you older than Fearn?'

He nodded. 'Three years.'

She did a rapid calculation, at some point Alicia had mentioned that Fearn was only nineteen, so that meant he was twenty-two. Pouring herself a glass of Pimms she offered the jug to him.

'I'll get you a glass,' she offered but he shook his head.

'If it's all the same to you I'll have a beer.' He stood up and walked across the patio, through the kitchen garden to the main house. A few minutes later he returned with a can of Budweiser.

Hillary glanced at the can and laughed. 'I don't know why but I just assumed you'd come back with some obscure Scottish brew.'

'Not likely, it's all pretty bad. I prefer this stuff.'

He let his head fall backward as he took a long draught of the cold beer and Hillary took the opportunity to have a proper look at him. He was certainly good-looking but not in the conventional sense. All his features were exceptionally well defined but each so strong that they seemed to clash, rather than complement each other. He also looked quite different depending upon the angle from which she viewed him. On one side his face seemed soft and round, almost childlike. Yet from the opposite profile his face was almost entirely composed of angles, with a sharp brow, a pointed jutting chin and a well-chiselled nose.

One feature which was consistent was the amount of dark hair he sported – from collar-length tousled locks, thick silken eyebrows and eyelashes, down to a generous layer of stubble. From where she was seated she couldn't see the colour of his eyes but even from a distance she could see they were genuine, smiling eyes and his mouth too was slightly up-turned at the corners and generous, with full, blood-red lips. After a quick assessment, Hillary decided that despite his slight air of mystery she liked him and had nothing to fear.

She drained her glass and poured another, enjoying the way the seemingly innocent cocktail snaked its fiery way down her throat to the pit of her stomach, igniting small sparks along the way. Torran still didn't appear inclined to indulge in idle conversation so she put on her sunglasses and settled her head back against the headrest, turning her face up to the sun.

Every so often she would sneak a look at the young man from between half closed lids, the sunglasses covering her voyeurism. She was slightly disappointed to note that he seemed intensely interested in his newspaper, reading each page with careful deliberation so that it was a good half an hour before he turned over to the next.

What she didn't realise was that he saw her looking at him and as soon as she closed her eyes he would return to observing her, his young eyes raking her near-naked body with undisguised longing. Presently, lulled by the soporific combination of heat and alcohol, she drifted off into a light, dreamless sleep. Torran smiled to himself and put down the newspaper, now he could allow his eyes and his imagination full rein.

Ever since he had arrived at Harwood Hall he had been assailed by overwhelming feelings of unrequited lust. The two women who met him at the entrance, the uptight blond and the other one, Chloe, had shown more interest in him in the space of five minutes than the handful of girls back in his own village had ever exhibited. Of course, these women were older, richer and more sophisticated but it didn't alter the fact that he wouldn't have to make all the running with them, or risk having his face slapped for attempting to steal a kiss, let alone anything more physical.

He removed his jacket and leaned back in the chair. This one was a bit different to the other two, he had recognised that straight away. She was slightly younger for a start and less, less . . .? He groped around in his mind for the right description, less 'tarty' he supposed, for want of a better word.

But also he sensed that he could really talk to this one if he wanted to, about important things like life and ecology – anything. He would have been shocked if he'd known she was a teacher – he hated teachers as a rule. They came under the heading of authority and he despised authority of any kind. At heart he was a rebel, a rebel without a brew he grinned ruefully to himself, shaking his empty beer can, the sound of the ring pull rattling against the sides until it roused Hillary.

It took a few moments for her to come to and remember where she was. A split second later she remembered Torran and glanced over to where he'd been sitting. His chair was empty. With a slight feeling of regret she looked at her watch, it was just after midday. This time, she decided, she wouldn't be caught out in the noonday sun.

Rising awkwardly from the low sun lounger she noticed first Torran, making his way back through the kitchen garden and then, coming from the opposite direction, the tall, rangy figure of Darius. Her heart skipped a beat at the sight of him. Although, to be honest, the sight of both men sent small darts of desire shooting through her. She gave herself a mental shake,

116

wondering if she was simply becoming a nymphomaniac.

Torran arrived a second or two before Darius and automatically sat down again in the same chair. With a deliberately casual air he opened the fresh can of beer, noting the interaction between the girl and the man he detested most in the world, his half-brother.

Wishing that this time she was wearing something a little less revealing, Hillary stepped forward to greet Darius politely. 'This is a pleasant surprise.' She genuinely meant it.

Darius almost smiled, trying hard not to stare at her scantily clad torso. 'I came to check that you are fully recovered.' He glanced in Torran's direction and raised an eyebrow enquiringly. 'I hope you are not pestering our guests, you know the converted wings are out of bounds to you?'

Hillary eyed the two men, feeling slightly embarrassed. 'It's okay, I invited him.' She stared challengingly at Darius, aware that there was more than a little friction between the two men.

Torran stood up. 'I should be off,' he said, but although his body seemed to be leaving, his voice was unenthusiastic.

Recognising his unwillingness to go and nervous at being left alone with Darius, Hillary was quick to intervene. 'No, please stay.'

Torran nodded his thanks and sat down again. Darius glowered but said nothing. Desperate to break the ice, Hillary asked Torran where he worked.

'Most of the time I work on the estate.' He glanced around and sipped his beer, looking at Darius who nodded imperceptibly. He continued. 'Although I'll be spending the next couple of weeks working at the Caithness glass works near here. I'm going to be training some of the new apprentices.'

'Oh, of course.' Hillary remembered seeing Caithness signs on the way from King's Lynn. 'And as you're

117

from Caithness in Scotland you know all about blowing glass?'

'Something like that.' Torran smiled. 'Caithness babies are not born with a glass blowing tube in their mouths, you know. I had to train for four years and I'm still learning now.'

'Pardon me, I stand corrected.' Hillary waved her arm in the general direction of the kitchen. 'I'd like to get out of the sun for a while, would either of you like a cup of tea, or something stronger perhaps?'

Both men nodded and followed her into the house. Darius accepted her offer of a cup of tea but Torran shook his can of beer.

'This'll do me for now, thanks,' he said.

As she waited for the kettle to boil, Hillary couldn't help sneaking a glance at the two men seated at the kitchen table, wondering what their connection was, if any. Both were equally dark and quite sinister in their own way and although Torran seemed much more open and friendly than Darius, Hillary suspected he had a dark side that could be quite frightening.

Darius, of course, was just a complete enigma as far as she was concerned. Mostly serious and unsmiling she felt he also harboured innumerable secrets. It seemed unlikely but, if it wasn't for the striking difference in their accents, Darius and Torran could almost be taken for father and son, she thought.

Under Darius's firm insistence, Torran opened up about himself, regaling them with stories of his childhood and the village where he was brought up and was currently bemoaning the lack of female company in both his home village and Harwood.

'That's one of the drawbacks to living in a close-knit community,' Darius was saying. 'You can't go around deflowering the local virgins wihout everyone knowing about it.'

A slight flush rose on Hillary's cheeks but Torran blushed even harder and in that instant she realised that for all his macho swagger and bravado he probably hadn't had much experience with girls, or with women at any rate.

'You need a special dispensation from the Pope just to kiss one of them.' Torran laughed ruefully and glanced at Hillary.

Suddenly their eyes met and she felt as though the room was receding and Darius along with it. All she seemed able to focus upon were Torran's serious, hazel eyes, the irises mottled with muted colours like pieces of broken glass – Caithness glass, she mused thoughtfully.

She had tied a sarong around herself when they'd entered the house, feeling the need for a little modesty but now she felt as though the brightly coloured material was restricting her somehow, stifling her body when all she wanted to do was throw off her clothes and make love to Torran like he'd never been loved before. All of a sudden she experienced a primitive urge to show him how real women enjoyed sex, not little village girls bound up by tradition and inhibition.

She knew he sensed it and felt that he could almost read her mind. Then she caught Darius staring at her too and realised, with a deep feeling of shock and embarrassment, that he could also see inside her head and translate her most basic, carnal thoughts. Whatever Torran thought he could see there, Darius knew for certain.

As if to torment her, Darius stretched out a hand and stroked his finger down her bare arm. 'You're developing quite a tan. Those who scoff at the idea of holidaying in Norfolk just aren't in the know, are they?'

Unable to speak, Hillary shook her head. She couldn't bring herself to look up at Torran, nor Darius. His finger was burning a path across her shoulder.

'Have you been away on holiday yet, Torran?' She felt desperate to keep the conversation going.

'Not away, no, I always spend my holiday weeks back home.'

Despite herself, Hillary was incredulous. 'Do you mean you've never been abroad?'

The young man shook his head. He didn't seem particularly bothered by his lack of worldliness. She thought about all the countries she had visited but then remembered that she hadn't really started to travel until she was in her twenties.

'There's plenty of time I suppose,' she muttered. Darius had stopped stroking her much to her disappointment.

They were silent for a few minutes then, as if on cue, they all looked at their watches. Hillary laughed nervously, wondering who would be the first to leave. Neither man moved an inch.

'Shall we go back outside?' Hillary suggested to no-one in particular.

Darius and Torran rose from their seats, both waiting for her to lead the way. She found another garden chair for Darius and resumed her own seat. Uncapping the bottle of suntan oil she began to anoint her limbs all over again. Both men followed her movements with their eyes but said nothing, each lost in their own private thoughts. A few minutes later they were startled by the sound of a car in the driveway.

Hillary cocked an ear and said, 'That sounds like Odile and Theo. They've been ballooning you know.' She smiled at Darius as he was the only one of the two men who had actually met Odile before.

As Odile walked out of the kitchen door onto the patio Torran sat up straight – he hadn't met this one before and she looked worth meeting. With her long red hair she looked a bit like the girls back home but much more sophisticated. He rose and offered her his chair. Suppressing the urge to smile at his chivalry, Hillary introduced them.

'Chloe and Alicia told me you had arrived yesterday but I was otherwise engaged.' Odile blushed prettily, causing Hillary to stifle another smile. By all accounts Odile had done very little but make love to Theo ever

120

since he had arrived – in fact it was a miracle that they'd actually gone out for the day.

At that moment, Theo, the object of this passion, appeared in the doorway holding a bottle of Mexican beer. 'Anyone want a beer?' He waved the bottle in the air then looked straight at Torran who just sat open mouthed.

Hillary couldn't help wondering if he had ever seen anyone quite as striking as Theo before, there couldn't be that many black, Parisian men in the wilds of Scotland. Odile beat her to the introductions this time. Neither Torran nor Darius had met Theo previously.

After ten minutes or so of small talk, Darius rose to his feet. 'I hate to break up the party but I still have some work to do, please excuse me.'

Hillary glanced at her watch for the umpteenth time that day. Surprised to note that it was almost five o'clock she said, 'I hadn't realised it was so late. Chloe and Alicia should be back soon.'

She wasn't sure if it was the thought of Chloe and Alicia that alarmed him but Torran jumped to his feet too. 'I must be going too. I promised to meet some friends at the pub,' he said.

Hillary sighed inwardly. Only a short while ago she had been enjoying the company of two very sexy men and now they were both about to leave. The prospect of an evening at home suddenly filled her with gloom and she was almost tempted to ask Torran if he had any objections to her accompanying him to the pub. She looked up but he was already halfway across the vegetable garden and Darius was nowhere to be seen.

As it turned out, the evening was not as bad as she feared. Considering they had been forced to spend the whole day together, Chloe, Alicia, Clive and Gus were in remarkably good spirits. They had brought some take-away Chinese food with them and as soon as she started to help Alicia unwrap each dish, Hillary realised how hungry she was. Perhaps it was because Gus and Clive were due to leave early the next morning but

Alicia and Chloe were on amazingly good form, making remarks that were genuinely witty instead of a thinly disguised bitch about someone they knew, or even each other, and treating their husbands with easy affection.

Hillary looked around the table happily. Odile and Theo had returned to their room 'for the last time for ages,' as Odile tearfully pointed out. But the other two couples were there, as large as life, laughing and joking and taking every opportunity to include her in their fun. After dinner Gus suggested a game of Trivial Pursuit and, being by far the most well informed of the group, Hillary won easily.

'You cheated!' accused Gus genially, leaning back so far in his chair that Hillary was afraid he would topple over.

'How could I?' She laughed in response.

'Easy,' he leaned forward again, drawing her to him conspiratorially, 'you spent all day reading the questions just so you'd win.'

'Aah, you found me out Gus, I give in.'

'Yes, I hear that's quite a common occurrence for you.' A deathly silence fell over the room and Hillary looked up to see who had spoken. It was Darius.

'I let myself in,' he explained, inclining his head toward the open kitchen door. 'You were all having such a good time I didn't really want to intrude.'

'Nonsense, you're very welcome.' Alicia fluttered around him like a bird of paradise, albeit one that was a little worse the wear for alcohol.

As Alicia pulled out a spare chair and poured him a glass of wine, Hillary eyed him thoughtfully over the rim of her glass, she was still smarting at his remark and wondered what he had meant by it.

He glanced in her direction and their eyes met, his smiling face suddenly becoming very serious. She tried in vain to hold his gaze but faltered and looked down at the table. The others had returned to cracking jokes and every so often Darius would interrupt with one of his own. Only Hillary remained silent. There was no

122

point trying to question him while there was so much activity going on around them; she would have to wait until they were alone. Oh, God! A strange trembling started deep in her belly just at the thought.

She knew she was drinking too much but she couldn't help herself, she felt so nervous in Darius's presence. Occasionally she would glance up at him and catch him staring at her, at other times it seemed he was the life and soul of the small gathering. She glanced surreptitiously at Chloe and Alicia. He was certainly the centre of attention of every other woman in the room at any rate.

'I met Torran by the way,' she blurted out suddenly, her voice sounding strangely loud even to her own ears.

'Oh did you? Isn't he lovely?' Chloe sat down next to her, ignoring the look of annoyance on Gus's face.

Hillary took a large sip of wine. 'I quite fancied him.' She giggled and almost fell off her chair.

Darius looked like thunder. 'I would say that boy needs a girl of his own age, wouldn't you?' He looked at Clive and Gus for support.

Alicia laughed throatily. 'We know exactly what he needs.'

Chloe snorted rudely at her remark and Hillary blushed hard. She desperately wished she hadn't mentioned Torran. Now Chloe and Alicia had grasped the subject with both hands, taking it in turns to describe just what they would do with him given half a chance.

Hillary couldn't bear to look at Darius because she was so embarrassed, and she felt incredibly sorry for Clive and Gus. It was obvious from their expressions that their wives didn't perform half the antics with them that they claimed they would love to do with the young Scots lad. Just as their imaginations were becoming far too outrageous, Darius stopped Chloe and Alicia in mid flow.

'Actually, ladies – well all of you really.' His sweeping glance took in Clive and Gus as well. 'I came to invite you to a party, or at least to give you prior warning. I

123

daresay you'll get an official invitation from my secretary.'

Alicia and Chloe looked at each other and grinned. Chloe clapped her hands. 'Oh goodee! I love parties. When is it?'

'Next Friday. I'm holding it here. Well not here exactly,' he amended quickly, noticing Alicia's look of panic. 'It will be in the main Hall, the part that's usually closed up.'

Despite her drunken and confused state, Hillary couldn't help feeling excited at the prospect of a party, especially one that was almost on their doorstep and where Darius would be the host. 'I'll come,' she slurred, nodding her head sagely.

'What a relief for all of us.' Darius's tone was tinged with sarcasm but when she looked up she noticed, with profound relief, that he was no longer glaring at her. She forced her lips into something resembling a smile in return.

Darius stood up. 'I must be off now. Thanks for the drink.' He nodded at Chloe and Alicia who simpered and giggled, then he turned to Gus and Clive. 'I hope we'll see you at the party, I know you spend the week in London but as it's on a Friday?'

'We'll be there, mate,' Gus assured him, the influence of liquor causing his carefully controlled accent to slip a little.

'Wild horses and all that,' confirmed Clive, raising his glass in Darius's direction.

It seemed to Hillary that Darius took all the spark from the evening when he went. She stared remorsefully into her glass of wine, wishing she didn't feel so drunk. She could hear Chloe and Gus rowing in the hallway and even Alicia was subdued.

'I think I'll go to bed.' Hillary stood up and wobbled a little, holding on to the edge of the table for support.

Clive locked the back door and Alicia turned off the light, mumbling, 'We'll sort out this mess in the morning.'

Hillary looked at her sister closely, wondering if she was referring to the remains of their Chinese meal, or the additional damage her ill-guarded remarks about Torran had done to her marriage.

'I'll help you,' muttered Hillary, falling through the open doorway to her bedroom. Under the circumstances, it was just as well she didn't hear Alicia's reply.

Back in his own room, Darius cursed himself for his unguarded remark. It wasn't like him to allow his feelings to show, or for that matter, to even have such feelings. As far as Hillary was concerned it had not been a good day for him. First of all he had found her in the garden, half naked and flirting with Torran. Then, to add insult to injury, the village grapevine had finally reached his ears. Knowing the object of his desire had already been well and truly taken by the remarkable Norwegian, Haldane, was almost too much for him to bear.

For over an hour he had paced the great Hall ranting and raging, until Ilona had begged him to stop. Finally, she forced him to listen to the voice of reason.

'Be sure, Darius, that their coupling was a passing thing. You are the one destined to break her in properly.' And it was she who, in a flash of inspiration, suggested the party. 'Leave the details to me Darius, just make sure she attends.'

He nodded, his expression concealing the churning excitement he felt within him. This would be the first such party Harwood had seen for many, many years – the last had been held by his own father and resulted in the final subjugation of Ilona herself.

He considered the older woman thoughtfully, remembering what he could of that momentous occasion almost twenty five years ago to the day. His father had been old then, already well into his sixties and he, Darius, had been at a particularly awkward age. Caught between childhood and manhood and beset by puberty, he had been a maelstrom of conflicting emotions. Ilona then must have been maybe nineteen or twenty – about the same age as Fearn but far more knowing even then.

He hadn't actually been allowed to attend the party, of course, but he would never forget the indefinable air of tension that hung over the house as the preparations took place. And then, on the great night itself, he had sneaked into his father's study, drawn back the heavy drapes intending to stare out at the clear night sky and found himself confronted, not by a window but a two-way mirror and beyond that the answers to all the questions that had tormented him thus far.

Throughout the long night, as the band played and the sound of laughter and the occasional smashing glass filled his ears, his eyes were glued to the bed beyond the mirror and the scenes enacted on it. Men with women, women with women, men with men, one at a time or all together. His introduction to the mechanics of sex was comprehensive and the best eduction a boy of his position could receive.

Darius shook his head and rephrased the thought, it was the second best. The best of course was when his father ordered Ilona to teach him personally. Just returned from their honeymoon, although his father and Ilona were never formally married, Ilona had sent for him. Using a maid to prepare him first she had gently instructed him in the ways of the flesh. He shivered, remembering that night as if it were yesterday, and his cock stirred in response to the recollection. Glancing at Ilona's profile as she stared thoughtfully out of the window he suddenly felt as though he were fourteen all over again. It was time to relive some memories.

Chapter Eight

Not surprisingly, Hillary awoke the next morning with a raging hangover and a terrible feeling that she had done, or said, something she would regret. Gradually the events of the previous day slowly unwound in her memory like a video film. She paused when she got to the part where Darius arrived for the second time, replaying the scene over and over again in her head. Whatever he had meant by his opening remark, it was obviously a thinly veiled reference to her sexual exploits. Well, damn him, the arrogant bastard! What business was it of his?

Her anger gave her fresh impetus and she leaped from the bed, showered and dressed in yet another bikini and sarong, this time in black and white. She found Alicia and Chloe sitting in the kitchen looking strangely subdued. From the silence that permeated the rest of the house she guessed Clive and Gus had already left for London.

Pausing only to pour a cup of coffee for herself, she sat down next to her sister. 'Cheer up, Alix, he'll be back next weekend.'

'I know. That's why I'm miserable.' Alicia managed a wobbly smile and Hillary grinned back.

Chloe piped up. 'Actually we're doubly miserable because we've arranged to meet them mid-week.'

'Really, why?'

'It's that damned horse,' Alicia explained. 'In a fit of temporary insanity Chloe and I agreed to go and take a look at it. It's stabled somewhere near Newmarket and Clive and Gus are going to meet us there on Wednesday.'

'Oh,' Hillary said, surprised. Flicking through a copy of Horse and Hound occasionally was about as near as Alicia had ever got to horses.

'Well, we do have a teensy-weensy ulterior motive,' Chloe admitted.

Hillary laughed. 'I thought there had to be something else. Go on then, what is it?'

'Well.' Alicia was all smiles now. 'Do you remember the boys mentioning that they only owned half the horse?'

'Yes. The other half is owned by a pair of brothers isn't it?'

'That's right, well,' Alicia said, pausing for effect, 'this is what they look like.'

She placed a photograph on the kitchen table and Hillary leaned forward to take a proper look. It depicted a very impressive looking horse and what looked like a couple of Argentinian polo players, both kitted out in tight white breeches that didn't leave much to the imagination.

Hillary used her hand to wipe imaginary perspiration from her brow. 'Phew, that's a pretty impressive sight.'

'I'll say,' said Chloe, grabbing the photograph and practically drooling over it. 'And the racehorse looks quite healthy too.'

'Boom, boom!' All three laughed in unison.

'You have to admit, these are seriously gorgeous guys, are they not?' Alicia tried to keep her laughter under control.

Nodding enthusiastically, Hillary took another look at the photograph. 'Are they polo players?'

'No, not as far as I know anyway. I think they just fancy themselves in the clothes.'

'I'm not surprised, I fancy them in the clothes. I just can't wait to see what they look like out of them as well.' Chloe looked deadly serious.

'Well, I'll bet you can't wait for Wednesday.'

Alicia smiled at Hillary, then she had a thought. 'Why don't you come with us, Hillary? It'll be a good laugh and we can all go in my car and stop at a pub or something on the way. What do you say?'

'Oh, I'd love to.'

She felt quite excited as she'd only ever seen race-horses on television. Funnily enough, she didn't feel particularly thrilled about meeting the two brothers. They looked far too vain and sure of themselves and, anyway, she had enough man problems to be going on with.

'They're Italian by the way.' Alicia nodded at the photograph. 'Not Argentinian or anything. Their names are Carlo and Guido if I remember rightly.'

Suddenly their attention was distracted by the sound of footsteps outside on the patio, the back door opened and Torran's silky dark head appeared.

Alicia and Chloe were both instantly flustered by his unexpected arrival and made a great show of adjusting their bathrobes and combing their fingers through their tousled hair – only Hillary had showered and dressed so far that morning.

Torran smiled disarmingly, his eyes twinkling. 'I'm sorry to disturb you, ladies, but I was wondering if you needed anything from the village? I'm just on my way down there, you see.'

Hillary spoke for all three of them. 'No, thank you. I think we have everything but it was nice of you to offer,' she added graciously.

'Okay, see you later.'

It seemed incredible how much more relaxed and cheerful he seemed compared with the day before. Of course, as soon as he had left Alicia and Chloe soon found their voices.

'Isn't he lovely?'

'Did you see that bum?'

'. . . and that hair?'

'. . . and those lovely eyes?'

Hillary let them carry on for a few minutes, then coughed politely.

'Oh, sorry, Hillary, we were miles away.' Alicia took a sip of her cold coffee. 'Ugh, disgusting, I'll make some fresh.'

Choe glanced at her watch. 'No time darling, Odile will be back in a minute and she'll expect us to be ready to go.'

'Go? Go where?'

'Out, Hills. We're all going out for the day. We're on holiday, remember?' Alicia spoke to her as if she were a small child.

'Am I included in this trip?' Hillary asked.

'Of course, why wouldn't you be?' Alicia looked surprised that she could think anything else.

'Well, it's just that you didn't actually mention it to me, that's all.' Hillary grinned.

'Really?' Alicia looked at her, incredulous. 'I thought we all discussed it last night.'

Hillary felt instantly sheepish. 'Oh, in that case perhaps you did. I was well out of it, if you remember.'

'So you were,' mused Chloe. 'What was all that about between you and Darius by the way?'

'I don't know what you mean.' Hillary began uncomfortably.

Just then, to her intense relief, they were interrupted by Odile who, having returned from taking Theo to the station, was now looking forward to their day out together.

'Oh, come on you guys!' she wailed, looking dismayed at Chloe and Alicia's dishevelled apearance.

'Two secs, Odile, honest.' Alicia dashed out of the kitchen, followed by an equally guilty looking Chloe.

The young woman sat down heavily at the kitchen table and Hillary poured her a cup of coffee. She sipped it then smiled gratefully at Hillary.

130

'Thanks, I needed that.'

'Did Theo get off alright?' Hillary asked, wondering if it was safe to mention his name.

'Yes,' Odile sighed. 'I will miss him terribly. But,' she added, brightening, 'soon I will be going to Paris to join him and we will have the most wonderful time together.'

Hillary smiled wistfully, it was nice to see two people who were genuinely happy together.

Amazingly, Chloe and Alicia reappeared before Odile had the chance to finish her coffee.

'Are you going to come with us, Hillary?' Odile looked enquiringly at her.

'I don't even know where you're planning to go.' Hillary laughed.

'Shopping in King's Lynn, or perhaps Norwich, followed by a film, followed by dinner, followed by – who knows what?' Chloe ticked off each item on her fingertips.

'It sounds hectic.' Hillary grinned. 'I think I'll stay here.'

'Don't you ever get bored with your own company?' Chloe asked, amazed.

'I think perhaps Hillary is hoping not to be alone for very long.' Odile winked at her.

'Oh, that big Norwegian you mean.' Alicia's tone was deliberately dismissive. 'Well, don't do anything I haven't tried yet will you, Hilly?'

As much as she loved her sister, Hillary couldn't help breathing a sigh of relief when she and Chloe finally left although she half wished Odile hadn't gone with them. The house suddenly seemed too quiet and she would have loved the opportunity to get to know Odile a little better as she felt instinctively that they had lot in common. As if deliberately trying to recreate the previous day, Hillary fixed herself a jug of Pimms but this time took two glasses out to the patio. Just in case, she told herself. She also rummaged around in Alicia's room until she found a couple of magazines that she hadn't read and took those out too.

She glanced around, hoping to catch a glimpse of Torran, then she remembered he had gone to the village. With a sigh of disappointment she lay down on the sun lounger, rolled onto her stomach and unhooked her bikini top, then, with an air of bravado she removed it completely and dropped it on the flagstones. When Torran finally returned, he found her prostrate, struggling to coat her back with suntan oil.

'Here, let me do that for you.'

Hillary almost sat up in surprise, then remembered that she was topless and sank down into the mattress as far as she could. She sensed him approach her, then he took the bottle from her trembling hand, poured a little of the oil into his palm and began rubbing it into her sun soaked skin.

For an uncultivated country boy he certainly had a gentle, rhythmic touch, she thought to herself dreamily, almost moaning aloud as he inadvertently brushed his fingertips over a particularly erogenous zone. As he moved up her back he lifted her hair; she raised her arms and held it over her head, exposing the full length of her neck. Inexplicably, she felt as though she had just revealed an extremely intimate part of her body to him.

Eventually she found her voice. 'Have you done this before by any chance?'

'What? Covered a beautiful woman in suntan oil? No, I have not, I'm afraid.'

She noticed that his accent was very pronounced today and wondered if he was more nervous than he appeared.

'Don't worry, you're doing a wonderful job.'

She squirmed luxuriously as he massaged the oil into her shoulders and turned her head to one side so that she could see him. Unlike the dark, almost austere, trousers and jacket that he'd been wearing the day before, he was now dressed in a pair of black denim jeans and a white cotton vest. As he poured a little more oil onto his palm she noticed that he wore a silver ring on the middle finger of his right hand bearing a design of a coiled serpent.

'I noticed your friends were all at home today.' His tone was light and conversational. She marvelled at the change in him overnight.

'Yes, I mean, no.' She, on the other hand, seemed to be having a little more difficulty organising her thought processes.

'Which is it to be then, yes or no?' He kneaded the tightly clenched muscles at the base of her neck and the last vestiges of her hangover disappeared as if by magic.

'Oh, God, that's better,' she groaned, then added. 'In answer to your question, they were here earlier but they're not here now.'

'I see.'

He continued to massage her in silence for a few more minutes, then he replaced the lid on the bottle with a decisive 'snap'. She couldn't help feeling a little disappointed that he'd finished so soon.

'Would you like a drink?' She gestured toward the table which bore the jug of Pimms.

He noticed there were two glasses but said nothing and simply poured out a drink for each of them. Now she was in a quandary. She wanted to take a sip of her drink but couldn't do so without sitting up. For a moment or two she groped around surreptitiously for her bikini top then, to her horror, she noticed that it was hanging on the back of his chair. He must have picked it up when he arrived she thought, her mind whirling. She had no choice but to sit up.

Hoping that she was exuding an air of graceful ease she pushed herself up with her arms, then turned over and stared him straight in the eye. There was no doubt her sudden movement had an impact upon him – his face flushed and she could tell he was trying desperately to keep his eyes trained above her shoulders. Reaching across to the table to take her glass, she noticed his eyes followed her and thought she heard him inhale deeply. She sipped her drink and searched her mind for something innocuous to say.

'Darius, I mean, Mr Harwood, stopped by here again last night. He's invited us all to a party. Will you be there?'

'He fancies you, y'know.' Torran spoke matter of factly.

'What?' His words took Hillary completely by surprise. In her confusion she took a large swallow of her Pimms and almost choked, her breasts shuddering as she struggled for breath. She had to give Torran credit for pretending not to notice.

With a totally inscrutable expression on his face he repeated his statement. 'Darius. He fancies you, anyone can see that.'

Hillary blushed. Feeling extraordinarily pleased and excited, she could sense the familiar tingling sensation deep in her belly.

'Mind you, I can't blame him,' Torran continued, obviously feeling a little bolder. 'You're a fine looking woman.' At last he allowed his eyes to travel across the bronzed, naked globes of her breasts, then continue on their journey.

She glanced down her body, seeing herself as he saw her, tanned, slim, with long athletic legs. Nevertheless, she couldn't help noticing that he referred to her as a woman rather than a girl.

For the second time in as many days, she felt as though she were sitting opposite a man, not a boy and she desired him as a man. She opened her mouth to speak but Fearn's lilting call carried over the short expanse between the two wings of the house.

Torran jumped up hurriedly, almost spilling his drink in the process. 'I'd better be going.'

Hillary nodded, watching him thoughtfully until he reached the far side of the kitchen garden, then he disappeared from view. Although she expected him all day, he didn't reappear. Eventually she went inside the house, desperate for another shower to cool her down and wash the oil and perspiration from her sun soaked flesh. She padded into her bathroom and stepped out of her bikini bottoms. When she turned on the shower nothing happened. Cursing quietly under her breath she turned it off and on again a couple of times but still nothing happened.

'That's all I need,' she muttered to herself angrily.

Wrapping herself in a short white towel she tried Alicia's shower, then Chloe's and finally Odile's. None of them were working.

'Damn!' She surveyed her surroundings for a few seconds, tapping her foot and wondering what she should do next.

She picked up the telephone and dialled the number Darius had given them for such eventualities. Although he wasn't there she spoke to his secretary who assured her that it was probably just a case of temperamental plumbing.

'It's probably working perfectly okay everywhere else,' the woman added brightly.

Hillary thanked her, put down the receiver and thought about her words for a few minutes – if what she said was right there was a chance that the showers were working perfectly in the main house. Pausing only to collect her washbag, she walked decisively down the hallway and pushed open the swing doors that connected the two parts of the building. She had expected to hear some sounds, possibly of music or Fearn's vacuum cleaner, but everything was bathed in total silence. She opened the first door she came to but the room was completely empty, as were many of the others she tried.

'Hello!' She called quietly, then a little more loudly, 'Torran! Fearn! Anybody!'

She marched on down the hallway trying door handles until she came to a room similar in layout to the sitting room in her own quarters where she found Torran sitting alone watching a tennis match on TV.

If he was surprised to see her standing there clad only in a short towel, he didn't show it. 'Are you looking for someone in particular?'

'Where is everyone?'

Torran stood up and faced her, his palms turned toward her in a gesture of friendliness. 'What's the matter, Hillary? Can I help?'

It was the first time he had actually used her name and it sounded strange coming from his lips. Suddenly feeling self conscious she struggled to maintain her equilibrium. With a falsely casual air, she waved the wash bag in front of her. 'The showers in our wing have packed up and I was wondering if yours were still working.'

He smiled, his hazel eyes forming deep creases at the corners. 'Let's see.'

He led the way to the nearest en-suite room and she looked quickly around. From the few masculine bits and pieces scattered about it looked as though he had chosen his own room. He reached into the shower cubicle and it immediately gushed into life.

'No problem here,' he said, shaking water droplets from his arm.

'Do you mind?' Hillary gestured toward the shower, the fall of clear water looked so inviting she forgot all about her reservations.

He stepped back. 'No, feel free.'

She waited but he seemed in no hurry to leave. Finally, she raised her eyebrows and looked directly at him. 'Do you mind?' she said again.

He backed out of the room, embarrassed. As soon as he had left she looked around again. Damn! She might have known the lock on the door would be broken. After a few moments hesitation she dropped the towel on the floor and stepped into the cubicle, the breath catching in her throat as the sharp jets of water hit her naked body.

As she soaped herself she hummed quietly, thinking once again how glad she was that she had decided to come on this holiday. She thought about school but it all seemed far away, as though teaching and London were part of a different life altogether. Just then her thoughts were interrupted by a loud rap on the bathroom door, quickly she turned off the water and held her arms protectively around herself. She didn't need to ask who it was.

'Would you like anything to drink?' Torran's voice called to her through the closed door.

'Yes, please,' she called back. 'a little white wine if you have it.'

'I think so,' he mumbled.

It was several minutes later when she heard him return just as she had finished showering and was rinsing conditioner from her hair. The shower had invigorated her. Now she felt relaxed and happy, positively glowing and more than a little aroused.

'Why don't you bring my drink to me?' she called provocatively as Torran rapped on the door a second time.

She could sense him hesitating, struggling to amass all his powers of control before entering. It wasn't vanity on her part as Torran had made it quite clear how he felt about her, although she suspected that it wasn't her that interested him in particular, simply women in general. Briefly she wondered if he was a virgin – that could be interesting, she thought.

She stayed under the shower as the door opened slowly, listening intently to his footsteps as he walked across the bathroom and the sound of a glass being placed on the window ledge. She opened the cubicle door a fraction and looked at him over her naked shoulder. He was just standing there, a mixture of anticipation and fear upon his young face. Suddenly she felt very grown up, a woman of the world. She took a deep breath and smiled. 'Come here, Torran.'

He stepped forward and as he did so she turned around and opened the cubicle door completely, revealing her naked body to him as it glistened still slick and steamy from the shower. He sucked in his breath and stared at her, looking her up and down with long, sweeping strokes, his eyes taking in every inch of her as she stood proudly before him. He started to speak but she put a finger to his lips, enjoying her role. 'Ssh, don't say anything.'

With one swift movement she grasped his T-shirt and pulled it over his head, then she knelt down in the shower tray and unbuttoned his jeans, holding his eyes with her own as she pulled down the zip. She rubbed a hand over his crotch, feeling the bulge swelling and growing beneath the thick black denim. Now it was her turn to catch her breath as there was no mistaking his desire for her. She pulled the material over his hips and clasped his buttocks using her forearms to ease his jeans further down his legs. She was slightly surprised to find that he wore nothing underneath.

He helped her then, kicking off his jeans and moving closer still. Fortunately he was barefoot and was able to step into the shower straight away. She closed the door once again but still didn't rise to her feet. She wanted to take him in her mouth, to thrill him in every way possible. Now she truly was the teacher and she was going to make sure her student passed with honours. Using one hand to cup his testicles she grasped the base of his penis with the other, aiming the glans toward her lips.

The water from the shower kept him moist as she ran her tongue up his shaft, encircled the ridge around his glans a couple of times and then snaked her tongue down the other side of his solid erection. As her tongue continued to tease him, she realised he wouldn't be able to hold out for very long. Eventually, as she licked and kissed and caressed his sex, he gripped her hair tightly between his fingers, his rising passion evident in more ways than one. Not ready to allow him to ejaculate in her mouth, she turned her head slightly at the last moment so that his semen was washed away in the flow from the shower. For a brief moment the simple act reminded her of another time and another man.

Swiftly she banished the memory, smiling up at Torran instead. To her surprise she saw that he looked a little disappointed and she hastened to reassure him. 'That's not it, Torran.' She smiled and tantalised his flaccid cock with her tongue until it sprang back into life.

With a sigh of relief he released her slick, wet hair and stroked it for a few minutes, his expression blissful. Then she rose slowly to her feet, running her hands lightly up the enticing musculature of his thighs and buttocks as she did so. She was particularly pleased with his body. Despite looking thin and gaunt in his clothes, his muscles were surprisingly well toned, although his body was nowhere near as hard or impressively defined as Haldane's. She gave herself another mental shake, this was no time to be thinking about past lovers and, until there was a next time, that's all Haldane was.

Swiftly, she came back to reality. Torran was stroking her breasts, teasing her nipples with a childlike fascination, his fingers circulating her aureole again and again then skimming lightly across the hard pink buds, smiling as they tightened even more.

'Do you like my breasts, Torran?'

For answer he bent his head and kissed first one rosy tip, then the other.

A thrill of excitement ran through her each time he touched her there and she moaned softly, 'That's wonderful.'

Sighing with pleasure, she ran her fingers lazily through his thick dark hair – now that it was wet it had gone quite curly. She kissed the top of his head then placed her hand under his chin and gently raised his face to hers. Wrapping her arms around his neck and body she kissed him deeply, enjoying his initial resistance as she probed his mouth with her tongue. She felt his hardened cock brushing against her belly and suddenly felt weak with desire.

Sensing that he needed more guidance, she took his right hand and placed it on her sex, using her own fingers to gently part her labia and urge his exploring fingertips to the core of her excitement. He was a willing pupil and a gratifyingly quick learner. Within seconds he began to alternately rub and stroke the demanding bud of her clitoris until she reached the brink of her own climax. Then to her frustration he moved his fingers away, returning his hand to cup her breasts once again.

She was enjoying the novelty of the shower but soon realised that it was not the best of locations for his first time – if it was his first time. She still wasn't sure he was a virgin.

'Let's go into the bedroom,' she murmured softly in his ear.

They kissed under the powerful spray for a few more minutes then, with a slight feeling of reluctance, Hillary turned it off and pulled back the cubicle door.

Darius returned to the Hall, sat down in his leather chair and turned on the monitor bank just as Hillary and Torran appeared naked from Torran's bathroom. He did a double-take, intrigued that the randy young lad had at last found himself a girl, then paled when he recognised the female companion. Quickly he called for Ilona to come, pointing wordlessly to the screen as she perched on the edge of the chair next to his. The couple leaned forward, each of them fighting a different set of emotions as the scene unfolded before their eyes.

Hillary and Torran padded hand in hand across the thickly carpeted bedroom, stopping to rub each other's bodies dry with thick, white monogrammed towels before collapsing onto the comfortable bed together. This time Torran controlled the action.

Perhaps he just wasn't used to vertical fucking, Hillary mused as he teased and stroked every part of her body, his tormenting hands sliding lower and lower down her torso until she was almost begging him to touch her between her legs. Opening her thighs wide she urged her pelvis upward, almost brushing his chin with the glossy curls of her pubic hair.

Steadfastly ignoring her encouragement he continued to lick her navel and the taut expanse of her belly, his tongue going around and around frustratingly in concentric circles. She tried to sit up so that she could at least caress him in return but he pushed her gently back against the pillow.

'I am exploring you, leave me be,' he commanded softly.

So she lay, moaning and writhing in mounting ecstasy as he discovered every part of her, front and back. When he'd finished, and only when he'd finished, did he allow his fingertips to drift across her lower belly, to create a path that divided the curls on her pubis to the natural division between the soft pink lips of her sex. Then he knelt on the floor, spreading her thighs wide and sliding his hands under her buttocks, pulling her toward him so that her lower body was level with the edge of the bed and his view of her was perfect.

She held her breath and waited, knowing that he was feasting his eyes upon her sex as she lay wide open to his view and desperate for his touch. As the minutes ticked by agonisingly slowly she toyed with her own nipples, desperate for release that would not come.

Then, so lightly that at first she thought it was a slight breeze through the open window, she felt something caress the outer edge of her vagina. She tensed her thighs until they trembled, her whole body was aflame. She wanted to scream the words, 'Touch me, damn it!' But he was young and had all the time in the world.

Then she felt a finger tip inside her and another. Gradually she felt herself being filled up by him and ground herself against his palm as he probed inside her relentlessly. She could feel her vagina moistening and expanding to accommodate him and close by the burning, urgent flesh of her clitoris swelled and throbbed. He had not touched her there since the shower and she felt she would scream aloud if he didn't offer her some release from the lust that had been building within her for the past couple of hours.

Strangely enough she didn't quite know the best way to communicate this need to him. She seriously doubted that he had ever performed cunnilingus before. Then she remembered that she was the teacher and it was up to her to show him how to please a woman. With a little difficulty she sat up and gently removed his hand from between her legs.

Torran looked hurt. 'Wasn't I doing it right?'

She smiled weakly. Between her legs she could still feel the legacy of his fingers. 'Good God, yes. But there are other ways to excite a woman, you know.'

He shook his head. 'No I don't. Tell me.'

She patted the bed next to her, then when he was seated beside her she pushed him gently backwards until he was laying flat on his back, his cock pointing at the ceiling.

'Do you remember when I did this in the shower?' She took his penis between her lips again, sucking and lapping it with her tongue as though it were an oversized lollipop.

He nodded, his eyes slightly glazed.

'Well,' she continued, 'you can do the same thing to a woman.' With uncharacteristic boldness she straddled him, her sex directly infront of his face, and then she delicately parted her labia. 'Lick me here,' she ordered softly. 'That's it, nice and slowly, up and down, around and around. Ahh! Ooh!' She could feel her climax building very fast – there was something very beneficial about telling a man exactly what you wanted him to do, she decided.

He stopped and looked up at her as she was about to mount the first wave of ecstasy. 'Am I doing okay? You seem a little uncomfortable.'

She shook her head vehemently. 'Oh, no, Torran, you're doing absolutely great, just don't stop again until I tell you. Whatever you do, don't stop.'

She couldn't believe her good fortune, here was a young man fresh and untrammelled, ready and eager to satisfy her every desire. Of course, no sooner had he discovered how to really arouse her than he began to caress her over and over and over. Finally, she had to stop him for a moment. 'Torran, this is great, it really is – but it's getting late. My sister and her friends will be home soon and they may come here looking for me.'

In all honesty, she seriously doubted it but she couldn't be sure, sometimes Alicia could surprise her with sudden inexplicable bouts of sisterly concern. He propped his head on one hand and regarded her with a serious expression, his dark hair flopping into his eyes.

'Do you want to go, is that it?' he asked.

'No Torran, far from it, I just,' she hesitated and gazed out of the window at the darkening sky for a few minutes, then she looked him squarely in the eye saying, 'I want you to fuck me.'

He looked bewildered. 'But isn't that just what we've been doing all the while.'

She couldn't believe he was so naive. 'Do you have any condoms, Torran?'

He nodded. 'A friend gave some to me before I came down here this time. He couldn't believe I hadn't scored yet. He said southern girls were much more forward. I think he was right.' He grinned, opened the cupboard next to the bed and rummaged around until he found a pack. 'I don't know how to put them on properly or anything.' He smiled at her apologetically but somehow she got the impression he had just overstepped the bounds of credulity.

'If I find out this innocence is all an act I'll, I'll . . .' She could hardly open the packet for laughing.

'You'll what?' he said, 'Withhold your favours? Fat chance.' Before she could think of a suitable retort he rolled her over, slipped on the condom and plunged into

143

her. Each time he penetrated her a little deeper, all the time mumbling into her hair. 'You loved every minute of being the teacher. If I hadn't played hard to get? Did you honestly expect me to be a virgin at my age?'

And so it went on. Hillary didn't know whether to laugh or scream, he was so full of himself – so aggravating, so cocksure. One thing was for certain though, she thought to herself as he sent her senses soaring on the crest of a monumental orgasm, he certainly knew how to fuck.

All the time that this went on, Darius and Ilona watched the heaving, perspiring bodies, each of them lost in their own private thoughts and reminiscences.

'I've definitely lost her now, Ilona.' Darius sighed with uncharacteristic despondence at the moment Hillary came with Torran inside her.

'Nonsense.' The older woman was brusque, although secretly she too marvelled at her son's finely honed technique for pleasuring a woman.

They both watched as Hillary unwound her legs from around Torran's torso and lay replete and smiling, her slightly damp hair fanned out around her, her arms thrown carelessly over her head.

'Perhaps it should skip a generation, perhaps he should be the one to sire the next Harwood heir?' Despite himself, Darius found he couldn't tear his eyes away from the intriguing sight of Hillary's sex. Reddened and swollen, it almost beckoned to him. 'Whatever the outcome, I have to have her, at least once.' He glanced sideways at Ilona waiting for a change in her expression. To his surprise she remained inscrutable.

Inside, Ilona fumed. Inside she was screaming words of hatred and abuse at the lovely young girl who had stolen both her son and her lover. She would make her pay. Somehow she would see to it that Darius would not want her after all. Thoughts and plans jostled inside her mind for pride of place but she knew she still had time. The party on Friday would suit her well enough.

Chapter Nine

*H*ours later, Hillary left Torran reluctantly to go back to her own quarters, making it with about five minutes to spare. No sooner had she shut the bedroom door behind her than she heard the screech of tyres on the gravel driveway and soon the heavy blanket of silence that hung over the house was shattered by Alicia and Chloe's piercing voices. Quickly, Hillary dived into bed and pretended to be fast asleep when they came in. As she expected there was a lot of giggling and the sound of someone stumbling about in the passageway, then her bedroom door opened a fraction and she heard Alicia's voice. 'Shh, everyone, Hillary's fast asleep.'

As soon as the door clicked shut again she smiled a secret smile and snuggled further into the warmth of her bed; compared with every other night for the past couple of weeks the air held quite a chill. She imagined Torran as he lay in his own bed, the sheets tangled and drenched with perspiration from their intense session of lovemaking.

Carefully she slid a hand between her legs, wincing slightly as she gently probed the tender, throbbing flesh. She still wasn't sure how much he had already known about sex but the outcome was what mattered most and she was certain that they had both benefited from her instruction. She lay awake for ages simply thinking and remembering, waiting for the sounds in the house to gradually die down and when they did she drifted off to sleep with a smile on her face.

The following morning started off pretty much like all the others. Odile and Hillary were the first ones to wake with Chloe and Alicia less quick to put in an appearance. Eventually they all drifted together and sat convivially around the kitchen table, drinking coffee and discussing their plans for the forthcoming day.

'Well, after yesterday I certainly don't want to do anything too energetic,' Chloe declared, assuming an air of exhaustion.

'All shopped out are we?' Hillary murmured dryly, adding, 'Where did you guys get to in the end?'

'Believe it or not only as far as King's Lynn,' said Odile. 'As you say we shopped, took in some local sights, had a meal, a drink, another drink . . .'

'I get the picture.' Hillary smiled. 'That's pretty tiring stuff. In that case why don't we all go down to the beach.'

Alicia groaned. 'I never thought I'd say it but I'm getting a bit tired of the beach.'

As if on cue, the other three women reeled back in mock horror.

'You cannot be serious!' exclaimed Odile.

'Well it's all right for you,' Chloe complained. 'You've spent most of the past few days locked in your room with Mr Universe, no wonder you fancy getting out in the open air.'

Odile pouted. 'That's not fair, we went ballooning.'

Chloe leaned across the table toward her. 'Tell me honestly that you didn't do it in the balloon.'

The young woman was silent, Chloe looked around at the others, a triumphant expression on her face.

'Okay, we did,' Odile admitted, a small gurgle of laughter catching in her throat. 'But only the once.'

'To quote your boyfriend dear, "Quelle horreur!"'

Hillary snorted and Alicia frowned at her friend. 'Oh,

Chloe leave the poor girl alone for goodness sake, you're only jealous,' she said.

'Too right I am.' Chloe picked at a piece of varnish flaking from her fingernail. 'Gus and I only did it once all the time he was here, can you believe it?'

Odile tutted and Hillary looked sympathetic but Alicia dismissed her complaint with a disdainful wave of her hand. 'Clive and I managed it twice, but . . .' She held up her hand to silence her friend who had opened her mouth to protest. 'But both times were so quick I hardly had time to put down the book I was reading.'

Hillary looked incredulous. 'You don't mean you read during foreplay?'

Alicia nodded, looking perfectly serious. 'Oh yes. At least if you can call it foreplay. If Clive ever learns to turn me on properly I'll buy a bookmark.'

Odile caught Hillary's eye and shook her head surreptitiously. Obviously, Hillary thought, she and Odile were the lucky ones. What bothered her the most was that both Alicia and Chloe seemed to take a rotten sex life for granted, as though sex with their husbands was something to be endured rather than enjoyed. Odile explained to Hillary later that she had given up trying to talk to Chloe about it, she simply didn't understand why she owed it to herself to make sure Gus knew how to please her in bed as well as out of it.

'And here I am with more sex than I can handle,' Hillary pronounced gravely.

'Oh, yes, tell me more.' Odile looked interested but just then they were interrupted by Alicia.

'Chloe and I are ready when you are.'

They had finally agreed to go to the beach again but this time they would take a detour to the naturist beach. This was Chloe's suggestion. They also decided to travel by taxi for a change as Alicia complained that she always ended up being the driver and so had to stay sober. None of the others were keen to volunteer so they called a local firm who dropped them at their usual parking spot near the wooded area where the two paths converged. They arranged for the driver to pick them up again at three o'clock and, each loaded down with bags and towels, set off down the path leading to the left.

At first they were agog – everywhere they looked men, women and children of all ages were sunbathing and swimming entirely in the nude. Some of them were even playing games, or walking the dog. Despite their apparent sophistication, none of the women really knew where to look and averted their eyes hurriedly every time someone walked past them.

'I can't believe how well hung some of these old chaps are,' Chloe whispered incredulously from the corner of her mouth.

Hillary was shocked and looked at Odile who stifled a giggle. She looked around them. 'This seems a good spot to me,' she said.

With a sigh of relief they all dropped their burdens on the burning sand and stared around them. A little way off a middle-aged couple were playing with a frisbee and one lone child was diligently building a sandcastle but apart from them their immediate surroundings were deserted. Alicia started spreading out the towels while Chloe, naturally, rummaged in the cool bag for a bottle of wine and a corkscrew. They took turns to cover each other with sun tan oil then Chloe poured the wine.

'Don't you feel a bit conspicuous sitting here wearing a bikini?' They all turned to look at Hillary who had spoken.

Alicia was the first to reply. 'Well, I suppose it does seem a bit prudish.' With an air of bravado she reached behind her and unhooked her bikini top.

Slowly, Chloe, Hillary and Odile followed suit. They looked at each other in silence for a few minutes then Chloe said. 'Who's going to be daring then?' The other three women stared back at her, blushing profusely.

Chloe wriggled out of her bikini bottoms and sat ramrod straight on the towel, her thighs clenched firmly together, staring directly ahead at the sea. After a few seconds she spoke between clenched teeth. 'Come on, I don't intend to be the only one to bare my all.'

Hillary glanced around. There was still no-one within a hundred yards of them so she quickly removed her bikini bottoms too and shortly afterward Odile and Alicia did the same. If they had expected crowds of spectators to suddenly appear, or a film crew, they were able to breathe a sigh of relief. Even when the odd person did pass them by they gave no more than a fleeting glance, or a friendly nod. Gradually, the women relaxed and began to enjoy the unique sensation of the hot sun caressing their naked skin. Hillary rolled on to her stomach and shyly asked Alicia if she would mind coating her behind with suntan oil. Soon they were all anointing each other and, their inhibitions loosened by the wine, the sun and the lack of clothing they all admitted to feeling aroused.

'What wouldn't I give for a group of nice hunky guys to come up to us now,' wailed Alicia.

Chloe blushed. 'Do you know who I can't stop thinking about?'

'No, go on,' Odile urged.

'That boy, Fearn's brother. Have you seen him in jeans? He's got a divine bottom.'

As she lay back on her towel and stared at the sky, Hillary couldn't help noticing that her nipples had become erect. She felt excitement bubbling up within her at the thought of him, she knew just how Chloe felt.

'I could teach that boy a thing or two,' Alicia asserted smugly, adjusting her sunglasses as she turned to face the opposite direction.

'I doubt it,' Hillary blurted out. She instantly regretted her slip of the tongue as all three women sat up and stared at her.

'Is there something we should know about, Hillary?' Alicia's voice was quiet and controlled.

Hillary trembled. This was a sure sign her sister was

about to exert her authority but none of the women were going to let her remark pass.

'Okay, I'll tell you. But promise not to tell Torran I said anything,' she protested feebly. At that moment she felt about six years old again.

'Yes, yes, we promise.' Chloe was impatient. 'Just tell us what happened between you and Torran. I take it something has happened?'

Hillary nodded, failing to conceal a grin. 'Yes, yesterday, when you were all out. Our showers weren't working so I went to the main house, Darius and Fearn were out but . . .'

'But Torran was there, eager for someone to play with,' Alicia finished for her, unable to hide the wistful tone in her voice.

Hillary nodded, wondering what the hell she had to feel guilty about. Suddenly she faced them all, her expression defiant. 'We had sex for hours and it was really fantastic and I hope we get to do it all over again.'

'Well,' Alicia said, pausing to allow her sister's admission to sink in, 'I just hope I get to do it with him too.' At that she threw back her head laughing and soon they were all falling about helplessly. Of course they wouldn't give up until Hillary had told them every single detail and then they wanted to know about Haldane as well.

'Is there anyone else?' Chloe asked.

'Not yet,' Hillary admitted.

Chloe squealed. 'Did you hear what she said? Not yet. Oh, my God, I feel like a nun!'

'Sorry, can't see any around,' Odile quipped, sending them all into fresh gales of laughter.

'Are you ladies having a good time?'

The deep voice was unexpected. Thinking it sounded slightly familiar Hillary looked up. It was Haldane. He too was naked and looking even more magnificent than she remembered.

Chloe and Alicia went bright pink with embarrassment when they saw him, but Odile grinned openly and waved a bottle of wine in the air. 'Would you like some?'

He nodded and sat down on the edge of Hillary's towel. Hillary noticed that Chloe couldn't take her eyes off his penis so after a few minutes she kicked her in the ankle.

'Ouch! Oh, sorry, Hilly.' Chloe pouted and rubbed her leg.

'What have you been up to?' Haldane asked.

It was a rhetorical question but Hillary blushed guiltily and stammered a reply. 'Just hanging around the Hall, sunbathing and so forth.'

Chloe snorted when Hillary said this, only blushing when Hillary flashed her a warning look.

Haldane sipped his wine and smiled openly at Hillary who was still red faced. 'I'm not checking up on you.'

They all sat around talking and drinking wine for a little while, then Haldane suggested a walk. Much as they fancied him, Alicia and Chloe shook their heads, They weren't mentally prepared to parade down the beach stark naked.

Odile was not embarrassed but sensed that Hillary would prefer to be alone with him. 'You two go, we'll just stay here and soak up some rays.'

Haldane took Hillary's hand and they walked for about half a mile in silence when suddenly he stopped and stared down into her face, his expression serious. 'Do you wish that we didn't meet any more, Hillary?'

'No.' She shook her head vehemently. 'Far from it. I just didn't want you to think that I was chasing you, or putting pressure on you.'

He nodded gravely. 'That's very perceptive of you, Hillary.' He stared out to sea for a moment or two, shielding his eyes from the sun with his free hand. Then he spoke, his words travelling out to sea on the ozone laden air. 'It's true I don't like to feel tied down, I am a free man, a free spirit.'

'I know that, Haldane and I'm not looking for any ties either, just some fun.'

'I know what sort of fun you like best, Hillary, remember?'

He ran his finger lightly down her spine and she shivered, her clitoris starting to tingle as though it had not been touched in ages. She looked around but the beach where they were standing seemed quite crowded.

'Come on!' Haldane took her hand again and started to run toward the dunes.

They slowed down and walked by the side of the high banks of dunes for a few hundred yards until they came to a place where they could climb up. Haldane pushed his large hand against the underside of her bottom, helping her upward.

Hillary smiled to herself. He was such a gentleman; a gentleman who never passed up an opportunity to touch her.

As soon as they had both reached the top of the dunes, Haldane held her and they kissed deeply for several minutes, running their hands over each other in a feverish attempt to quell their growing lust. Hillary glanced around. The dunes were so high where they stood, in a low dip, that they were completely hidden from view. Suddenly, a dark cloud passed across the sun and she shivered, feeling her nipples harden. All at once she felt unaccountably primitive, like a child of nature, and couldn't deny an overwhelming urge to possess him there and then. One look at Haldane told her he felt the same way. They both knew there was no time for preamble; voices could be heard in the distance and the sound of children playing overlaid the rhythmic pounding of the surf against the shore.

He ran his hand over her belly and suddenly swooped between her legs, taking her unawares. His fingers were cool against her hot flesh and they soothed each desperate, throbbing part of her with deft strokes then hovered for a few seconds before plunging deep inside her, catching her breath from the inside.

While he caressed her, Hillary reached between their hot naked bodies, grasping his shaft in both hands and squeezing hard. She ran her fingers up and down the length of it, teasing the tip until the first drops of fluid appeared and coated her fingers. Then she held them up to her lips and sucked each one in turn, savouring the saline flavour before rubbing her lips across his chest. He tasted of the sea inside and out.

Behind her was a large, flat-topped dune about waist height. Haldane spun her around and pushed her forward unceremoniously. She gasped as her stomach and breasts came into contact with the hot sand, then cried aloud as he entered her. Holding her hips firmly he thrust into her eight or nine times, smiling with satisfaction at her cries of passion which were drowned out instantly by the squalls of the seagulls wheeling overhead.

She thought he would let her go as soon as they climaxed but she was wrong. Pinning her to the dune with one massive hand spanning her back, he slid the other between her legs. Gently he parted her labia, rubbing cool fingers over her burning clitoris. Then, using his pelvis, he forced her body forward, moving his hand at the last minute, so that her exposed bud was pressed against a tuft of marram grass, the spikes immediately prickling her delicate flesh.

Hillary moaned at the unexpected contact. Used only to the sensation of pliant flesh against the most sensitive parts of her body, she suddenly felt a primeval yearning for more of the same.

Haldane must have read her thoughts, she mused, as she saw him scan the area of sand around their feet. A few inches away, on top of another tuft of grass, lay a long smooth stone, its rough edges polished to a shine by years of tossing about in the tide. They both seemed to notice it at the same moment and Haldane swiftly bent and picked it up before returning immediately to his position as captor. For a few moments he weighed the stone in his hand, considering the possibilities. It had obviously been recently picked up by a seabird and dropped because it was still cold and salty wet from the sea.

The first thing Hillary felt was its cool slick dampness stroking her buttocks, occasionally sliding between the cleft and over her throbbing sex. Haldane's cock was no longer inside her and she wondered how he would use the stone, if he would use it to penetrate the place he had so recently vacated. The thought excited her but, at the same time, the dimensions of the inanimate object were nowhere near as impressive as the Norwegian's own member.

Haldane seemed in no rush to make a decision. He extended the path of the stone, trailing it up and down the length of her spine as he continued to stimulate her sex with his hand.

All movement ceased for a moment, then he spoke. 'If I let you go you will stay in that position.' His words were a command that Hillary wanted to obey. She nodded, her stomach tightening with fresh excitement.

As Haldane took his hand from her back, she pressed herself further forward over the sand dune and clasped it with both arms. A wisp of chill air whipped her exposed sex and she moaned with renewed desire, rubbing her swollen nipples against the hot grains of sand. She could sense him looking at her, considering what to do next.

Suddenly she felt his massive hands on her buttocks, spreading her wider and wider as his fingers teased the pink puckered skin. Despite her embarrassment she squirmed under his touch, then jumped as the tip of the long smooth stone nudged the rosy opening inside her cleft. 'Haldane?' she murmured. Her voice was tremulous. He was going to do what she dreaded and desired the most.

'I won't hurt you, Hillary,' he replied, his tone reassuring.

Carefully, he pressed the stone against the tight muscles surrounding her opening, using the fingers of his other hand to probe her vagina, arousing her to

154

such an extent that her body automatically yielded to the new invader. With great delicacy he used the stone to mirror the actions of his fingers. Probing, turning, withdrawing a little.

Gradually she relaxed into the rhythm, her mind and body totally consumed by the unprecedented sensations invoked within her. As her moans turned to screams of ecstasy Haldane was forced to urge her into silence. The sounds that were reverberating around them were approaching a crescendo that was sure to attract the attention of others.

After a few more minutes he withdrew the stone, replacing his fingers with his rock hard shaft. Once more they took delight in each other's bodies, until they both exploded in a final, glorious climax.

Afterwards, Hillary sank to the ground, as limp as a rag doll, her breathing laboured. Using every ounce of her remaining strength, she turned her head to smile at Haldane who also sat on the sand, his back to a high dune. 'I've realised what's different about you, Haldane,' she said, when she had recovered her breath a little.

'Yes?' He smiled contentedly.

'Every time I think it can't get any better between us, it does.' She paused, wondering if she had overstepped the mark somehow, perhaps by making it sound as though she was looking for some sort of commitment from him. She hastened to reassure him. 'I don't want anything from you, Haldane, it's just an observation, that's all.'

Without replying, he unfurled his massive frame and rose to his feet, pulling her upright along with him.

With a serious expression he looked into her eyes. 'I told you already, Hillary, I am a free spirit.'

'I know, I didn't mean . . .'

He silenced her with a brief shake of his golden head. 'Do not worry, I want you to become a free spirit too. I want you to return with me to Norway. We will have some good times there, I promise you. A little adventure for the two of us perhaps,' he added, smiling.

Hillary was struck dumb. It was the last thing she had expected him to say. She wanted to explain that she liked him a lot and desired him like crazy, but to go to Norway with him? That would mean turning her whole life upside down and she had only known him a few days, they hadn't even spent a whole night together. She explained all this to him, as gently as she could, adding that despite all her reservations she loved the idea and would appreciate some time to think about it.

'Of course.' He nodded gravely. 'I understand, but I plan to leave by the end of next week. Either you go with me then or we say goodbye.'

They left the cave and walked back along the beach in silence, each consumed by their own thoughts. By the time they reached Alicia, Chloe and Odile, it was almost three o'clock. The women had already packed up their things and were waiting for her, looking more than a little disgruntled. Alicia tossed Hillary her bikini as she approached.

'I'm sorry I cut it so fine.' Hillary said apologetically, feeling as though she should say something by way of appeasement.

Haldane whispered something in her ear and she nodded. He looked around at the others. 'Bye everyone.'

They waved until he was out of sight, then Chloe turned to Hillary, her face agog. 'Did you? While you were walking, I mean?'

Hillary sighed and stepped into her bikini bottoms, then tied the halter top around her neck. She felt confused and was becoming a little tired of people choosing to live vicarious sex lives through her; consequently she felt a little snappy. 'Not while we were walking along, no.'

Chloe pulled a face and Odile caught her eye, shaking her head as if to say, 'Leave it alone.'

The older woman shrugged, picked up a couple of bags and started making her way back up the beach to the car park, the other three following silently in her wake. About half a mile from the beach they decided on an action plan for the evening which basically involved eating a lot and getting very drunk. During the drive back they ordered the driver to stop in the village where they stocked up with more wine, some bread, cheese, pate, salad and fruit. By the time they arrived back at Harwood Hall they had managed to recover their high spirits completely.

As soon as all their purchases were stacked in the fridge, the four women went outside to the patio. It seemed a little crowded with four sun loungers but soon they were once again stripped, oiled and laying prostrate under the sun's rays.

'Do you think we should sunbathe in the nude here?' Hillary said glancing round nervously but Alicia laughed.

'Relax, Hilly, there's no-one here. Fearn has gone to Cromer for the day, Darius won't come here because his secretary said he's at a farm auction in Suffolk and Fearn's brother is working in King's Lynn.'

Hillary was impressed. 'Do you keep tabs on everybody?'

Her sister nodded blithely. 'It just takes a little practice and a bit of effort, darling. Mind you, it comes naturally to me now, I've honed my skills on Clive.'

Hillary laughed but presently their conversation dried up and they concentrated on improving their tans. The soporific effects of the sun and wine quickly lulled them into a blissful, dreamy state and, as a result, they were all completely unaware that they were being watched. Not via hidden cameras but in person.

The unexpected voyeur was Torran, who had returned to the Hall early. One of the apprentices had failed to grasp even the basics of his craft and so, by mutual agreement, he had left the glass works early and for good. With no-one else to instruct there was no reason for Torran to stay until the end of the shift.

The telephone was ringing as he entered the Hall. It was Fearn calling to let him know that she would be staying in Cromer for the night. Torran wasn't bothered by his sister's absence as in truth they didn't really have much in common. He agreed to convey her message to their mother and to Darius, changed out of his work clothes, showered and dressed again in a pair of cut-off blue denim shorts. Then he made a sandwich, opened a can of beer and switched on the television but there was only ten minutes of tennis left to watch.

As he watched the players flick the ball backwards and forwards across the net, he wondered idly what Hillary was doing. Although he longed to repeat their encounter from the day before he seriously doubted that they'd get the opportunity. Not with Darius watching his every move.

He had accepted long ago that his half-brother was a strange character and not beyond being cruel or ruthless in his quest to get what he wanted, therefore it worried him that such a man should set his sights on someone as basically naive as Hillary. Perhaps he could get his mother to intervene, he mused, she at least had some vestige of control over Darius.

With concentrated determination, he pushed all thoughts of Darius and his other family members from his mind, acknowledging that the heady combination of a hot day and someone as luscious as Hillary was making him feel horny as hell. He glanced at his watch and frowned. As it was still too early to go down to the village pub, the only thing left for him to do was catch some rays. Grabbing a second can of beer from the fridge on his way through the kitchen, Torran opened the back door and stepped outside, pausing for a few seconds to breath in the heady scent of herbs coming from the kitchen garden.

He looked through the archway to the patio where he'd discovered Hillary the previous day and almost choked on his beer. Hillary was there, along with the other two women, plus the girl he'd seen with the French boyfriend. The best bit was, they were all sunbathing stark naked.

He hesitated, unsure of his next move. The scene before him was the answer to any man's prayers yet he felt awkward about approaching them. What should he do, simply saunter through the garden and say hello? He knew he didn't have the balls for that. He took another gulp of his beer and thought for a moment. A plan came to mind.

Unfortunately, or not, depending on which way one looked at it, he never got the opportunity to put his plan into action. While he was still hovering at the entrance to the kitchen garden, Chloe opened one eye, saw him and screamed. Instantly the other three sat up and looked around. Hillary spied Torran, who was now blushing even harder than Alicia and Chloe.

She waved and called to him. 'Hi there, would you like a drink?'

'Hillary!' Alicia hissed a warning under her breath but Torran was already striding toward them.

The women's apparent embarrassment made him feel a little bolder. He surveyed them all slowly, his eyes finally coming to rest on Hillary's amused face.

'This must be my lucky day.' He smiled and sat down on his usual chair. Accepting Hillary's offer of wine, he poured himself a glass then topped up the others. 'Bottoms up.' He smirked, his eyes skimming insolently over each woman's pubic mound.

Inside the house the telephone rang and Odile jumped up. 'That will be Theo, he promised to ring me. I'll take it in my room.'

If Torran was disppointed that the young woman had left he didn't show it. Alicia had rolled over onto her stomach when Torran looked at her but now she was obviously having difficulty oiling her back. Hillary was just about to offer her assistance when Torran knelt down by Alicia's side and took the bottle from her hand. 'Please, let me,' he said.

He poured a little of the liquid into his palm and began massaging her shoulders, increasing the pressure of his strokes until Alicia started to moan contentedly. Torran glanced across her back and winked at Hillary who instantly returned his smile, although she felt a little resentful; only the day before she had been the sole object of his attention. She conveniently chose to forget about her satisfying encounter with Haldane that same afternoon.

Chloe too was watching Torran's expert manipulations with undisguised envy. 'Do me next, please,' she said, pouting.

'Your wish is my command.' Torran grinned. Oh boy, was he going to make the most of this!

By the time he had finished oiling both Alicia and Chloe his arousal was obvious. Chloe had insisted that he anoint both sides of her body and he had great difficulty controlling himself as his hands slid sensuously over her breasts. Hillary was now waiting expectantly for him to oil her too yet he knew that once he touched her familiar, willing curves he would be lost completely. He took a huge gulp of wine to fortify himself. 'I – ' he said, hesitating.

'Please, Torran.' She looked so beguiling laying there, naked, deeply tanned and with her silky hair fanned out on the pillow of the sun lounger.

He drew in his breath and, with a huge amount of self control knelt beside her and began to knead her supple flesh. He could tell that she was as aroused as he. Her breath was coming in short gasps and her nipples were as hard as bullets, swollen to twice their normal size. He let his fingers drift across the tops of her thighs, conscious of the other two women watching him. From their conversation he now knew which was Chloe and which was Alicia and he had also gathered that Alicia was Hillary's older sister. That bothered him a little but what he really didn't like to think about was that both Chloe and Alicia were married.

Suddenly he felt a hand snake between his legs, encompassing his cock. Naked breasts were pressing against his back. It was Chloe. He swallowed hard, almost holding his breath as she withdrew her hand momentarily before encircling his waist with both arms, her fingers fumbling with his button-fly.

'Damn! Now I know why zips were invented.' Chloe had broken a carefully cultivated fingernail.

Hillary giggled at the other woman's complaint. 'No pain, no gain, Chloe.' She was surprised to find that she didn't mind Chloe touching Torran, as long as he was touching her. Eventually, as Chloe continued to fumble, Torran took pity on her and removed his own shorts. Again he wore nothing underneath, Hillary noted. She glanced at her sister who was staring at Chloe and Torran with unconcealed fascination. Chloe was now kneeling in front of Torran, teasing his cock with her lips.

'I didn't know you knew how to do that, Chloe,' Alicia commented matter of factly.

Chloe mumbled, her mouth too full to reply.

Alicia walked over to the couple and kissed Torran hard on the mouth, he responded by cupping her small breasts in his hands, teasing the nipples with his thumbs until they were as hard and swollen as Hillary's. All Hillary could do was watch them wondering where it would all lead.

Suddenly Odile appeared in the kitchen doorway, she was fully dressed in white cotton trousers and a T-shirt. 'Would anyone like some real food?'

At the mention of food, Chloe looked up, kissed the tip of Torran's penis and smiled sweetly at him. 'Later, darling, I'm famished.'

Hillary also rose to her feet and hovered uncertainly. Torran and Alicia were still groping each other like a couple of sex starved teenagers. After a few minutes she shrugged and stepped inside the kitchen. Out of

161

the corner of her eye she just caught a glimpse of Torran pushing Alicia back onto the very sun lounger she had just vacated.

Odile had prepared a lovely spread and despite a slight feeling of disquiet, Hillary realised she was extremely hungry. They sat eating in silence for a few minutes, then Chloe smiling brightly, inclined her head toward the back door. 'No need to guess what those two are up to.'

Odile noticed Hillary frowning and asked, 'Does it really bother you? You hardly know Torran after all.'

Hillary shook her head, realising something as she did so. 'It's not that Torran is screwing someone else, it's just that the someone else happens to be Alicia.'

Odile nodded sagely. 'I know what you mean.'

Chloe obviously didn't. 'So you don't mind if I have him after Alix then?'

Hillary laughed and shook her head. 'No, Chloe, feel free.' Then she looked enquiringly at Odile. 'I take it you're not planning to join the orgy?'

The young woman shook her head. 'I couldn't. Theo means too much to me and anyway – ' She suddenly hesitated.

Hillary was about to ask her to carry on when she saw Torran in the doorway. 'Come and have something to eat, you must be starving,' she said.

He noticed Hillary was laughing as she spoke but didn't miss the fact that her voice also held a trace of sarcasm. 'Thanks, I am.' He sat down at the table and helped himself to some cheese and salad.

Alicia sidled into the kitchen and they all looked up expectantly but she dashed to her room. A few minutes later she reappeared wearing a short, red sun-dress. Red was Alicia's favourite colour.

'I was feeling a little chilly,' she said by way of an explanation.

'Oh!' Chloe looked at Hillary. 'I feel a little under-dressed now, don't you, Hills?'

Hillary nodded and stood up. They too both dashed

out of the kitchen, threw on some clothes and returned to their meal. Like Alicia they were wearing short cotton T-shirt dresses, a white one for Hillary, whilst Chloe chose beige. Against the background of her tan she still looked almost naked. After they had finished eating they went back outside to sit on the patio, sip some more wine, and enjoy the balmy evening. Only Odile begged off, saying she wanted to write to Theo.

'But you just finished speaking to him on the 'phone.' Chloe was dumbfounded.

Instead of choosing to sit in his usual seat, Torran sat down next to Hillary on her sun lounger, leaned back comfortably and put his arm around her shoulders, his fingertips casually brushing her breast. A moment later she felt an unfamiliar touch upon her thigh. Opening her eyes she saw that Chloe was seated at the foot of the lounger with her arms wrapped round Torran, kissing his back and shoulders. Hillary felt slightly annoyed at her intrusion but said nothing as she conceded defeat. She rose stiffly to her feet and went inside the house.

As it turned out the evening continued in a much tamer fashion. Chloe and Torran finally resurfaced about an hour later, Chloe looking more relaxed and happy than Hillary had ever seen her before. In their absence the wine had finally run out, so Hillary and Odile made a huge pot of coffee which they took into the sitting room. There they all lounged around listening to music, talking and finally they played Scrabble. Hillary decided it was the strangest orgy that she'd ever been to, then she realised that she'd never been to one before so she had nothing concrete to go on.

Considering the differences in their ages and personalities, they all got on extremely well together, finding that they had quite a lot in common after all. Of course, Hillary thought wryly, with the exception of Odile, they all had Torran in common for a start. Just before midnight, Alicia looked at her watch and reminded them that they were due to drive to Newmarket the following day. 'We need to make an early start,' she warned.

Hillary laughed. 'What do you call early, Alix?' She knew full well that her sister didn't believe the world existed before eight o'clock in the morning.

'You may well scoff, Hillary, but I'd like us all to be ready to leave by nine at the latest.'

'Oh well, in that case we'd better turn in now.' Hillary knew she was being unnecessarily sarcastic but couldn't resist adding. 'We are only going to Newmarket, Alicia, not the North Pole.'

'I know, but we might get lost and I said we'd meet the boys before lunch.'

Hillary sighed. She couldn't bear the thought of being cooped up in a car with Alicia and Chloe, especially when Alicia didn't know where she was going. Then there was the prospect of meeting up with Clive and Gus. She didn't know how the other two women were feeling but she felt guilty enough for both of them. She fervently hoped neither of their husbands would ask her any potentially embarrassing questions.

Wondering if she could get away with feigning a headache in the morning, she showed Torran the way back to the main house throught the swing doors on the upper floor, then said goodnight to Alicia, Chloe and Odile. She noticed that Chloe seemed reluctant to go inside her bedroom and wasn't surprised when she heard the sound of the swing doors opening and closing about a quarter of an hour after everyone had supposedly gone to bed.

Chapter Ten

*H*illary awoke feeling on top of the world, which was more than she could say for Chloe who staggered from her room after the third call looking like death warmed up.

Alicia eyed her suspiciously. 'Did you get any sleep at all last night?'

Chloe sat at the kitchen table, her head in her hands. 'Please don't do this to me, Alix.' Just then Odile appeared, looking as fresh and perky as ever. Chloe looked up at her friend and groaned. 'I think I hate you.'

'What's up with wonder woman?' asked Odile. She opened one of the kitchen cupboards and took out a clean mug. With a surreptitious grin Hillary inclined her head in the general direction of the patio, pointed to her own crotch and then faked an elaborate yawn. Odile nodded, understanding immediately but Alicia wasn't quite so subtle.

'She's been screwing that Jock with the cock all night, I've got no sympathy for her.'

Odile caught Hillary's eye and raised her eyebrows. Hillary laughed and fought desperately to resist the temptation to put into words what they were both thinking, that Alicia was jealous.

Despite Chloe's general sluggishness they managed to be ready and on the road by nine-thirty, a little behind schedule but a lot earlier than Hillary had expected. The drive was uneventful. Alicia was behind the wheel as usual with Chloe as her navigator, and Odile and Hillary seated in the back staring silently out of the window at the passing countryside. Eventually they crossed the border into Suffolk and in no time had reached the outskirts of Newmarket. Everyone agreed that they were feeling thirsty and a little peckish so Alicia proposed that they detour into the town itself and find a tea shop before continuing on to the training yard – the vote was unanimously carried.

Although she wasn't a horsy person Hillary was very taken with Newmarket. Her first impression was of a quaint, cobbled-together town fringed by gracious old trees and surrounded by vast areas of rolling heathland. As they drove into the town centre she admired the large, almost palatial, houses with their wide sweeping lawns and impressive driveways, relics of a bygone era yet still very much inhabited. And, of course, horses pervaded everything, from the first glimpses of shadowy riders galloping across the heath to the High Street itself, chock-a-block with horse boxes, lorries piled high with manure and signwritten delivery vans proclaiming different types of horse feed.

As Alicia searched for somewhere to park, Hillary looked about her eagerly. The shops were intriguing, every third one it seemed having some connection with horses. There were the obvious ones selling riding clothes and equipment, and bookshops whose bow windows boasted vast displays of riding literature, and then there were the insurance companies offering bloodstock insurance rather than the usual life, or buildings and contents cover, horse transport agents and, last but not least, the Jockey Club building itself.

Fortunately the town also enjoyed its fair share of cafes and tea shops and they were soon relaxing over bottomless pots of tea and sinfully large toasted teacakes dripping with melted butter, and indulging in one of their favourite pastimes – people watching. Of the smartly dressed people who strolled along the streets with casual aplomb, at least half of them were sporting an enviably flattering uniform of tight jodhpurs and long, shiny leather boots, the boys looking every bit as good as the girls. On the whole they seemed very young, probably no older than their early twenties, Hillary thought to herself, although she realised afterwards that their size automatically made them seem younger than they really were, most of them having the standard jockey's build.

'We really should think about pushing off.' Alicia glanced agitatedly at her watch for the third time in as many minutes.

Hillary looked down at her own wrist; it was almost eleven thirty and they had promised to meet Gus and Clive before lunch. She threw a few pounds into the kitty in the middle of the table and stood up, smoothing the creases from her dress as she did so. She hadn't been sure what to wear for such an excursion but knowing that in the heat she would be uncomfortable in anything too restrictive she had settled on a short navy-blue cotton sundress, buttoned all the way down the front, worn with low-heeled, tan leather sandals. She looked disparagingly at Chloe's own choice of footwear, wondering what sort of mind thought high heels were appropriate for visiting a stable-yard.

Alicia picked up everyone's contributions and went to settle the bill. When she returned she was smiling. 'Right, I now have proper directions so let's get this show on the road.'

As it turned out they were only ten minutes from their destination and soon the car was heading up a long tarmac driveway, bounded on either side by carefully tended lawns.

Chloe was smiling. 'This certainly isn't what I was expecting. It reminds me of that soap opera you and I used to like watching, Alix, you know the one with all the expensive ranches and hunky men.'

Alicia pretended unsuccessfully that she didn't know what Chloe was talking about. Hillary grinned to herself, her sister was such a snob that she professed only to watch television for the news, documentaries and other suitably highbrow programmes, to admit to watching a soap opera was anathema to her.

A wooden sign pointed the way to the visitor's car park and on the way they passed a couple of empty stable blocks. From what they had seen so far the whole place seemed deserted. Just as they were getting out of the car a large, red-faced woman approached them. Hillary tried hard not to stare as the woman was dressed in an extremely strange assortment of clothes, from her brightly coloured, knitted bobble-hat, to her mauve stocking-clad legs and pink fluffy bedroom slippers, her appearance was tramp-like but with definite overtones of eccentricity. Alicia stepped back alarmed as the woman thrust our her hand and said, 'Jolly good to meet you, good journey I hope?'

Alicia mumbled noncommittally, craning her neck in a desperate attempt to spot Clive and Gus. She pushed Chloe forward as she spoke. 'We're supposed to be meeting our husbands.'

Chloe stumbled in her heels on the uneven ground. 'Yes, we've come to see our horse, it's being trained here,' she said, also looking around. There were no horses to be seen.

'Perhaps we've got the wrong place,' Odile muttered in a low voice.

'No, I followed the directions the man in the tea shop gave me, besides – ' Alicia added indignantly, 'there was a huge sign at the entrance, remember? This is definitely the right place.'

The woman interrupted them. 'I should have introduced myself. I'm Mrs Houghton-Sewell. I own this joint, for my sins.' She gave a rueful grin, displaying a badly fitting set of dentures.

Chloe and Alicia flashed each other horrified looks as the woman asked them their horse's name. The four women looked at each other, temporarily dumbfounded.

'Oh, it's so stupid of me.' Alicia stammered, embarrassed. 'I don't actually know its name.'

Just at that moment they were interrupted by the clattering of hooves and they turned their heads to see about thirty or so horses and riders trotting majestically up the driveway. One by one the riders dismounted and led their steeds to an empty stall, their arrival suddenly transforming the whole place into a hive of activity. A few minutes later a couple of Range Rovers rolled up and came to a halt next to the group of women. Clive and Gus were seated in one of them, Alicia noted with relief.

Mrs Houghton-Sewell walked around the nearest vehicle and had a brief word with the driver who nodded his head and waved his hands in the air in response. In a much louder voice she issued a series of instructions to a group of stable lads who were standing around talking and smoking. Hurriedly the smokers put out their cigarettes and rushed to do her bidding.

Hillary watched the exchange with interest. It was apparent, at least to her, that despite her strange appearance Mrs Houghton-Sewell was a force to be reckoned with. Later she learned that this odd lady was, in fact, one of the most respected trainers in the business and a millionairess to boot.

Being totally oblivious to this fact, Alicia and Chloe did their best to ignore her. As soon as Gus and Clive stepped down from the Range Rover the two women latched on to them and insisted on being taken straight to see their horse. Much to their annoyance, Mrs Houghton-Sewell interrupted.

'You have decided to visit us on a working morning, which means all the horses are taken out to the heath to be put through their paces, to see how they're shaping up and all that. Your husbands have just been watching the horse make a trial gallop.'

She looked at Clive and Gus for confirmation, both men nodded eagerly and Clive chipped in. 'I don't know much about racehorses but he certainly looked impressive.'

'Which one is he?' Mrs Houghton-Sewell inquired.

'Hang Seng,' said Gus, looking slightly embarrassed at the name.

The older woman looked at him sideways. 'Work in the city, am I right?'

Gus nodded. 'We both do, but the horse was already named when we bought him.'

'Yes – we bought our half from a Japanese dealer, you might remember him,' Clive added.

At that moment another group of horses arrived, their riders looking tired but exhilarated. Odile commented on this to Mrs Houghton-Sewell who smiled kindly, obviously appreciating the young woman's interest. 'They have every right to look tired, it's a five thirty start here and woe betide anyone who fancies a lie-in.'

Chloe gave a low whistle, impressed. 'My goodness, five thirty! Why last night I didn't even . . .,' she trailed off hurriedly but not before Gus had flashed her an enquiring look.

Hillary decided she'd better cause a diversion. 'Is one of those horses ours?'

Mrs Houghton-Sewell nodded. 'Yes. See the grey near the back, the one just having his hooves checked?'

They all craned their necks and nodded and Alicia and Chloe smiled at each other like cats who had just been given the cream. Thank goodness the poor beast met with their approval, Hillary thought.

For a while they all stood and stared at the colt as the stable lad, who turned out to be a girl, rubbed him down, settled him in his stall and gave him something to eat and drink. She smiled at Clive and Gus. 'He's got a lot of potential you know,' she asserted encouragingly.

Both received her words with gratitude. They'd been dreading their wives' visit and any expert encouragement such as this would go a long way to smooth over any bumps in the post-mortem which was bound to take place over lunch. Alicia and Chloe were obviously already bored and even Hillary had to admit that she would rather be sitting in a country pub somewhere than standing under the intense heat of the midday sun close to a pile of rotting horse dung.

Just then they were interrupted by the arrival of two dark skinned men dressed identically in tight white jodhpurs and red polo shirts. Alicia jabbed Hillary hard in the buttock, needlessly hissing. 'They're the ones in the photograph.'

Hillary felt her breath catch. She'd already realised who they were, although she had to admit that they certainly made an impressive sight and looked even better in the flesh, so to speak.

Gus introduced them. 'Everybody, meet Carlo and Guido, our partners in crime.'

The one who turned out to be Carlo looked around him with an expression of mock horror. 'Please,' he urged, 'there are already too many villains in the horse racing fraternity for that to be considered a joke.'

'And,' Guido said, 'there are those who believe racehorse syndicates are controlled by the mafia, obviously with our heritage – well, need I say more?'

The four women stared at them open-mouthed. With their Italian good-looks and pronounced London accents they certainly could be mistaken for crooks, albeit very handsome ones. Chloe, surprisingly, appeared more interested in her wristwatch than the two men standing in front of her. She was studying it intently.

'Gus darling, I'm famished and its after one, look!' She thrust her arm at his face.

Guido looked at his brother who nodded, then he

spoke to the group. 'Please, let Carlo and I take you to lunch. One of our cousins has a restaurant not far from here. I hope you all like Italian food?'

Chloe perked up immediately. 'Oh, we love it, don't we, Alix?'

Alicia nodded enthusiastically, as did Hillary and Odile.

'Then it's settled.' Guido smiled, satisfied. He spoke directly to Clive. 'If you, Gus and your wives would like to follow us in your car, Carlo and I would be happy to drive these gorgeous young things in ours.'

Realising that Guido meant them, Hillary and Odile gave each other a quizzical look and each smothered a smile. Nevertheless under the circumstances it seemed the most sensible solution. They all trooped back to the car park and Carlo walked straight to the second Range Rover, not the one Gus and Clive had travelled in. He unlocked all the doors and gallantly stepped back so that Odile and Hillary could climb in. The floor of the Range Rover was quite high and Hillary couldn't help feeling his eyes on her legs as she hitched up her skirt. Guido walked around to the other side and jumped in the passenger seat as Carlo settled himself behind the wheel. Soon they were all speeding back along the now familiar route towards Newmarket.

Despite their arrogant appearance, Hillary had to admit that the two brothers were extremely entertaining and good fun to be with. All the time they were driving and throughout the meal they kept up a continuous and highly amusing patter, bouncing witticisms off each other like a comedy double-act, or at the very least, Hillary thought, like two people who knew each other extremely well and enjoyed each other's company.

She couldn't help glancing surreptitiously at them during the meal. Guido had said he was older than Carlo by exactly one year and one month but in truth they looked more like twins and absolutely Italian in every way. Their olive complexions made the perfect canvas for proud foreheads, Roman noses and the limpid, black pools that were their eyes. And she had already had the opportunity to admire their physique. Lean, hard and tight was the best way she could describe them, due no doubt to rigorous training and daily bouts of horse riding of all kinds. Too tall to be jockeys, Guido explained that he and Carlo enjoyed various other equestrian pursuits, particularly polo, hunting and eventing.

Hillary kept on smiling and nodding throughout the constant banter but most of the time had no idea what they were talking about. Equestrian slang and terminology seemed a completely different language. One aspect that she did manage to keep pace with was the amount of wine being consumed. The cousin who owned the restaurant couldn't do enough for the two brothers and their guests. So copious amounts of wine flowed constantly at their table, although Carlo drank less than the others, being the driver.

Straight after the main course, Odile had asked if anyone minded her slipping away for a few hours to sightsee and to do some shopping saying she would make her own way back to the training yard by six o'clock at the latest. It would be another two hours before the rest of the party would leave. Two more hours of drinking wine.

At first, Hillary had tried to stay reasonably sober, covering her glass with her hand at every other top-up, however, being sensible proved too much of an effort and she eventually lost count of the number of glasses that she had consumed.

Whilst they were all seated at the table she felt fine and still perfectly sober, but as soon as she got to her feet Hillary wobbled disconcertingly. Guido put out a hand to steady her and she gripped it with both hands, holding on for dear life. She smiled up at Guido in gratitude and, without warning, found herself trapped in his steady gaze. She saw something in his eyes that she'd been trying to ignore ever since they first met – pure lust.

Whether she'd been attracted to him originally or not made no difference to her now. As far as she was concerned, it was always an enormous turn-on when a man made it obvious he was interested in her. Disconcertingly, Carlo looked at her in exactly the same way as he helped her climb back into the Range Rover. Telling herself that it was simply because they were brothers, she nevertheless wondered how she could feel equally attracted by two men at exactly the same time. Stepping outside the restaurant into the fresh air was almost her undoing as the effects of the wine suddenly hit her like a lightning bolt and it took all her strength of will to remain seated upright on the return journey to the training yard.

When they pulled into the car park they found Mrs Houghton-Sewell waiting for them, arms crossed, her cheeks more flushed than ever, although in deference to the scorching heat she had at least removed her bobble hat. 'Thought you might fancy coming up to the house and talking a bit of business over some afternoon tea,' she boomed affably.

Hillary almost groaned at the thought of more food but Alicia, Chloe, Gus and Clive accepted immediately.

'I think I'll stay out here in the fresh air, if you don't mind,' Hillary said in a small voice. Groping behind her until her hands came into contact with a low brick wall, she sat down unsteadily.

Carlo and Guido exchanged glances. Carlo spoke for both. 'Don't worry about the young lady Mrs H. We'll take care of her.' They sat down either side of Hillary in a protective manner.

Mrs Houghton-Sewell grunted. 'Now I am worried about her.' But there was a distinct trace of laughter in her voice that dispelled Alicia's initial concern for her sister's well-being.

As soon as the others were out of earshot, Guido turned to Hillary. 'Would you like a guided tour?' Noticing Hillary's doubtful expression he quickly added. 'You'll soon feel better when you start walking around.'

Despite her slightly confused state, Hillary could see the sense in what he said and rose to her feet uncertainly. 'Do you mind if I hold on to your arm?' She directed the request at neither one in particular but both were quick to snake an arm around her waist, holding her firmly from both sides. Carlo winked at Guido over the top of her head.

She was surprised to find that Guido's prediction about her soon feeling better was quite right, in no time at all she was feeling pleasantly relaxed rather than drunk and perfectly in control of her faculties. Still, she reasoned, there was no reason to let the brothers know that just yet. She pretended to stumble and smiled to herself as both Guido and Carlo tightened their grip on her, now that she no longer felt ill she was starting to feel very sexy.

After about half an hour Guido asked her if she'd seen enough. In all honesty, she had had her fill after the first five minutes but she pouted and replied that she supposed so and was there anywhere nearby where they could sit in the shade? Carlo pointed to a large barn that stood alone some distance from the main stable blocks.

'We'll be comfortable in there, as well as out of the sun. It's where they store all the fresh hay,' he explained.

Inside the barn it was cool and shadowy. Hillary dropped down onto a pile of hay with a sigh of relief. She fanned herself with her hand then pulled the neckline of her dress away from her body and blew down it. 'Phew, I didn't think it was possible for the weather to get this hot in England.' She glanced down. Her dress had ridden quite high up her bare thighs and Carlo was looking at them again. She shivered with anticipation and felt her stomach clench. Something was definitely going to happen between them and she was now certain that she was going to let it.

Since they began their walk she had been having an argument with herself about the possibility. Telling herself on the one hand that Haldane and Torran were more than enough for any woman and, on the other, that they weren't around at that precise moment and Guido and Carlo were. She lay back against the straw and stared at the ceiling of the barn, if something was destined to happen between them then so be it.

A quarter of an hour later she was starting to arrive at the conclusion that nothing was meant to happen. A small uproar had broken out next to one of the stable blocks sending the brothers dashing out of the barn to see what the problem was. So far they hadn't returned. Hillary moved restlessly on the straw, she still felt very hot and couldn't get comfortable so in desperation she undid a couple of the buttons on the front of her dress, just enough to ease the constriction around her thighs and allow a little more air to her chest. After a few minutes she undid another couple.

By the time Carlo and Guido returned she had fallen asleep, one bare breast almost exposed, her body slightly twisted at the waist, her legs carelessly splayed to reveal the faintest hint of white lace knickers atop firm brown thighs. The two Italian men drew in their breath simultaneously – she was so stunning they wanted to sit and stare at her forever.

Hillary was aware of their return – the barn door was old and creaky, their footsteps heavy and their breathing heavier still. Nevertheless, she didn't feel inclined to waken properly just yet, she would rather let nature take its course with her the innocent participant. For a long while nothing happened, at least nothing tactile. She fought to maintain the steady pattern of her breathing and resisted the temptation to steal a glance. Neither Carlo nor Guido spoke, not even in whispers, although she had already come to realise that they possessed a gift of communication through their eyes and expressions alone. It didn't occur to her that they might have fallen asleep themselves.

176

As it turned out, the men were quietly studying her, their reticence adding to the eroticism of the situation. It was only when the lengthening shadows made by the sun through the cracks in the wooden barn door reminded them the afternoon was fading quickly that they began to feel a sense of urgency.

The first touch is always the sweetest, Hillary thought poetically, wilfully bastardising the words of a song she'd first heard many years before. She didn't know whose fingers were upon her, although she guessed they both touched her at the same time. A slight brush against the swell of her partially exposed breast coincided with a long sweep of fingertips the length of her left leg. Both were tentative, exploratory, stirring the natural responses of her body.

Her nipples hardened, her clitoris tingled, a rush of wetness suddenly soaked her knickers. She couldn't pretend to stir very slightly. At her movement the caresses stopped for a moment until, obviously satisfied that she was still asleep, the men resumed their exploration of her body. From time to time she shifted, or moaned a little, just enough to be convincing. But it no longer interrupted them, they were past caring anyway and suspected that she would be too, by the time she woke up.

Someone was removing her knickers, carefully easing them down her thighs. She conveniently choreographed her movements to assist their smooth passage. At the same time other fingers were undoing the few remaining buttons on the front of her dress, peeling back the damp, creased cotton to completely expose the naked body that lay beneath. She almost weakened then, almost opened her eyes to catch the moment when they first revealed all of her to their gaze. It was one of her favourite parts of a first encounter but one that she would have to forgo or else break the illusion of sleepy acquiescence.

Soft, silky hair brushed her naked skin, across her breasts and at the top of her thighs, a few stray curls tickling her belly. The men's touch was all over her now, hands stroking everywhere, twenty fingers probing into crevices, opening her up like a flower, stimulating the most sensitive parts of her body. Knowing their eyes were directed below her face she dared to open her lids a fraction, glacing down under cover of thick lashes. As she thought, one brother was stroking and kissing her breasts, the other caressing her between her legs but, from her viewpoint, it was impossible to distinguish one from the other.

She knew she couldn't keep up the pretence much longer, her arousal was deepening, her expressions of ecstasy becoming ever harder to conceal. They spoke now, in low voices, discussing her. Soft fingers spread her labia, one voice asking the other to look. Her breasts lost the sensation of hands upon them as their caresser moved position. Hands were now opening her sex wider, fingers spreading the edges of her vagina while other fingers dipped inside, stroking, twisting, turning.

Helpless under the manipulations of the two men she quickly became a writhing, moaning, carnal being, straining for release. Suddenly there was a hand back at her breast, teasing the nipple just as its hardness had started to subside. Hillary gasped as the fingers pinched her hard, the pain swiftly followed by a fresh burst of pleasure, then they did the same with the other nipple. Arching her back towards the tormenting hands, Hillary felt fingers drawing back the little hood of skin that protected the delicate bud of her clitoris. Then she felt the wetness of a tongue upon it and she was lost completely.

As the sultry afternoon wore on, the enjoyment they wrung from her body was enduring, all-encompassing, the simple act of giving pleasure bringing its own reward. She had not laid one finger on either of their bodies, nor taken them inside her to return the gift of orgasm.

Perhaps if there had been more time, if the sound of footsteps and voices coming closer to the barn had not made them wary, the encounter between the two brothers and Hillary may have been consummated. But, the same fingers that had deftly aroused her time after time now just as deftly buttoned her dress and hastily sought her discarded knickers. As it turned out the footsteps and voices passed by the barn and away into the distance but by that time all three realised that the spell had been broken.

Hillary slowly opened her eyes and smiled at each of them. Without saying a word, the two brothers stood up and Guido stretched out a hand and helped her to her feet. Her legs still felt shaky but she knew that this time the wine had very little to do with it. She expected them to say something about what had passed between them but they acted as if they had just entered the barn minutes before and their erotic interlude had never taken place. Joining in their charade, Hillary said nothing and simply strolled with them up to the main house, their journey taking them across the training track to save time and effort.

Just as they approached they met Clive, Alicia, Gus and Chloe who, having just said goodbye to Mrs Houghton-Sewell, were talking about going their separate ways. At that moment a taxi pulled into the yard, dropping off Odile and at least a dozen carrier bags.

Hillary turned to Guido and Carlo feeling, and looking, more than a little regretful. 'It looks as though we're leaving already.' She spoke loudly, half hoping that one of the others would suggest a drink at a local pub. She felt as though she was about to leave behind some unfinished business. The Italians looked at their watches at exactly the same moment.

'We have to be off anyway – , we're due to meet someone in town in ten minutes.'

Carlo started the sentence and Guido finished it.

Hillary just stopped herself from asking them if they always did everything together. With an inward blush she realised she already knew the answer to that one.

Clive and Alicia, Gus and Chloe stood a little way off,

saying goodbye to each other. The men had already explained that they were due back at work the next morning without fail and wouldn't be able to make it back to Norfolk until sometime on the Saturday. Alicia complained that it would mean that they would miss Darius's party on the Friday night but Chloe didn't look too distraught at the news. Either she was planning a replay with Torran or was hoping to entice Darius himself, Hillary thought glumly.

After a last, quick check on Hang Seng they all climbed into their various cars. Clive and Gus spoke briefly with Guido and Carlo before the two brothers sped off to keep their appointment, then blew kisses to their wives. Slowly Alicia backed her Mercedes out of the car park and headed for the main road that would take them back toward the north Norfolk coast. For a while everyone was silent, lost in their own thoughts. Chloe yawned.

'Oh God, don't do that you'll set me off,' Odile warned.

Chloe swivelled around in the front passenger seat so that she could look at Odile. 'I take it you shopped 'till you dropped.'

'Something like that.' The young woman laughed. 'You wouldn't believe how many interesting things I found to buy. I even splashed out on a couple of silk shirts for Theo.'

'Oh! Buying him clothes now? It must be love.'

Hillary marvelled at the way Chloe managed to make the most enjoyable of human conditions sound like a disease but Odile simply smiled and nodded contentedly, closing her eyes sleepily to ward off any further criticism her friend may have had in mind.

Alicia caught Hillary's eye in the rear view mirror. 'What did you get up to while we were having tea with Mrs Houghton-Sewell?'

Hillary was deliberately vague. 'Oh, not much. I just wandered around the yard talking to Guido and Carlo.

I even dozed off at one point,' she added ruefully, giving a little laugh.

Alicia wasn't about to be fobbed off. 'I noticed you were with those two Italians when we came out. Were they making a nuisance of themselves, Hilly?'

'Oh, no, of course not.' Hillary was quick to leap to their defence, a little too quick she realised with a sinking feeling.

'It sounds as if there was more to your afternoon than you're letting on,' Chloe remarked incisively.

'Not really, we just talked – they're a nice couple of guys.'

To Hillary's relief Chloe and Alicia seemed satisfied with her response and only Odile gave her a knowing look when no-one else was watching. Hillary blushed and stared out of the window but no-one spoke until they reached Harwood Hall.

As soon as they arrived back at the Hall Chloe dashed up the stairs and through the swing doors to the main house, ostensibly to ask Fearn if she could do some ironing for her. She came back looking glum.

'Isn't Torran there then?' Alicia said, smirking.

Chloe flashed her a venomous look. 'I went to see Fearn.'

Alicia nodded. 'Of course you did. So, was he?'

'No.' Chloe flopped into the nearest armchair looking despondent. 'And to make matters worse, Fearn said a girl had telephoned him and ten minutes later he said he was going to meet someone at the Baker's Arms.'

'That's the pub in the village, isn't it?' Odile asked.

Chloe nodded. 'As far as I know. She stood up decisively. 'Does anyone fancy going for a drink?'

Alicia looked horrified. 'You're not serious are you, Chlo'?'

'Of course I am. Why shouldn't I go to the pub for a drink? Odile's been there, even Hillary's been.'

Hillary wanted to ask her what she meant by 'even Hillary' but Odile interrupted her.

'I wouldn't mind a stroll down to the village and they do quite a nice selection of food at the Baker's Arms.'

The mention of food obviously swayed Alicia, although she still sounded doubtful. 'Okay, let's all go. But I'm warning you, Chloe, if you show us up –' The unspoken threat hung in the air between them all the way to the village.

Chapter Eleven

At first Torran wasn't anywhere to be seen but then Hillary spotted him sitting in a corner booth next to a very pretty girl who was slim, with long blonde hair and undeniably young. She knew Chloe wouldn't be at all happy when she saw her rival and as soon as she heard the tell-tale hiss in her left ear she knew she was right.

'Look at him sitting there with her,' Chloe said bitterly.

Hillary tried to sound placatory, after all she had bedded Torran before Chloe and therefore she should have been feeling the most aggrieved. 'They're not doing anything wrong, Chloe.'

The older woman snarled. 'Is anyone getting the drinks in?'

Hillary sighed. Chloe really was taking this situation to extremes and if she wasn't careful she'd end up making a complete fool of herself and embarrassing them all. In an effort to defuse the situation she took her by the arm and guided her to the other side of the cosy bar where a table had just become vacant. Taking Hillary's cue, Odile offered to get everyone's drinks and asked the barmaid for a couple of menus.

'I've lost my appetite.' Chloe stared at the menu, uninterested, her voice deliberately petulant.

Hillary's fingers itched to slap her. 'If you don't line your stomach with something then you'll just end up drunk and you don't want Torran to see you like that, do you?'

She'd said the right thing, and Chloe perked up at last. When Chloe ordered a rare roast beef salad, Odile and Hillary said they would have the same, whilst Alicia finally decided on prawn quiche. Halfway through their meal Hillary noticed that Torran and the girl were preparing to leave. Chloe had just got up to use the lavatory and Hillary prayed that they would be gone before she got back. God must be asleep, she thought to herself despondently as she watched Chloe run slap bang into the couple halfway across the room.

The three women strained to hear what was being said. Surprisingly no voices were being raised and Chloe appeared amazingly relaxed and in control. When she returned to their table she was beaming from ear to ear. Without a word she sat down and resumed her meal, enjoying the suspense that she was creating.

Finally Alicia gave in. 'Well?'

Chloe smirked, picked up her napkin and dabbed her mouth. She looked at the expectant faces of her friends. 'She's just an apprentice, nothing more.'

Alicia let out a low whistle. 'Thank goodness, now perhaps we can relax and enjoy the rest of our meal.'

'You must be joking.' Chloe was already rising from her seat. 'He said he'd meet us back at the Hall in ten minutes.'

As it turned out, Chloe never did get to meet up with Torran that night. When they arrived back at the Hall she was met by a worried looking Fearn who said that there had been an urgent telephone call for her from her husband. By the time Chloe got through to Gus and found out that his crisis amounted to nothing more than being unable to find a favourite tie, it was well past midnight and Torran had gone to bed. Although she didn't say anything the next morning, Hillary suspected that Chloe had lain awake most of the night waiting for him in vain.

Reports on the radio promised another scorching hot day and the possibility of thunderstorms by evening. Alicia said she couldn't face another day on the beach, not even the naturist one and suggested a trip to Norwich. Chloe and Odile agreed but Hillary shook her head. She knew it would end up becoming yet another shopping trip and couldn't bear the thought of tramping along dusty pavements in the stifling heat trailing in and out of endless shops.

'Oh, Hill, you're such a party pooper,' Alicia complained. 'Apart from going to Newmarket yesterday you haven't wanted to go anywhere other than the beach.'

Chloe bit into a piece of toast, speaking with her mouth full she exclaimed. 'You can't blame her, Alix, not when she knows that muscle bound Viking is likely to be waiting for her.'

Alicia nodded in agreement.

'Haldane is not a Viking,' Hillary protested, although she had to admit Chloe had a point. 'Besides,' she mumbled, almost petulantly, 'I wasn't planning to go to the beach today.'

'No? Oh, but I forgot, if you lay around her long enough you're bound to run into some young stud who'll screw the arse of you.'

'You bitch!' Hillary started to rise from her chair, she had come close to slapping Chloe a few times during the past week, perhaps now was the right time.

Alicia put a placatory hand on her shoulder. 'Calm down, Hilly, she didn't mean to be nasty.' Then she turned to Chloe, the barely controlled anger evident in her voice. 'That was totally uncalled for, Chloe, I think you should apologise to my sister right now.'

Despite the anger bubbling away inside her, Hillary couldn't help smiling to herself at Alicia's use of the words 'my sister'. They may have had their differences over the years but any attempt by an outsider to denigrate one of them automatically resulted in Hillary and Alicia closing ranks.

Chloe smiled wanly. 'I'm sorry, Hillary. I seem to have a bit of a blind spot where Torran is concerned.'

Hillary nodded. That was true enough. She suspected that for all her posturing and bravado Chloe was not the femme fatale she made herself out to be and it was obvious she couldn't accept that what had happened with Torran was a one off, nothing more than a bit of fun. Deciding she could afford to be magnanimous, Hillary returned Chloe's smile with one of genuine friendship and assured her that there was no harm done.

Shortly afterwards the four women drifted off to their respective bedrooms to dress in whatever they considered most appropriate for their planned activity. In Hillary's case this meant her customary bikini and sarong.

As soon as the others had left she settled herself on a sun lounger on the patio. At Odile's request she kept the cordless telephone on the table next to her, in case Theo should ring to say he could come over to England at the weekend after all. She also had a jug of iced fruit juice and a book that she borrowed from Alicia's room.

At first all was silent. Everyone from the main house was out: Torran at the glass works and Fearn gone by taxi to the nearby resort of Hunstanton. She read her book for a while until, enervated by the heat, she put it down, removed her bikini top and simply lay back and toasted herself.

She had just fallen into a half-doze, dreaming that she was adrift on a desert island, her every whim being attended to by a tribe of virile young natives who all looked Italian, when the telephone buzzed harshly beside her. Groggily she reached out and brought it to her ear.

'What are you wearing?'

The voice was smooth and deep, as sultry as the air around her. For a second she wondered if she was still dreaming but the same question issued forth from the receiver. Her body tingled in response as she recognised the speaker as Darius, the situation reminding her of a scene in a film she had once seen where a girl had described her near naked state to her lover over the telephone, arousing herself as she did so. She stretched voluptuously and put on her sexiest voice.

'I'm not wearing very much at all, just a little pair of knickers, my breasts are completely naked and . . .'

Darius's voice interrupted her, this time he sounded much less sensuous. 'I think you misunderstand me. Hillary isn't it?'

Hillary nodded, then, finding her voice, squeaked into the telephone that it was indeed her.

Darius's response was terse. 'I thought so.'

'What did you want, Darius?' Hillary snapped, her previous feelings of irriation with him resurfacing.

'I actually wanted to enquire what you intended wearing to my party tomorrow night. I thought it only fair to let you know that it will be quite a dressy affair, just in case you and your southern friends were labouring under the misapprehension that Norfolk society is comprised of hicks and yokels.'

'I, we never . . .,' Hillary broke in but Darius was still in full flow.

'The last thing I want is for you all to turn up dressed for a beach barbecue, or city disco, you'll only embarrass yourselves.'

All he's worried about is that we won't embarrass him, Hillary thought to herself angrily – how dare he! She almost felt like telling him where to stick his invitation but she knew if she did that Alicia and Chloe would never forgive her.

She fought to control her tone. 'Your concern is touching but I can assure you we are perfectly capable of dressing and conducting ourselves with decorum.' If she could have put her hands down the telephone and throttled him she would have done so.

'Good, then I'll look forward to seeing you

187

tomorrow,' Darius concluded tersely. Just as she thought his call was over he spoke again, only this time his tone had softened considerably. 'I hope I haven't upset you, Hillary.'

'Of course not,' she answered stiffly. Damn him! For some inexplicable reason she actually felt relieved he had said this.

He apologised again and also apologised for disturbing her, then rang off leaving Hillary plagued by a seething mass of conflicting emotions. On the one hand Darius Harwood was a charming, handsome man, extremely eligible and desirable and, although he was the total opposite of Haldane she felt drawn to him sexually. In complete contrast to this charming, sexy self, he was also aggravating and insufferably patronising, often inciting disturbingly angry and violent thoughts within her. In some ways, she thought, she would be relieved when her holiday ended and she could put some distance between herself and Darius. Hopefully it would be a case of out of sight being out of mind.

Lost in her thoughts she didn't hear the front doorbell ring and was startled to hear heavy footsteps approaching through the gardens. Shading her eyes with her hand she craned her neck to see who it was, concerned that she was hardly dressed to receive a visitor. It was a man, but the glare of the sun made it impossible for her to see his face. She used her other hand and arm to cover her naked breasts. 'Who is it?'

'I came to apologise again, in person.' It was Darius.

Now that he was standing closer to her she could see him clearly, although the moment he spoke she recognised his voice. He sat down easily on one of the garden chairs and stared openly at her. Hillary felt her mouth go dry and her cheeks glow with embarrassment. Why did he always make her feel at such a disadvantage?

'There was really no need.' She was referring to his most recent apology.

'I thought there was,' he stated in a tone that dared

her to contradict. Then he said a wicked smile touching the corners of his mouth, 'When you told me on the telephone how little you were wearing I couldn't resist coming over here to ogle.'

Despite her better judgement, she found her anger with him receding, his words and the way he looked at her sending small thrills of erotic excitement coursing through her near naked body. She looked at him, then quickly looked away – his expression was disturbingly insolent, obviously mirroring his thoughts.

Rising from his chair he took two steps toward her, knelt in front of her and with slow deliberation removed the arm that shielded her breasts. As soon as he had exposed her to his gaze he gave a low murmur of appreciation.

Hillary felt herself growing warm as he gave her a long, lingering stare.

'You have a superb body, but I expect many men have told you that already,' he said.

Hillary sighed, wondering if she was being over sensitive as she picked up his use of the word many. Her mind instantly jumped back to a few days earlier when he had entered their kitchen and remarked on her sexual excesses. Who, and however many, she chose to sleep with was really no concern of his.

She was just about to tell him so when he stood up, smoothing the creases in his trousers. Smiling down at her, he informed her that he really couldn't stay, his explanation being that he had to go to a local tree nursery and pick out some saplings. Hillary felt deflated. He always seemed to deliberately stir up her emotions, whether lust, anger or whatever and then leave her high and dry. She felt tears of frustration prick the backs of her eyelids and, not trusting herself to speak, merely nodded silently.

After he had left she picked up her book once again, determined not to give him another thought. But, against her will, his image hung around in the back of her mind, taunting her until finally she slammed the book shut, rolled over onto her stomach and willed her mind to go completely blank. Eventually she fell into a deep, dreamless sleep.

By the time Chloe, Alicia and Odile returned she had awoken feeling totally rested, read almost all of the book and was cheerfully preparing dinner for them. A walk to the village in the late afternoon had restored her spirits and she had returned laden with good things to eat.

'Mmm, this is a lovely surprise.' Alicia peered into the casserole dish that Hillary had just removed from the oven. 'Ooh, chicken chasseur, my favourite.'

Hillary smiled. She had decided to cook that particular dish by way of an unspoken thank you to her sister for supporting her at breakfast against Chloe's uncalled for attack. Although she had to admit that even Chloe was looking much more relaxed – she offered to peel the potatoes which Hillary knew to be one of her least favourite chores. All in all, it was a happy band who sat down around the scrubbed pine table that evening to enjoy the simple pleasures of good food, fine wine and light hearted conversation.

Odile was just describing how Alicia had nearly run over a policeman's foot as she was trying to park in an awkward space when the first bolt of lightning lit up the sky. A few minutes later it was followed by an ominous roll of thunder. Large drops of rain spattered against the window, their momentum gathering until there was a torrent. They stared out at the patio which was beginning to look more like a swimming pool.

'Thank goodness we had the foresight to put the garden furniture away,' Alicia muttered.

Chloe put a hand to her head. 'Storms always give me a headache,' she complained to no-one in particular.

After a few minutes they returned to their meal but the constant interruption of the thunder and lightning made conversation impossible. They finished eating in silence and adjourned to the sitting room where they attempted to play Scrabble.

'It's no good, I just can't think.' Odile flopped back in her chair, exasperation showing on her face – she had just tried to spell the word 'brick' using the letter 'k' twice instead of 'ck'.

'Okay, well let's play something else.' Hillary opened the door to the sideboard and considered their options, Trivial Pursuit, Monopoly or Ludo.

Alicia put her hand on Hillary's arm. 'I don't think any of us are really in the mood.'

Hillary nodded and shut the door again, gathering up the Scrabble tiles without another word.

Alicia and Chloe both rose to their feet, yawning. 'I'm off to bed,' they said in unison.

Without looking up, Hillary nodded, finished picking up the Scrabble pieces and stowed the box away in the sideboard before sitting down heavily in the armchair Alicia had just vacated. She gave a tired sigh and glanced at Odile. The young woman was as white as a sheet.

'I hate storms, don't you?' Hillary offered kindly. In reality she rather liked the unrestrained drama of them but she could see that Odile was petrified.

The young woman nodded, curling her legs under her until she looked as though she was trying to revert back to the womb. Hillary picked up the book that she had been reading earlier. Alicia had complained at first about Hillary borrowing it before she'd even had a chance to read it herself but then relented and said it didn't matter because she had bought another book in Norwich that she was dying to start. They sat in companionable silence until, about an hour later, the telephone rang. Hillary stretched out a lazy hand to answer it. The caller was Torran asking for Chloe.

A few minutes later Chloe herself popped her head around the doorway. 'Worst luck, Torran rang to say that he was going to stay with a friend tonight. He didn't fancy travelling back from King's Lynn in this weather – the roads are treacherous by all accounts.'

Hillary marvelled at the way Chloe's mind worked.

'Well, thank you for the bulletin,' she remarked sarcastically. Obviously Torran and Chloe were now an item.

Odile stood up. 'I think I'll go to bed,' she said in a small, tight voice.

The book held Hillary's attention for another half an hour or so and then she closed it, with a sigh, deciding to give in to the storm and go to bed like everyone else already had. She took the book with her to her room, undressed, climbed into bed and opened it again.

She looked at the pages with unseeing eyes as thoughts of Darius intruded on her mind once again. Eventually she gave up trying to read, switched off her bedside lamp and lay back against the pillow, staring at the ceiling. Presently she felt her eyelids begin to droop.

Some time later she sensed someone climbing into bed beside her; the mattress dipped slightly then the silence was broken by the sound of light breathing that wasn't her own. Keeping her eyes tightly closed, Hillary considered the possibilities: she was still asleep and therefore dreaming, the house was haunted, or someone was genuinely occupying the space next to her in bed. Dismissing the first as impossible and the other two options as highly unlikely she ponderd what to do, then a hand touched her leg. Immediately she sat up and switched on the bedside lamp. She found herself looking into Odile's frightened face.

'I'm sorry, Hillary, I know its stupid of me but I was afraid. I couldn't sleep on my own.' Then she added. 'I didn't mean to wake you.'

Despite her surprise Hillary breathed a sigh of relief then she turned off the light and lay back against the padded headboard, looking down at Odile through the gloomy half-light.

'It's okay. You just gave me a fright that's all, I thought you were a ghost.' Hillary gave a rueful laugh and Odile smiled crookedly.

'I'll try not to disturb you,' she promised, moving right over to the edge of the bed.

They lay still and unspeaking for a few minutes with

Hillary feeling inexplicably tense. She reasoned that it was because she hadn't shared a bed with a person of her own sex since she and Alicia were children and had been forced to double up when relatives came to stay at the family home. She didn't like to admit the real reason for her disquiet. After a few moments she closed her eyes tightly and prayed for sleep. Slowly, their release unbidden, memories floated through her brain, snatches of conversation sounding as real to her ears at that moment as if the words were being freshly spoken.

It was the first time all four women had gone to the beach together and they were laying on the hot sand talking about men and sex and themselves. Odile had said Theo was only her second male lover, making it clear that she was bisexual. At the time Hillary had laughed at Alicia's and Chloe's shocked faces but now she felt gauche, uncomfortable with the knowledge that Odile had the capability of finding other women sexually attractive.

She tried to reason with herself that Odile was straight now. She had Theo and they enjoyed a very vigorous and satisfying physical relationship. Hillary laughed inwardly. She was making the classic assumption that gay or bisexual people would prey on anyone who happened to be around, which she knew logically was not the case at all.

Odile must have been reading her mind. 'I'm not planning to seduce you, Hillary.'

Hillary laughed aloud but even to her own ears it sounded false. 'I – I know, I wasn't . . .,' she trailed off, embarrassed.

Turning on her side to face her, Odile said, perceptively, 'You were remembering that day on the beach.'

Almost unwillingly, Hillary looked into her pale green eyes. 'Yes. I'm sorry, I just couldn't help wondering.' She felt the warmth rise in her cheeks.

'Do you want to know what it's like to make love to a woman, Hillary, is that it?'

Hillary shook her head vehemently, shocked at the

suggestion. Then she felt herself overtaken by the realisation that Odile might have uncovered something she hadn't been prepared to admit even to herself.

'I don't know,' she said honestly. 'It's not something I've ever thought about consciously but I've enjoyed the odd fantasy, every woman does. That doesn't make me a lesbian does it?' Deep down she knew the answer to that one but nevertheless her question finished on an uncertain note.

Odile smiled reasurringly. 'I'm not a lesbian either, Hillary.' She laughed then. 'Look at Theo for goodness sake, do you think a man like him would tolerate a relationship with a dyke?'

Hillary had to admit that she had a point. She stared straight ahead and tried to make sense of her thoughts before she spoke again. Before she had chance to say anything else. Odile broke the silence between them.

'You're probably feeling a little foolish right now but you shouldn't you know.' Something in Odile's tone captured Hillary's attention, deep within her she could feel a faint fluttering.

'Why?' Hillary's voice was barely a whisper.

'Because I am attracted to you, that's why.' Her admission came out in a rush and then she sighed deeply. 'And now I suppose I should go back to my own room and chastise myself for ruining our friendship.'

Hillary trembled, acknowledging that deep down she had known what Odile's reply would be. Had she hoped for it? She put out a hand, tentatively touching Odile's arm and feeling the soft, warm skin under her fingertips where the light downy hairs stiffened as she spoke. 'Don't go, Odile.' She wasn't sure if the young woman would take her invitation at face value, or use her feminine intuition to see past the thin barriers Hillary had erected around that so far undiscovered facet of her sexuality. Odile didn't speak, nor did she move. Hillary closed her eyes and tried not to think about the young woman laying next to her in the warm comfort of the double bed. They were all alone, she thought, cast adrift in the middle of a storm.

She was reminded of the dream she had been enjoying earlier as she sunbathed, before Darius had turned her thoughts upside down. Thinking of Darius made her wonder why she bothered with men at all, perhaps lesbians were the wise ones? In her dream she had been physically attended to by natives but not all of them had been male, she now recalled. One of them, the one who brought her most pleasure, was a young girl, slim, long legged, with lustrous auburn hair. Smiling at the recollection she turned to look at Odile. Their eyes locked.

Hillary held her breath, conscious of the ferocity with which her heart was hammering in her chest. Slowly, deliberately, Odile sat up and pulled her nightgown over her head. Shaking her mane of hair free of tangles, she waited until Hillary had composed herself. It was obvious to Odile that her companion was stunned by the sight and proximity of her now naked body. Unabashed she allowed Hillary to satisfy her curiosity, sitting upright while Hillary stared at her. Although they had sunbathed naked before, she appreciated that this wasn't quite the same.

Finally, Hillary followed suit and pulled off her nightdress, feeling acutely embarrassed as she sat next to Odile, her nipples tightening under the young woman's open gaze. This can't be happening, she thought to herself, its just part of my dream. In her dream though she had not felt the intense churning in her stomach, nor the throbbing anguish between her legs. In her dream she hadn't been able to smell her own arousal.

When she thought Hillary was ready, Odile put out one slender, well-manicured hand and touched her shoulder, running her fingers lightly down Hillary's arm until they were level with her breast before moving across to stroke the softly swelling flesh. Despite her trepidation Hillary moaned, her pleasure increasing as Odile rubbed her thumb lightly across her nipple. Then she moved her hand to the other breast and did the same. Hillary waited, half of her mind enjoying the sensation of Odile's hand upon her body, the other half wondering what she should do in response.

Eventually, curiosity overcame her reticence. Tentatively, she mirrored Odile's actions, feeling the natural resistance of the other woman's breast as she touched with her fingertips. Then she too stroked the soft flesh, moving around and around the smooth globes until she dared to touch a nipple. She enjoyed the way the puckered flesh instantly stiffened under her touch, a reaction much more pronounced than on a man. She looked up at Odile's face, noting how her eyes were glazed, her lips slightly parted revealing the tip of a soft pink tongue. Suddenly she wondered how that tongue would feel on her body and shivered, realising that it would probably not be long before she found out.

They lay on their sides facing each other and for a long time the two women contented themselves with stroking the upper half of each other's bodies. Odile wanted to make sure that Hillary was completely relaxed and ready before moving on to the next stage. There was no hurry, they had all night.

Gradually, as she stroked the length of Hillary's back, Odile let her fingers drift a little lower, skimming the upper swell of her buttocks. Hillary inhaled deeply, it was happening, it was really happening. The realisation that they were set on a course released Hillary from the last of her reserve. Feeling quite bold, she ventured her hands a little further, stroking them over the whole curve of Odile's taut behind, enjoying the way the muscles quivered beneath her fingers. She trailed her fingers down the cleft between them, her long nails slightly stimulating the sensitive flesh. Odile moaned loudly and, despite her good intentions, thrust her pelvis toward Hillary's feeling the soft down of their pubic mounds mesh together.

Hillary stiffened, startled at first. Then she relaxed again, it really was quite a nice feeling. With a slight sigh of contentment she urged her body even closer to Odile's until their breasts made contact too. At that point it seemed the most natural thing in the world for them to kiss – two pairs of soft feminine lips touching for the first time. It was sublime, the sweetest kiss she had ever had, Hillary thought. When she went over the whole thing in her mind later, she realised that what she had enjoyed the most was the softness and gentleness of the whole encounter.

Men, she decided, could be unnecessarily rough, even when they were trying hard to be considerate. It wasn't their fault, they just didn't realise their own strength. And, of course, a woman had the added advantages of being an instinctive lover and of knowing precisely how she liked to be pleasured herself. Therefore it stood to reason that she could interpret another woman's needs much more accurately than any man.

They kissed for some minutes then Hillary relaxed back against the pillow, her body language issuing an open invitation for Odile to explore further and introduce her to all the delights a female lover had to offer. She closed her eyes, allowing each new sensation to sweep over her in waves.

The first thing she felt most keenly was the luxurious caress of Odile's soft, silky hair, the long auburn tresses trailing over her body as the young woman began to kiss her throat, her shoulders, her chest, and then her breasts. She sucked and licked each nipple in turn, rolling them around her tongue like boiled sweets. Then her tongue trailed lower, across her rib-cage and down her stomach, leaving a wet zig-zag trail across Hillary's burning flesh. It paused for a while at her belly as Odile inhaled the heady, musky aroma of her friend's arousal, then continued downward, becoming entangled in the thatch of hair that covered her pubic mound.

Hillary felt her mouth go dry – every nerve ending was tingling, sending urgent messages to her brain for release. Using only her tongue, Odile probed between Hillary's labia, finding the source of her desire and opening the floodgates with one simple flick of the soft pink tip. Moaning, Hillary forgot all her inhibitions and spread her legs wide to invite the young woman's tongue to enter her most secret, tempting places. She felt Odile's sweet breath upon her inner thighs and sought to open herself still wider. Now that she had given in to the power of their encounter, there was no way she could hold back.

Desperately she clutched her own breasts, kneading them, rolling the hugely swollen nipples between her fingers. She flung her pelvis upward and Odile caught her, a buttock in each hand, raising Hillary to her lips as if her throbbing vagina was a precious goblet, filled with nectar. Then she licked and sucked and drank, oblivious to the other woman's screams of glorious agony.

All through the sultry, storm-wracked night the two women alternately slept and pleasured each other always finding new ways to stimulate and excite. Hillary, tentative at first about touching Odile intimately, soon discovered to her amazement that it opened up a whole new realm of sensuous, erotic enjoyment. For Hillary, nothing would ever exceed the pleasure of discovering the other woman for the first time. With shaking fingers she had lightly spread the fleshy pink outer labia, then the darker inner fold of flesh, exposing the hard bud of her clitoris and the deep, dark tunnel of her vagina.

Much later, Hillary had dared to venture into that moist velvety place, first with her fingers and then with her tongue. What surprised her the most was how sweet Odile tasted, not harsh and salty like any of the men she had sought to sample but delicate, almost succulent and very, very moreish.

Odile undulated gently at first under Hillary's gentle probing then, as her friend became bolder, her touch more assured, she writhed and moaned with abandoned ecstasy. And so their pleasure continued. Eventually, as the first fingers of dawn's early light prodded their entangled, dozing bodies, Odile said she should go back to her own room.

'I doubt if either Alicia or Chloe will be awake for hours yet,' Hillary smiled, contentment written all over her face.

'Even so.' Odile was firm, she didn't want to embarrass Hillary or herself for that matter and if Theo ever found out she'd been unfaithful, even with another woman. She sighed.

Hillary noticed Odile's troubled expression. 'What's up?'

Odile looked down at her hands, suddenly feeling embarrassed. 'Hillary, you won't ever tell Theo about this? I mean about last night?'

'No, of course not. I won't tell a soul if you don't want me to.' Hillary looked Odile squarely in the eye. 'You don't regret what we've done do you?' It seemed crazy that she should be the one asking that question.

The young woman shook her head and smoothed the creases in her satin nightgown. 'No, never in a million years. It's just that to Theo it would seem a betrayal, just as if you'd been a man.'

Hillary said she understood, although she couldn't quite accept that by sleeping with her Odile had been unfaithful to Theo. 'By the way, he didn't telephone yesterday,' she said.

Odile sighed. 'I wasn't expecting him to really, I just hoped that's all.'

Hillary smiled sympathetically, suddenly everything was back to the way it had been before, with Odile fretting and missing Theo like crazy and herself reminded about the previous day and therefore about Darius. Logic had told her that things could never be quite the same between herself and Odile but she now doubted that they would turn out to be that different after all.

Chapter Twelve

*H*illary stared at her reflection in the mirror, marvelling that the woman who gazed steadily back at her was scarcely recognisable. Tall, elegant and carefully coiffured, she was a vision in a thin white sheath of fluid silk. She turned this way and that, admiring the way the garment clung to her body covering everything from shoulder to ankle yet revealing all.

The dress had been Odile's choice. She picked it from her own wardrobe and handed it over with an instant generosity that typified her. At first Hillary had been doubtful. Despite her assurances to Darius that she knew how to dress for such an occasion, a quick glance in her own wardrobe that morning had confirmed her worse suspicions, she had brought nothing remotely suitable to wear to his party. Of course, both Alicia and Chloe had harangued her about not going shopping with them.

'You only have yourself to blame,' her sister had asserted self-righteously. 'You were invited on our shopping trips but you preferred to stay here and lounge around in the buff.'

Hillary bit back several retorts knowing that nothing would silence Alicia. Instead she agreed, albeit reluctantly, to go with the three other women to a beauty parlour in King's Lynn. The party was important enough in Alicia and Chloe's estimation to warrant an all-day session. In Hillary's case this included a sauna, a facial, leg and bikini line waxing, a manicure, a pedicure, full make-up and, in every way the crowning glory, a new hairstyle.

Much to her surprise, far from finding the experience tedious, she actually enjoyed it. Wallowing in all the attention and pampering, she felt as though she was being prepared for something momentous. Idly, her mind had drifted to a film she had once seen where a young virgin girl was undergoing preparations to marry the Prince of some exotic desert kingdom. In the film, the other wives in the harem busied themselves about her body, washing and drying it carefully, anointing it with oils and finally dressing her in wedding finery. Obviously the elaborate ritual was destined to make her feel and look her best for her husband-to-be.

Now Hillary felt much the same. At each stage of her own preparations she had closed her eyes and imagined the eventual outcome of all the effort and expense she was currently going through. She could just see Darius and picture his look of amazement and approval as she swept into the great hall turning all the other men's heads and leaving hordes of envious women in her wake.

He would come straight to her of course and, ignoring the pleas of others to talk and dance, would stay with her all evening, filling her plate with tasty morsels, her glass with the finest champagne and her ears with delectable words of passion. In the end she would yield to her own desire for him and take him upstairs, away from the noise and the people and the chatter, to a place where they could be totally alone to discover each other with languorous rapture.

Each time she changed location in the salon the scenario would change slightly too, mostly for the better, although the outcome was always a little more erotically charged than her earlier visualisation of events.

Every person attending to her asked a variation of the same questions. 'Are you going somewhere special? The theatre? – A party – ? Do you live locally? Where are you staying? Oh, Harwood Hall.' A note of surprise and a slight change of tone indicated that the speaker was now impressed. 'Is it nice there? I've only seen it from the outside. Is that where the party is being held?' And, the final question, 'Do you know Darius Harwood well?'

Hillary would be forced to smother a lewd grin at this point. How would the speaker respond if she said Darius had tied her to a tree and caressed her body and that she was intending to get to know him even more intimately by the time the night was out? She hugged her secret close. It added to her excitement, this uncertain certainty of that which was to come.

Her already turbulent emotions were severely rocked, however, by the older woman who attended to her body waxing with a zeal bordering on enjoyment. Although it was neither what she did, nor how she did it that caused Hillary's stomach to tighten in painful knots. It was what she said.

'So you're going to the Harwood do, then?' the woman asked.

Hillary nodded happily, wriggling on the couch to find a more comfortable position in which to resume her fantasies.

'They say that that woman's there again,' the therapist continued, carefully positioning the first strip of wax on Hillary's waiting body.

Hillary had reached the point in her mind where she made her grand entrance, but she finally absorbed the question. 'What woman?' she said.

'That Ilona what's 'er name. Harwood's old mistress.'

Hillary forced herself not to sit up. 'Did you say mistress?'

'Oh, yes. She went with the old man for years, right

up until the day he died. Mind you she did alright out of it by all accounts.'

The relief burst from Hillary's lips. 'You mean she was Mr Harwood senior's mistress?' She opened her eyes in time to see the older woman nod in agreement.

'Yes, that's what I meant, right enough, although everyone knows she seduced the young Harwood as well.' She paused to rip the wax from the tops of Hillary's thighs. 'And there's some people that say that the boy, Torran, is Mr Darius's son, not his half-brother. Although you can tell the girl's not his she's much too fair.'

For a second or two Hillary lay mute, simply thinking – , 'Why not just rip out my heart as well while you're about it?' Then she let out a loud yelp of pain as the strip came off. Her mind was whirling. For one thing, she hadn't even known that Torran and Fearn were related to Darius in any way at all, let alone as half-brother and sister. As for the rest – she didn't dare contemplate the possibility of the woman's implication that Torran could be Darius's son. Eventually, she felt calm enough to speak. 'I didn't realise there was a family connection. I thought they came from Scotland.'

The woman nodded again, then went on to say that the Harwoods owned property all over the country, including a house near Caithness in Scotland. 'That Ilona woman inherited it when the old man died. That's what I meant about her doing well,' she added. 'And Torran and Fearn inherited part of Harwood Hall.'

'Oh, I see.' Hillary considered the woman's words carefully, then a thought occurred to her. 'She, Ilona I mean, must have a lot of influence in that family then?'

'About as much as anyone.' The woman ripped off the last strip of wax. 'Some say Mr Harwood can't make a move without her say so.'

By the time Hillary was ready to leave the salon she had managed to rationalise the new information, deciding that whatever had happened in the past was now well and truly water under the bridge. Obviously,

Darius felt obliged to let Fearn and Torran stay at the house and would naturally allow their mother to visit them. As for the rest of it? Well, it was probably based on nothing more than typical village gossip.

Leaning forward to peer at herself in the mirror for the umpteenth time, she caught sight of Alicia bearing down on her from behind although she still jumped as her sister spoke.

'You look lovely, Hills.' Alicia put out a hand and fingered one of the loose tendrils that framed her sister's face. 'I told you it would be worth coming here, didn't I?'

Hillary nodded and smiled at her sister's reflection. 'I still don't know if Odile's dress is really me though and I haven't any light coloured shoes to wear with it.'

Alicia tutted impatiently. 'There are three shops all within a stone's throw of this salon and if the worst comes to the worst I've probably got a pair. So stop worrying.' She stared hard at Hillary, noting her pinched expression. 'I thought you were looking forward to this party, one look at you and anyone would think you're about to go to the guillotine.'

For her own sake as much as her sister's, Hillary managed a tight smile. 'I'm just a bit nervous, I suppose. Unlike you, Alix, I don't get invited to grand parties all that often.'

Accepting her sister's explanation at face value, Alicia nodded and then waved as she caught sight of Chloe and Odile, both looking equally glamourous. Odile was also wearing her long hair piled on top of her head and Chloe sported her usual blonde bob but the cap of hair looked more sleek and shiny than usual.

By the time the four women returned to Harwood Hall, loaded down with yet more shopping bags, Hillary felt as though she barely had the energy left for a bath let alone a party. She eyed the dress still on its hanger and the new pair of matching white satin shoes that she had just bought, then looked at herself in the mirror.

Suddenly, she felt as though her body was being recharged, small sparks of energy shot through her, setting every nerve ending tingling with excitement. She was going to the party of a lifetime, she would look fantastic and no doubt end the evening in Darius's bed. How lucky could one woman get?

The heavily embossed invitation said, 'Cocktails at seven, to be followed by dinner and dancing.' Hillary turned the card over in her hand thoughtfully. She hadn't noticed it before but her's was the only invitation to be worded like this, those addressed to Alicia, Chloe and Odile merely said, 'You are cordially invited to partake of cocktails at Harwood Hall, between seven and nine pm.' In each case there was no mention of dinner or dancing afterward.

Alicia regarded the four cards with a haughty expression. 'I expect there's been some kind of mix-up. There's no reason why he should single you out for preferential treatment.' She glared at Hillary who stared back with wide eyed innocence.

'I don't understand it any more than you do, Alicia.'

Her sister sniffed and stooped to pick up her evening bag from the chair beside them. 'Let's go and find out then, shall we?' She opened the front door and they all trooped out into the warm evening air, walking the hundred yards or so from their wing to the imposing main entrance of Harwood Hall.

It seemed strange to see the driveway packed with cars, Hillary thought, eying the clutches of BMWs, Porsches and Mercedes, interspersed with the odd Rolls Royce, Ferrari or Aston Martin. She smothered a smile at the sight of Chloe and Alicia's expressions, an equal mixture of envy and lust. Nothing excited the two of them more than an obvious display of wealth.

She felt very grand as she walked up the wide stone steps to the front doorway, which stood wide open to reveal the marble flagged entrance hall in all its glory. Pausing at the threshold to savour the moment of her entrance she stared with wonder at the scene before her. Dominated by the sweeping staircase and a huge crystal chandelier, the majestic room was thronged with richly jewelled ladies decked out in all their finery and their escorts, men of all ages and sizes, most of them identically dressed in tuxedos.

Although the evening was balmy to say the least, many of the women still wore fur coats and jackets, dropping them carelessly into the waiting arms of an army of uniformed servants as they walked through the door. Obviously culled from the village, she thought to herself, realising that she recognised a few faces. Chloe and Alicia, of course, were absultely agog, although unlike Hillary they wasted no time standing and staring but dived straight into the throng.

A smiling Odile touched her arm. 'Shall we go in, Hillary?'

Hillary started with surprise. 'What?' Hastily she corrected herself. 'I mean, pardon?'

'Let's join the party Hillary,' Odile prompted gently, then added. 'I can't see him can you?'

Hillary blushed, realising straight away that Odile meant Darius. Realising it was pointless to try and pretend otherwise, she shook her head. 'I expect he's inside, greeting his guests as a proper host should.'

She soon found that she was right. As they crossed the hall and entered a large room to their left Hillary noticed him immediately. He was leaning casually against a huge grand piano, talking to a group of middle-aged women who appeared to be hanging on his every word. As she entered the room he looked up and caught her eye. It wasn't quite how she had visualised the moment but almost, with a lazy, practised eye he swept the length of her body, nodding with approval at her appearance. Almost against her will, Hillary found herself feeling extraordinarily pleased at his reaction.

In the distance she could hear Odile's voice but her senses were filled with him and the way he looked, so tall and dark and dressed not like the other men but in a stylishly cut grey silk suit, worn with a shirt of paler grey and a tie of muted greys and pinks. Even from a distance his voice too filled her ears. In low, seductive tones he charmed the women who clustered around him looking like brightly coloured jewels with their glossy hair and painted talon-like nails. And, she fancied, her nostrils were touched by the heady aroma of his masculinity, mixed in equal parts with the spicy citrus and pinewood fragrance she had come to associate with him.

Through her haze of lust she felt her fingers being prised apart and her palm forced to bear the weight of a heavy crystal glass. She tore her eyes away from his to glance at the drink which she now held, her expression almost uncomprehending, then looked into Odile's gentle face.

'Are you okay, Hillary? You look as though you've been hit by a thunderbolt.'

Hillary forced her frozen lips into something resembling a smile. 'Yes.' She felt her gaze slide away from Odile in the direction of the piano. Darius had gone from there and in his place stood a pianist about to earn his evening's wage. She looked back at Odile, a feeling of normality returning to flood her body. 'I'm fine. Shall we mingle?'

The two women drifted through the room, pausing every now and then to hover on the outskirts of a conversation which at first sounded rivetting but soon became as boringly predictable as the rest. Houses, cars, horses, money, who was having an affair with whom – there wasn't a lot of variation in the issues that mattered most to Darius's guests. She and Odile had just helped themselves to a second glass of champagne when a buzz circulated and the level of chatter dropped a few decibels as people craned their necks towards the door at the back of the room.

Hillary pushed her way in a none too subtle manner through a crowd of people who were blocking her view. As she stepped forward she gasped with surprise. The object, or to be more precise the objects of everyone's attention were Torran and Fearn who had just made their entrance. A split second later she noticed the woman standing behind them. Tall and majestic with hair like burnished copper piled high on her head, she stood and surveyed the room with a proprietory air. That must be Ilona, Hillary surmised correctly.

To her enormous consternation, Ilona's eyes alighted on her and she began to walk straight toward her. There was nothing Hillary could do except stand there and accept the woman's hand as it extended graciously, the skin so pale it was almost translucent. The woman was smiling, her deep green eyes sparkling with overt good humour. 'Welcome to Harwood Hall. You are Hillary, I believe?'

Hillary nodded, speechless for a moment while her heart thumped madly in her chest. For some indefinable reason she felt this woman could be a major threat. Nevertheless, the woman continued to smile an apparently genuine smile. 'I am Ilona, mother of Torran and Fearn.' She spoke as though she were reading her lineage aloud from an old tome.

'I guessed correctly then.' Hillary wanted her to know that her existence was not a complete surprise as far as she was concerned.

Ilona laughed. 'I take it there's been the usual gossip in the village? Oh, don't worry. There's no need to feel embarrassed,' she continued, as Hillary's cheeks started to redden. 'I've heard it all before countless times and in many different combinations.' She paused to accept a glass of champagne from a passing waiter. 'I doubt that the gossip-mongers can come up with anything new by now.'

Hillary decided to try and changed the subject. 'I expect Scotland is lovely at this time of the year?' It was the only non-controversial thing she could think of to say and, to her dismay, she noticed that Odile had wandered off so she couldn't depend on her to share the conversational burden.

Ilona's attention was wandering and she glanced at

her watch. 'My word it's almost nine already. Most of these people will be leaving soon, thank goodness.'

Her comment reminded Hillary about the differences between her invitation and those sent to Alicia, Chloe and Odile. She mentioned it to Ilona who explained that the cocktail party was a more or less regular event.

'Darius holds one every month but tonight, as it's his birthday, he's selected a few special guests to stay behind and help him celebrate in a more, shall we say, intimate fashion.' To Hillary's surprise she suddenly dropped her gaze in embarrassment.

Hillary broke the awkward moment of silence. 'I didn't realise it was Darius's birthday. I didn't bring him anything.'

'Oh yes you did.' the older woman murmured, almost under her breath, then she added in a normal voice. 'You brought yourself, my dear, that's what matters. Now then I must away and check that everything is organised for supper.'

She melted quickly into the throng before Hillary had chance to utter another word and seconds later Alicia appeared at her side looking more than slightly miffed.

'Apparently we are only invited for the cocktail party. Are you coming back with us, Hillary? We thought we'd go into town and find somewhere swish to eat so all our efforts don't go to waste.' She patted her hair and ran her hands across imaginary creases in her black velvet skirt.

Much to her sister's obvious annoyance, Hillary shook her head. 'I've been invited to supper here, apparently it's Darius's birthday.'

'Yes, he's thirty-nine. Doesn't look it though, does he?' It was Chloe, looking slightly rumpled, as though she'd been grappling with something, or someone.

Hillary did a quick calculation in her head; she'd assumed that Darius was only in his early thirties, at thirty-nine he could easily be Torran's father. But she couldn't bear to think about that now. Turning to Chloe she snapped 'Have you seen yourself in a mirror lately?'

Uncomprehending, Chloe returned Hillary's look with a blank stare until Alicia pointed out what Hillary meant.

'Oh, that!' She giggled. 'I bumped into Torran a little while ago and he seemed very pleased to see me.'

At least, thought Hillary with a rueful grimace, she had the grace to blush. For a moment, she felt as though she'd had enough of the party and of the Harwoods in general and she was just about to agree to accompany her sister and the others when she caught sight of Darius again. Their eyes locked and she melted inside.

'You all go and enjoy yourselves. I'll see you tomorrow.' Hillary could hardly tear her eyes away from Darius long enough to give her sister a placatory smile. 'You'll probably have a much better time than I will but it would be rude of me to leave.'

Alicia looked unconvinced but said goodbye anyway before taking Chloe by the elbow and propelling her towards the door when they met up with Odile. The three of them waved to Hillary who waved back absently. Now the room had cleared she was starting to feel a little vulnerable.

Fortunately Torran appeared beside her. 'You look incredible, Hillary.' Like Darius, he swept his eyes approvingly over her body, taking in every detail of her appearance, particularly the dress she had borrowed from Odile.

Although very plain and simply cut, the fluid white satin fell from shoestring straps to mould itself around her curves, outlining every part of her firmly toned body. As Hillary had soon discovered, anything worn under it simply ruined the effect so, with a slight tingling of excitement at her own decadence, she placed her underwear back in the drawer, allowing the sensuous material to slide over her naked skin; her only additions being a pair of flesh coloured hold-up stockings and a diamante choker with matching drop earrings. Finally, for the sake of modesty, she fastened a matching belt around her waist and three tiny diamante clips to hold the sarong-style skirt tightly around her hips.

It had seemed very strange at first to leave the house wearing no knickers, although she soon became accustomed to the sensation of fresh air tantalising her exposed sex and, once she had entered the Hall, all thoughts of anything but Darius had flown from her mind.

At this moment though, as Torran stood beside her his eyes stripping the thin layer of material from her body, she was reminded instantly of her nakedness underneath. Her stomach tightening at the realisation, she gazed levelly at him, a secretive smile playing about her lips. To hell with Ilona and the Harwoods' possible family connections. There she was at an exclusive party looking her absolute best and in the company of at least two superbly attractive men – she hadn't really bothered to look at the other male guests – this was no time to be fretting about the incidentals of life. She would go with the flow, let the party run its natural course and just enjoy everything as it happened, whatever that might be. As if to underline her decision a loud gong sounded, summoning everyone to the dining room.

Hillary looked around, unsure where to go but Torran was already guiding her, his hand placed firmly in the small of her back and the heat of his palm penetrating the thin material to scorch the sensitive skin beneath. She turned and gave him a broader smile, to which he nodded and slipped his hand lower to rest on her undulating buttocks. As they walked through the doorway, the first thing that struck Hillary was the size of the dining room. Almost as large as the room they had just vacated, it was dominated by a vast mahogany table laden with the finest china, silver and crystal, the latter reflected over and over again in the deeply polished wood.

Ilona stood just inside the doorway, greeting each guest and indicating where they should sit. Darius's place had been set at the centre of one side of the table, rather than at the head, and to her surprise and pleasure Hillary found herself seated to his right with Torran to the other side of her. Everyone stood until the last guest had found their place then, upon an imperceptible command from Ilona, the male guests gallantly withdrew the chairs for their female companions to be seated. Torran held Hillary's chair for her and she nodded gratefully, noticing with another jolt of surprise that Ilona was not seated on Darius's left as she had expected but across the table from him.

Darius sat down last of all and briefly thanked all his guests for attending. His penetrating blue eyes swept the room, looking around the table at the twenty or so couples who sat either smiling and contented, or nervously twitching. Hillary hadn't realised before but it was obvious now that a number of the women were not the wives of their male companions. As they started on the first course, she mentioned this observation to Torran who laughed deeply, then hastily silenced himself, whispering under his breath that most of the women there were prostitutes. Hillary stared back at him amazed, they all looked normal.

'Are you sure. How can you tell?' She persisted, resisting the urge to add the words, at your age, to the end of the question.

'Oh, it's quite normal for Darius to arrange such things for his friends,' Torran commented airily, pausing only to take a sip of blood red wine before adding. 'You and my mother are probably the only women here who aren't hookers.'

She gazed around the table once again, this time in open fascination. Now that Torran had mentioned it, she could see that they didn't have the same polish as the wives and girlfriends who had attended the earlier cocktail party. Finishing the last of her soup, she dabbed at her mouth with the corner of her napkin, then sat back in her chair and crossed her long legs, the gossamer material parting easily to allow her movement. Whether it was the actual movement or the sound of her nylon-clad legs sliding against each other, she couldn't tell but Darius immediately turned to look at her properly for the first time since they had begun the meal.

Hillary swallowed hard and gripped the edge of the table. Although she had been watchful about the amount of alcohol she was consuming that evening she suddenly felt light-headed. Of all their encounters so far this was the one that shook her the most. His very proximity made her giddy with a powerful emotion she had never experienced before.

More than mere lust, the sensation rocketed through her with the intensity of an orgasm, weakening her limbs so that she had no option but to allow her legs to uncross and slide apart. Immediately, she felt a draft of cool air waft over her tingling sex, then a hand upon her left thigh, kneading the flesh where it met the lacy stocking top.

Stifling a moan of desire, Hillary turned her head slightly to observe Darius's expression but he merely smiled thinly before turning to the man on his left and striking up a conversation about brood mares or some such equine subject. Despite his lack of visual attention to her, his hand remained in place, still gripping and releasing with hypnotic regularity. Desperately, she forced herself to concentrate on the second course which had now been set before her, a delicate concoction of salmon mousse garnished with scallops, prawns and caviar.

As she glanced up from her plate she noticed Ilona staring at her from across the expanse of dining table, her expression inscrutable. With a trembling hand, Hillary tried to transfer a small forkful of mousse to her lips. Darius's fingers had become more exploratory and the tips were now brushing the outer limits of her labia. Hastily, she ate the mousse then set down her fork and rearranged the edge of the tablecloth so that it covered her lap completely. Now only her expression could reveal that anything extraneous to dining was taking place.

Using one determined finger, Darius forced a path between her inner thighs, sliding it up and down the length of her pulsating sex. Still she concentrated on her plate, her heart thumping and her breathing shallow, and starting nervously every time someone glanced in her direction. Despite her best intentions she wriggled slightly and parted her thighs a little more.

Although she couldn't bear to contemplate the moment when he would surely withdraw his hand, the meal seemed interminable. Under the cover of long lashes, she eyed him surreptitiously. He was still talking animatedly to the man on his left. Picking up her glass she took a huge gulp of wine but, as she moved forward in her seat, two more of his fingers delved between her legs, thrusting inside the desperate moistness of her vagina. Gasping with surprise, she hastily turned the action into a cough although she straight away wished she hadn't. Noticing her discomfort Torran immediately patted her on the back until she assured him that she was okay. Glancing down she saw that Darius's hand could clearly be seen to be at work between her legs.

'Torran, do you think you could pass me the water jug?' It was the only thing she could think of on the spur of the moment and as soon as he reached for the jug she covered her lap once more with the tablecloth.

'Thank you.' She smiled gratefully at him and, much to his surprise, topped up her already full glass so that the water cascaded over the rim.

Her action immediately prompted a battalion of waiters to surround her, clearing away the mess she had made with the minimum of fuss. Under cover of their massed ministrations, Hillary allowed herself to submit to a powerful orgasm while burying her face in her napkin and faking a second coughing fit. With a satisfied smile, Darius withdrew his hand and solicitously enquired whether she would care for anything else. Blushing madly, Hillary shook her head. 'No, thank you. Perhaps later?' She added, a note of devilment creeping into her whispered response.

To her slight disappointment, the rest of the meal passed without incident, although this did give her ample opportunity to observe the other guests. Apart from Darius and Torran, none of the men there were remotely attractive to her. Most of them looked to be in their forties or older, a couple even fairly elderly she surmised, judging from their liver-spotted skin and shrivelled appearance.

The women, on the other hand, she found visually fascinating. Most looking as though the were only in their twenties, they all wore a similar air of controlled boredom. In appearance though they were vastly different. Some tall, some short, some reed-thin, others curvaceous to the point of plumpness, each women looked as though she had been designed, or at least chosen, according to a much more precise specification than her hair colour.

Gradually, people finished eating, cutlery was discarded and the plates were cleared. At a discreet signal from Ilona, all the guest rose from their seats and proceeded to make their way back to the room where they had been enjoying cocktails earlier and which had now been arranged for dancing. Aside from the piano, comfortable leather sofas had been positioned around the edges of the room to make space for the highly polished parquet of the temporary dance floor.

Hillary accepted a large brandy balloon from a passing waiter and looked around for Torran who, it appeared, had momentarily abandoned her. Unable to see him at all, she crossed to the far side of the room and sat down on one of the sofas, positioning herself opposite the doorway so that she could see everyone who entered. As she sat she could feel her stomach clenching and fluttering. There was no doubt about it, she was waiting for something momentous to happen.

Chapter Thirteen

*H*illary looked up as Ilona approached. She felt a distinct surge in the anxious tremors of trepidation that coursed through her body at the sight of the older woman's strange half-smile. She had to admit she found her disconcerting; even if one disregarded the village gossip she was still an enigma. A vibrant woman of indeterminate years, her beauty still intact, Ilona was cloaked by an aura of mysterious power. Hillary shivered inwardly as it was obvious from her determined manner that she had not come over to her with the intention of a casual chat.

The older woman sat down gracefully, lifting the hem of her emerald satin dress slightly as she did so to reveal a pair of slender calves sheathed in silver-grey silk stockings. For a second, Hillary thought, the scene seemed unreal, as though they had stepped back in time. All around them, men and women dressed in evening wear sipped cognac and talked quietly of the weather and the forthcoming harvest, or whose grand society wedding was next on the year's social calendar. She herself felt slightly removed from reality, as though anything that occurred that evening would not really be happening to her at all.

With a start she realised Ilona was speaking to her.

'I'm sorry, I didn't catch what you said.' The woman smiled, although the smile did not quite reach her eyes. I must watch out for her, Hillary thought to herself. She intends to hurt me in some way.

In the patient tone people usually reserve for children, Ilona spoke again. 'I said, I have solved your small quandary about Darius's birthday gift.'

'Oh, really? Well, that's good.' Hillary didn't know what to say. In all honesty, after her initial embarrassment she hadn't given it a second thought.

Ilona moved closer and put her mouth to Hillary's ear. Her breath was warm and doused in brandy like a Christmas pudding. 'There is a photographer here, a friend of mine as it happens, who would be delighted to take a special portrait of you so that you may present it to Darius as a gift.'

Her suggestion surprised Hillary. Although she hadn't known what to expect, she had not anticipated that Ilona would suggest something as innocent as a photograph.

'I see. That's very kind of him but I wouldn't want to put him to any trouble. I presume like everyone else he's here tonight to enjoy himself, not to work.'

Ilona waved her doubts away with a perfectly manicured hand. 'Nonsense, he would be happy to do it for me.' She coughed discreetly. 'That is – for Darius.' She rose from her seat extending her hand. 'Come. If we go now he can take the photograph and process it before midnight.'

Hillary hesitated. There was something about the situation she didn't like. For a start she didn't trust Ilona and there was something in the woman's expression that sent a shiver down her spine. Was it a challenge, or mockery of her presupposed cowardice? She expects me to refuse, Hillary thought wildly, and if I do she will have beaten me. But for what purpose?

Using the last of her cognac as an excuse to buy time, Hillary swilled the amber liquid around and around the heavy crystal glass, regarding its movement thought-

217

fully. Then making her decision at long last, she rose to her feet, threw back her head and tossed the fiery liquor down her throat, setting the glass on a side table with a finality that attracted the attention of the others in the room. At the sound Darius looked across at them, raising a questioning eyebrow to which Ilona smiled and gave an imperceptible nod.

Wondering just how much of a surprise the photograph would turn out to be, Hillary followed in Ilona's majestic path out of the door and along the corridor to a second room. She noticed straight away that it had been hastily equipped as a photographer's studio with several spotlights, a dark coloured backdrop and, of course, a camera on a tripod. All the equipment was arranged around an elegant chaise-longue which was deeply buttoned and quilted in a rich, burgundy coloured velvet.

It seemed to Hillary to be a very tasteful arrangement considering the haste with which it must have been set up. After all, it was supposed to be a spur of the moment idea, whatever would possess someone to go to a party equipped with an entire photographic kit? She turned to Ilona, prepared to ask that very question and to insist on being allowed to return to the party but instead found herself staring into a pair of solemn brown eyes.

Although they were more suited to a spaniel, the eyes actually belonged to a slightly Bohemian-looking man who appeared to be somewhere in his mid-forties but pathetically trying to look twenty years younger. His hair was long, although slightly thinning on top and he sported a bristly chin that was more than simply unshaven, yet not quite bearded.

'This is Serge, the photographer I mentioned.' Ilona introduced him with a proprietary air.

Nodding wordlessly in response, Hillary walked across the room and pretended to examine the camera. Although she didn't know much about photography the equipment seemed to be the sort a professional would use. Ignoring Hillary's actions, Ilona began chatting to Serge about a mutual friend of theirs. For several minutes no one mentioned the photograph until, eventually, Ilona asked Serge in an over-loud voice where he would like to start. Hillary looked around in anticipation of his response.

'I think we'll have the young lady here, on the chaise of course.'

He nodded to Hillary, who dutifully sat on the red velvet seat, her back straight, legs demurely crossed at the ankle. Serge took a few steps across the room and patted the corner of the chaise longue where the back and arm met.

'Please sit back here.' His voice bore a slight trace of a foreign accent, cultivated, Hillary assumed, to please his clientele.

She smiled and did as he asked, raising her legs so that she reclined full length along the seat, taking care to arrange her dress to cover them.

From her assumed position of authority behind the camera, Ilona tutted, crossed the room and moved the material of Hillary's dress so that it exposed her legs up to the thigh, as she did so she caught the faintest glimpse of the younger woman's silky thatch of pubic hair.

Serge nodded approvingly and took a couple of shots. A moment later Ilona stepped up to his side and whispered something to him to which she received a nod and smile of accord.

'Can we have the dress opened more and perhaps one leg bent? He shook his head as Hillary moved accordingly. 'No, the other leg.' He waited until she moved again. 'That is correct.' Then he peered at her through the camera and waved his hand agitatedly. 'No, that's still not right.' He ran his fingers through his hair apparently considering her pose. Finally he spoke again, his tone much more decisive. 'Let go of the dress.'

Hillary was clutching the material together, knowing

that if she released it she would be exposing more than she intended. Wishing that she had worn underwear after all she shook her head. 'I can't, I have nothing on underneath my dress. It would show.' As she spoke, she felt the slight air of tension in the room increase a hundredfold and the simple truth of the situation, a fact that she had been desperately trying to ignore, finally filtered its way into her slightly alcohol softened intellect.

'Let go of the dress.' Serge's tone was not pleading nor demanding, it simply called for her to obey.

With a small sigh of reluctance, Hillary did as she was asked, allowing the thin material to slip from her fingers. Like a pair of theatre curtains, it parted to reveal the neat triangle of hair.

Serge took a few more frames. 'Lovely,' he said, smiling at Ilona who nodded.

'You are a beautiful girl, Hillary. Darius should be pleased with your gift.' Ilona sounded sincere and a little wistful. 'I sometimes wish I could have my youth again.'

Obviously an admirer, Serge interrupted vehemently. 'But Ilona, you are so beautiful now, you have no need of youth to gild the lily.'

Ilona smiled, obviously pleased by his flattery but not convinced. 'If I were you, Hillary, I would take pleasure in showing off my body.'

'I do! I mean . . .' Hillary said, confused. She wanted desperately to jump up and run from the room but she felt trapped by her unwillingness to give Ilona the satisfaction of seeing her cowardice. Making the most of Hillary's moment of indecision, the older woman swiftly crossed the room to sit beside her and, one by one, began to unfasten the tiny diamante clips that held her dress closed.

With great delicacy she parted the material further and further, gradually revealing Hillary's smooth brown belly, then she reached up and eased the thin straps of the dress over Hillary's shoulders and down her arms until the firm, tanned globes of her breasts were similarly exposed. When this was done Ilona stood up to admire her handiwork.

'This is much better!' Serge exclaimed from across the room. He freed the camera from its tripod and walked around her, clicking away at random.

If she hadn't felt so nervous, Hillary would have chuckled. The whole episode was like a scene from any number of films. Gradually though she felt herself relax and enjoy the experience, her imagination taking her further forward in time, visualising Darius' reaction when he saw the finished prints.

Just then she was startled out of her reverie by a knock at the door. As it swung open Hillary moved quickly to cover herself but it was already too late. A young girl, with jet black hair cut in a short feathery style, had already entered the room. Hillary recognised her instantly as one of the prostitutes whom Torran had pointed out during supper.

'Mr Harwood said you wanted to see me.' the girl spoke quietly, glancing at Hillary's half-naked form with a dispassionate expression.

Hillary tried to return her look with an air of casual aplomb but failed miserably. She couldn't help wondering why Darius had sent the girl, or how he knew where she and Ilona could be found if the photographs were indeed meant to be a surprise. Considering this turn of events very carefully, she glanced around the rest of the room, her eyes coming to rest on her reflection in the large ornate mirror behind and to the left of the now discarded tripod.

Yet again she failed to recognise herself. This time it was not simply due to her unaccustomed hairstyle or make up but because she looked wanton, like a voluptuous Victorian maiden reclining half naked upon the richly upholstered chaise, her taut brown curves straining to escape the meagre confines of her virginal coloured dress. If only Darius could see me now, she thought.

* * *

'My, my, Darius, but you've excelled yourself again.' The slightly balding man reached across the table for the decanter, pouring himself a generous measure before returning his attention to the entertainment. Dressed identically to the other half dozen men in his company, his slightly rounded form was covered by a well-cut black tuxedo that looked as though it was suffering more than slightly at the seams. Settling back in the comfort of the leather chair, he sipped his drink.

His praise delighted his host, who took great pleasure in his renown for these intimate gatherings. Every couple of months or so he would invite a close-knit circle of friends and business acquaintances to an evening of wine, women and general debauchery. Needless to say, the events were very popular amongst those on the receiving end of invitations.

He looked around at the small gathering. Women were excluded from the entertainment part, unless they were involved in it of course and, with the exception of his own female companions, wives and girlfriends were ruthlessly exempt from these special evenings. In their place, Darius always saw to it that an interesting array of professional girls were selected to keep his guests company.

His contented smile took in every one of his companions. The small number who had managed to resist the temptation to seek individual gratification from their partner for the evening were all appreciative of his attractive new discovery.

'She's not a local girl is she, Darius?'

Darius smiled enigmatically at the speaker, he was not the first person to have prompted him for further details. Others had commented privately to each other that they thought Ilona was on her guard that evening, having recognised the first genuine rival to her special relationship with Darius. 'She'll do her best to humiliate that girl,' was the observation of more than one guest, not because they were particularly astute but because they knew Ilona of old.

* * *

From her position on the sofa, Hillary watched as the young girl started to undress. Unzipping her tight blue dress, she allowed it to drop to her feet to reveal shapely curves clad in ice blue satin camiknickers, her long slim legs covered by white lace hold-up stockings.

In the deeper recesses of her mind, she knew that Ilona had engineered this and that she was being set up for something she wanted no part of. Yet, on a more superficial level, she wondered if her imagination was becoming out of control. Instantly reaching a decision, Hillary sat bolt upright and started to pull one of her straps up her arm toward her shoulder, partially covering her breast again.

Serge put out a hand to stop her and looked pleadingly at Ilona. 'She cannot leave now, please!' He turned to face Hillary again, his expression so sincere that she dropped the strap and stared at him wordlessly.

She felt helpless, caught up in something that she didn't understand. Having her photograph taken had not been the terrible experience she had feared, at least not so far, and her insatiable curiosity was still determined to lead her down an unexplored path.

Recognising her indecision, Ilona moved toward the chaise longue and looked down at Hillary's half-naked form, her face desperately trying to soften into a smile. 'Obviously you have a choice, you can leave now. But I urge you to think of Darius, consider the added pleasure a slightly more, shall we say, erotic photograph would give him.'

To Hillary's ears her tone was persuasive, although the younger woman knew there wasn't an ounce of sincerity in it. After a moment's hesitation she nodded, looked across the room at Serge who stood poised, camera in hand, and then finally at the girl. 'Okay. Let's get on with it so I can go back to the party.'

Swiftly, before Hillary could change her mind, Ilona commanded the girl to sit beside her on the sofa. Her only instruction was. 'Do whatever comes naturally to you.'

For a few minutes the girl sat staring mutely at Hillary's half naked body, her clear blue eyes taking in every part of her, then she reached out a hand. At first Hillary resisted the girl's touch but, hating to give Ilona the pleasure of witnessing her discomfort, she gradually allowed the young woman to caress her legs and breasts. Her touch was so light, so similar to Odile's, that if she half closed her eyes she could imagine it was her friend there beside her and that they were on their own, locked away in private from the rest of the world, heedless of the violent storm that raged elsewhere.

For a long time all was quiet apart from the intermittent click of the camera. Despite her initial embarrassment, Hillary felt herself rapidly becoming aroused, easing her legs apart slightly in a reflex response to the girl's caresses. At once, Serge was at the foot of the chaise longue, clicking away at close range. She felt herself blush and moved to close her legs again but the girl stopped her with a gentle hand and a single, quietly whispered word. 'No.'

Leaning over the back of the chaise, Ilona reached down to unfasten Hillary's belt; the only device that now held the two sides of the wrap-over dress together. As she removed it so the dress fell away from Hillary's body, instantly revealing her total nakedness.

Conceding defeat in this respect, Hillary eased the dress from under her, handing it to Ilona who draped it carefully over the back of a chair before turning around to consider the younger woman's position.

'I think it would be attractive if you were to roll over onto your stomach, Darius is most appreciative of a well shaped bottom.' Serge spoke carelessly, revealing that it was not the first time he had photographed someone for Darius's pleasure.

Ignoring a further urge to call a halt to the proceedings, Hillary complied with his request, enjoying the sensation of the opulent velvet against her naked breasts and stomach. Despite her misgivings, she writhed sensuously on the chaise almost past caring that Serge was at once behind her taking shot after candid shot. Feeling suddenly wanton she rose to her knees, arching her back so that her body was displayed to its best advantage.

As soon as she changed position, the girl had moved away allowing Serge unrestricted access to photograph Hillary from all angles. But at his request she returned with a vengeance, stroking her hands along the length of Hillary's spine, over the curve of her hips and buttocks and down the backs of her thighs. Moving upward, she repeated her actions in reverse, deliberately allowing the tips of her fingers to stroke Hillary's exposed sex.

Instantly, Hillary's body responded, the tingling of excitement rapidly becoming an insistent throb. The moisture of her own desire glistened around the entrance to her vagina, forming tiny pearl-shaped droplets which quivered tantalisingly like dewdrops on the curly hair covering her swollen labia.

For several minutes the girl did nothing more than tantalise her until, heedless of the camera or the others in the room, Hillary moaned and writhed against the girl's touch. Desperately she used her own body to encourage the girl to explore further, to delve her magic fingers deeper into the churning cauldron of her anxious sex.

There was nothing she wouldn't do now. Her arousal was so intense that Serge could have jammed the telephoto lens of the camera up inside her for all she cared. Carnality taking over where sensitivity lay discarded, she rolled over onto her back, pulling the girl with her until they lay full length together on the narrow seat, their hands and mouths fully occupied with a fervent need to satisfy their own lust.

Hastily discarding roll after roll of film to reload his camera as fast as possible, Serge paid little heed to technical correctness. An artist at heart, he immediately realised he had embarked on the most challenging session of his whole career. The final outcome would be a triumph of erotica, the most passionately charged work he had ever produced.

In a brief second of respite he glanced at Ilona, expecting to receive a grateful smile in return but her expression shocked him to the core. Filled with anger and hatred, she stared at the writhing forms in front of her. She had not intended events to turn out this way. Hillary should have responded to the whole encounter with shocked horror before submitting to the indignity with mute acceptance, not throw herself into it with wild abandon. She had underestimated her rival completely.

Unable to bear witness to the scene any longer Ilona left the room, leaving a confused Serge to continue with his celluloid capture of the unbridled pair as they approached the climax of their passion.

When Hillary and the girl, whom she discovered was called Polly, finally returned to the party, they were surprised to find the room deserted apart from a dejected looking pianist.

'Where do you suppose everyone has got to?' Hillary asked, looking around in confusion.

'I dunno.' Polly walked over to a table which had been set up as a bar, she held up a bottle of gin. 'Want one?'

Hillary nodded, crossing the room to select a bottle of tonic water to go with it. Polly sipped her drink nonchalantly. 'I expect they're still recovering from the entertainment.' She laughed ruefully and grinned. 'Was that your first time with another girl?'

'No.' Hillary shook her head and grinned back. 'The second actually.' She stared at her drink for a few seconds while the rest of what Polly had said sank in. 'What entertainment?'

The words had hardly left her lips when she realised that she didn't need to hear the girl's reply – the answer was so obvious she wondered why she hadn't become aware of it earlier. Not only that, but she was also surprised to find that she felt strangely aroused by the knowledge that Darius and his friends had been watching her and Polly together, although she was intensely angry with Ilona for setting it up.

Gradually the other guests drifted back into the room. The pianist struck up a lively repertoire of tunes and the whole atmosphere became more festive than it had been all evening. It was as though the tension that had subtly pervaded the party all evening had dissipated. Glancing around, Hillary noticed that Darius hadn't returned. No doubt he's congratulating Ilona, she thought glumly to herself.

At that moment Torran appeared in the doorway, the movement out of the corner of her eye making her glance toward him. Torran, in turn, looked around the room and as soon as he spotted Hillary smiled broadly and began to walk over to her. As he approached, she sensed the much greater buzz of Darius's arrival and again looked across to the doorway in time to catch his eye. As secretive as Torran was open, his expression as he held her gaze was maddeningly inscrutable as usual.

With a start she realised the younger man was asking her if she wanted to dance. 'Oh, yes, thank you.' She smiled and followed him to the centre of the room. After a few minutes she found the courage to ask the question that had been troubling her ever since his reappearance. 'What did you think of the evening's entertainment?' She couldn't keep the sarcasm out of her voice.

Torran looked at her blankly for a moment. 'Entertainment?' Then, obviously realising what she meant he laughed. 'I'm afraid Darius refuses to allow me to take part in his party games. I'm not even allowed to have a girl of my own for the evening.'

Although a little surprised, Hillary laughed with relief at his response. 'By the way you said that, I take it you simply borrow someone else's?'

'One or two.' Torran grinned mischievously. 'I quite

like the look of that little brunette over there. I haven't had her yet.'

Fighting the urge to reply. 'Oh really? I have.' Hillary glanced at Polly who was dancing with a man who seemed fairly young in comparison with the rest of the guests. Just as the pianist approached the last few bars, Darius walked up to herself and Torran and took her by the arm saying, 'My turn, I think.' His determined expression prevented either of them from challenging him.

It was the first time Darius had touched her since their encounter at supper and Hillary felt herself becoming weak with desire all over again. It was a good thing that he was holding her so tightly, she realised, otherwise she might not have had the strength in her legs to support herself. Feeling his fingers burning through the thin material of her dress, Hillary allowed herself to imagine what it would be like to be fucked by him.

It was strange that she could never think of sex with Darius in terms of sleeping with, or making love with, as she did with other men. Her desire for him was so basic, so earthy, that she could only think in terms of fucking when she thought of the two of them together.

Wondering whether she had actually spoken aloud, or was still thinking, she said simply. 'I want you to fuck me, Darius.' Looking into his eyes she saw the first glimmer of a smile there, albeit one of triumph.

Without uttering another word he took her by the hand and led her from the room, guiding her down the same corridor where Ilona had taken her a couple of hours earlier, and then up several flights of stairs until they reached his own suite of rooms at the very top of the house. Without preamble he kicked the door shut behind them and pushed her against the wall, pressing himself up against her and kissing her hard on the lips until she thought her teeth would crack under the pressure.

Then he released her, leaving her where she stood, breathless and trembling with fear and desire. She didn't even have the self-possession to examine her bruised, swollen lips while he walked across the room to the window and drew the heavy drapes.

For a few seconds they remained apart, cloaked in thick darkness, the only sound that of their breathing – his was deep and controlled, while hers was shallow and uneven. Presently the spell was broken by the click of a lamp that bathed the centre of the room in a subtle rosy glow, picking out the red hues of the flowers in the richly patterned carpet.

Still without saying a word, Hillary stepped away from the wall, missing its support instantly. On shaking legs she crossed to a sofa and sat down heavily.

'Would you like a drink?' Darius's voice sounded strangely normal.

'I would, yes.' Hillary looked at her hands which were folded demurely in her lap. After all that had passed between them she and Darius were still total strangers she realised.

He handed her a glass of clear liquid then stood before her, his stance so self-assured and with his crotch only inches from her face. With a dry mouth she felt an overwhelming urge to bury her face in it and inhale the musky scent of his masculinity. Instead she sipped her drink and grimaced slightly, it was practically neat vodka.

Unmoving, he watched her expression. 'Is it alright? Would you like some more tonic?'

She shook her head. 'No, it's okay. I'm not really thirsty.' She looked around her for a table on which to put the glass.

Darius's strong fingers reached out and touched her hair, then drifted down her cheek to cup her chin, raising her face so that she was looking into his eyes. 'Come with me,' he said.

She rose obediently and he led her through another couple of rooms until they reached his bedroom. As she expected, Darius's bed was huge with ornate carved wood at its head and foot and four equally ornate

229

columns supporting an opulent canopy of raw red silk. The mattress was high, needing a couple of wooden steps to climb up to it and the coverlet and sheets were in the same red silk, only this time with a light pattern woven into them.

The entire piece of furniture looked womb-like and she found it easy to imagine Darius's pleasure at spending the night cocooned in the rich warmth of a woman's body. She was just about to make a comment about the bed when they were interrupted by the sharp rap of impatient knuckles on wood. Darius excused himself and left the room closing the door carefully behind him.

Hillary strained to hear the muffled voices. The uninvited guest was Ilona she decided, instantly recognising the force of tone rather than the voice itself. Giving up her efforts to make out their words, she passed the time by looking around the rest of the room and examining the many pictures on the walls, most of which turned out to be highly erotic scenes taken from a variety of cultures, both ethnic and western. She found one to be particularly abhorrent, although despite her revulsion she found herself drawn back to look at it several times.

It was a simple sketch on plain brown paper roughly nine inches by five, of an old man – so thin his rib-cage and pelvic girdle protruded through tightly stretched skin, his head draped with long thinning locks. The other character was a young woman, very tiny like a child although her well-rounded breasts and thick bush of pubic hair signified that she was some years past puberty. In complete contrast to his feeble appearance, the old man proudly bore a rigid, virile-looking penis of enviable proportions with which, by the way he held the young woman, he obviously intended to bugger her. The sketch was simply entitled "Playtime."

Drawn to it for the fourth time, Hillary searched in vain for the name of the artist. As far as she could tell there was no signature. She wondered if Darius had sketched the work himself and made up her mind to ask him on his return. However, when he did re-enter the room he was bearing a large brown envelope and all thoughts of the picture vanished from her head as he tipped the contents onto the bed with a smile of pure satisfaction.

She stepped forward and recognised the photographs instantly. They were the ones taken of herself earlier that evening. Even from a distance she could see that the majority of them were very good. Serge obviously knew what he was doing behind a camera. She picked one up and studied it – for the third time in twenty four hours she failed to recognise herself, her back arched, her head thrown back in wild abandon, her most intimate parts displayed in full glory, surely the girl in the photograph could not be her.

Darius took the print from her and looked at it with a serious expression. She felt her colour heighten as he peered closer then turned to look her up and down. 'Did you ever think you would prove to be so photogenic?' Using his fingertips he traced the curve of her buttocks on the glossy paper, his perspiration leaving a slight trail of moisture that looked for all the world like her own juices. He licked his lower lip and made a soft murmur of appreciation in the back of his throat.

Hillary felt her real self becoming moist, her nipples tightening under the thin material of her dress. She shifted her weight from one foot to the other and simply stared at the photographs on the bed, unable to meet his eye as he sifted through them. There were quite a few of her and Polly, of course, although to her eyes they looked less focussed, as though they had been taken too hastily. Nevertheless Darius seemed no less appreciative, perhaps what they lacked in technical merit they made up for in content, Hillary thought to herself perceptively.

From some distant hallway a grandfather clock sounded the half-hour, its loud gong echoing around the vast mansion and reminding Hillary where she was and how late it had become. 'I should be going.' She knew her tone was unconvincing.

231

Darius gathered up the photographs and began collecting chairs and sofas and moving them to the bedside, then he arranged a chosen selection of the prints upon them, propping the pictures against the arms and backs of the furniture so that they were properly displayed.

'Go, if you wish,' he said simply. 'Or stay and enjoy these with me.' He waved his hand expansively then stepped forward and clasped her upper arms tightly, his thumbs deliberately grazing the swollen buds of her nipples.

As though she hadn't already known before, she knew then she would be unable to resist him. Thoughts of the wonderful, golden Haldane and dark, mischevious Torran with whom Darius may or may not have had a paternal connection crowded her brain but she forced them out. Ever since their first meeting at the station, where he had penetrated her mind, she knew Darius was destined to penetrate her body also. Some aspects of destiny just could not be denied.

232

Chapter Fourteen

*H*illary found it difficult to discern what it was that made her feel particularly trapped. Was it Darius's hands still tightly gripping her arms, his deep, penetrating gaze which held her spellbound, or her own turbulent desire for the man who held her captive?

'Are you ready for me, Hillary?'

She shook her head slightly, not really understanding his question. 'I don't know.'

Pulling her firmly toward him, Darius pinned her lips with his own, prising her shocked jaw wide with the pressure of his own mouth and exploring her with his tongue. Relief combined with pleasure made her suddenly go limp, had his hands not been supporting her she would have dropped to the floor. Was it her imagination or had she honestly never been kissed like this before?

She yearned to wrap her arms around him, to trace the contours of his strong body beneath the immaculate grey suit, then loosen his shirt from the waistband of his trousers and run her hands over his unclothed back. Still he held her firmly but not painfully so, his leg now forcing its way between hers causing her to stumble slightly from the precarious dais of her high, narrow heels.

Her legs gave way, parting automatically and thereby allowing Darius's leg to slip between them, his thigh rubbing agonisingly against her uncovered sex. She could feel the firm muscle beneath the silken material that covered his limb, sense the tautly quivering dynamism of this singular part of his body. It seemed each individual part of him had the power to pleasure her and she wondered, with mounting excitement, how powerful he would be when the combined forces of his body were finally unleashed upon hers.

Writhing against his thigh, she moaned softly and kissed him harder, testifying her need for him. He released one of her arms then and brought his hand up between their tightly compressed bodies, feeling her breasts as they thrust urgently against the delicate material of her dress. She couldn't get enough of his touch, couldn't bear for him not to feel every part of her immediately.

'Please! Darius!' She didn't know how to convey her needs to him, they were strangers after all. He smiled into her eyes and with more than a faint trace of satisfaction in his expression he unfastened her dress, removing his other hand temporarily to allow it to slither unhindered over her curves and fall to the floor, pooling like liquid around her feet.

The temperature in the room was quite cool which she hadn't realised before. Now the slight chill air wafted over her denuded body, drying the thin film of perspiration that had accumulated on the surface of her skin. She looked at the photographs and the pictures on the walls, visualising her own appearance at that moment, her bronzed tight body clad only in stockings and high heeled shoes. With overwhelming narcissism she aroused herself.

If Darius was similarly aroused he didn't show it. Not even a surreptitious glance at his crotch could reveal the answer. Using her released hand, Hillary felt his bulge, breathing a sigh of relief that it was large and firm. She had begun to wonder if he was actually capable of being turned on like other men. There was no doubt in her mind that his sexual predilections extended some distance outside the norm. Despite her churning emotions she smiled to herself, who was she to determine what was normal and what was not?

With trembling fingers she tried to open his fly, fumbling for a zipper and finding buttons instead. With all the uncoordinated finesse of an infant, she managed to undo each one, sliding her hand into the uncharted warmth that lay beneath. Despite her exploration Darius's kisses did not miss a beat, nor did he stop rubbing her sex with his thigh, although she thought she sensed a slight quiver as she cupped the downy pair of peaches that were his balls.

Acknowledging that he had her well and truly hooked, Darius dared to release Hillary's other arm, sliding both his hands around her hips to clasp her buttocks. Gradually, imperceptibly, he manoeuvred her around so that her rear view could be seen clearly as a reflection in the mirror. With satisfaction he watched his fingers kneading the pliant flesh of her bottom, parting the cheeks so that the tantalising cleft between them was fully exposed.

With great deftness he worked one finger inside the tight, puckered opening, moving it around slowly so that she would open up to him more before adding its opposite number. For her part, Hillary moaned loudly as he entered her with his fingers, enjoying the singularly painful pleasure of being thus ravished. In return she grasped his penis tightly with one hand and his balls with the other, squeezing and working them in time with his own manipulations of her.

She clearly felt his excitement building, the throbbing shaft beneath her fingers was becoming more and more erect with the first droplets of semen issuing from the tip and dribbling down her fingers. Not wishing to release her grip but concerned about spoiling his suit, she murmured his name, hoping he would stop momentarily and allow her to disrobe him. In reply he merely delved deeper into her, her passionate response resulting in a harder squeeze of his balls. All at once he exploded, the semen bursting from him like a gushing well of clear, viscous oil, coating her hands and stomach.

'Your suit!' She exclaimed, glancing down at his saturated clothing.

'Do you care, Hillary?' he questioned, adding a third finger to his manipulations. 'I certainly don't.'

She was taken aback by his response and didn't know what to do with her semen covered hands. After a few moments' consideration she wiped them across her breasts, moaning as she spread the sensuous liquid over her soft skin. To her surprise, Darius bent his head, put out his thick, pink tongue and started to lick her clean.

'He obviously enjoys the taste of himself,' she thought with a slight feeling of shock, watching him lap at her breasts with relish. In all her experience, she had never known a man to do that before.

Cradling the back of his head in her hands, she gave herself up to the sensation of his mouth against her sensitive flesh, urging each of her swollen nipples into his mouth in turn. She felt as though there was a fire raging between her legs and longed for him to move his hands and mouth to touch her there instead. Trying to urge his head lower she applied a little pressure but his mouth would not leave her breasts.

Giving up the fight, she traced her hands over his shoulders and down his back, cursing the material that acted as a barrier between her flesh and his. She reached awkwardly under his jacket, freeing his shirt from the waistband of his trousers so that she could at least caress his naked back. His skin too felt like silk, she noticed and, as she moved her hands around to his stomach and chest she found, with a little surprise, that his skin was as smooth and hairless as a new born babe's.

With graceful ease he stretched himself upright once more, removing his fingers as he did so. Carefully he unknotted his tie and threw it on a nearby chair, then removed his jacket and likewise disposed of it. With rapidly mounting excitement bubbling up inside her at this new development, Hillary began to unbutton his shirt. He stopped her, holding her wrists and gazing deep into her eyes once more with the unique expression that almost drove her insane with desire. 'Climb on to the bed. I'll do this.'

Pausing only to kick off her shoes, she did as she was asked and lay on her side, watching him as he removed the last of his clothing. His body was everything she had expected it to be and more – firmly toned, well proportioned and with a rampant cock of more than ample proportions. At the sight of his completely naked body, Hillary sucked in her breath. He walked to the head of the bed and untied the thin silken cord that held the thick drapes in place, he did the same with the cord at the foot of the bed, then circumnavigated the monstrous piece of furniture to undo the matching cords on the other side.

Climbing on to the step, he leaned forward as far as he could and kissed her hard. Then, while she was still caught in the magic of his kiss he caught her wrists and swiftly tied them with the cords, doing the same with her ankles before she could protest so that she was helplessly spread-eagled before him.

The expression on his face as he surveyed his handi-work made her come. 'Go with it, Hillary, let it flow out of you.' He knelt beside her on the bed, watching her intently as she thrashed helplessly against the coverlet, riding the ecstasy as it gripped and shook her. Gradually, the waves subsided, leaving her limbs like water, a dull throb overtaking her entire pelvis.

Feeling temporarily sated she looked at him and blinked a couple of times, her eyelashes catching against the silken veil of her hair which, having broken free of its elaborate design, now lay draped partially across her face.

'I think you needed that.' He smiled and traced a lazy

finger across the tops of her thighs, immediately she felt a slight quiver deep inside.

With great delicacy he parted her labia and stroked the pulsating bud of her clitoris, leaning across her to examine the effect of his caress. He looked up at her face, noting with satisfaction the haze of renewed desire in her heavy lidded eyes.

'I want you to tell me what you feel, what you like and what you don't like.' He circled the outer edge of her moist vagina with his thumb. 'Do you like it when I do that?'

She nodded weakly, unable to do more.

He rubbed the flat palm of his hand over her sex. 'Does that feel good?'

Again she moaned quietly in response. A finger entered her, then another and another until she was full of him, at each juncture she testified to her appreciation by moving her head slightly or simply murmuring a single word. 'Yes.'

She could do no more than lie back and accept his caresses. Being bound hand and foot she had no option but to let him make all the moves. With a surge of renewed desire she ground herself against his hands, her buttocks writhing against the rich, red coverlet.

He removed his fingers and held them to her lips. Just for a moment she felt reviled, then remembering Darius's apparent enjoyment of his own juices Hillary sucked each one, becoming greedier and greedier as she went on. Darius smiled, pleased at her response and rewarded her by thrusting his turgid, latex covered cock deep inside her.

Oh, the bliss she experienced now the moment had finally come! 'Yes! Darius, yes!'

There was enough slack in the cords for him to kneel between her legs and raise her bottom on to his thighs. She felt the increased depth of his penetration, mumbling incoherently as he touched the magic place within her, driving her harder and harder toward another climax.

With his hands he again gripped her buttocks, his mounting passion making each caress a little less refined until she felt totally impaled upon him. Still the dual probing was exquisite agony and she felt herself come yet again with renewed vigour.

His self-control was phenomenal. Again and again he thrust inside her, moving around to penetrate her from different angles, varying the pleasure in as many ways as possible. She thought he was surely the perfect man. Then she remembered Ilona and Torran, allowing their images to drift across her closed eyelids like unwelcome black clouds.

Some time later, after Darius had eventually permitted himself to climax, he untied the cords that bound her allowing her to use her hands to discover the whole of his body. They lay almost content. Darius was on his back, his hands clasped behind his head with an air of satisfaction, Hillary was stretched out on her side next to him. Despite her temporary satisfaction she found she was unable to keep from touching him, her hands delicately smoothing and stroking each portion of his body. She plucked up the courage to ask him one of the myriad questions that had been plaguing her for the past eighteen hours or so. 'Darius, what is Ilona to you exactly?'

He looked at her askance. 'I'm not sure I follow you?'

'Yes, you do.' She gazed at him intently, watching his expression to see how much her question bothered him. 'Is she your mistress?'

He was silent for a moment, obviously considering his reply carefully. 'She was my father's mistress, not mine.'

'I know that.' Hillary started to wish she hadn't begun this line of questioning but still she pressed him. 'But some people think you took over when your father died.'

Darius sat bolt upright, dislodging her hands. 'I took over the estate.' He began cautiously. 'And, yes, I'll admit I have fucked her from time to time. She's a vibrant woman, with powerful needs,' he added almost defiantly.

Hillary was thoughtful for a moment, this was obviously a subject that could easily disturb his usual cool, calm exterior.

He gave her a sideways glance. 'There's more you want to ask me, isn't there?'

She was relieved to hear his tone. It was no longer angry or defensive, merely resigned. 'I suppose so.' She put her arms around his waist and nestled her head against his chest. 'I'm not bothered Darius, really,' she lied.

'Is that the truth?' He raised her chin so that she was staring deep into his eyes.

Unable to trust herself to speak, Hillary nodded in what she hoped was a convincing manner. Then after a while she murmured softly. 'What's past is past.'

Darius opened his mouth, obviously intending to say something else, then shut it again and kissed her instead, this time with more tenderness than before. Gently, he caressed her breasts, pushing her onto her back before entering her for a second time. Her response to him was instanaeous. She felt the fire rapidly building within her again and thrust her pelvis up to meet his.

Raising himself to his knees, Darius pulled her upward and toward him so that eventually they were seated face to face, his cock buried deep within her. Slowly they rocked together, enjoying the slow, rhythmic dance towards orgasm. Hillary pressed her breasts against his chest, wishing that she could enter his body. It was all so one-sided, she thought absently clasping his buttocks in her hands in the same way he now clasped hers.

Through a chink in the thick drapes she could see that dawn had broken, the sun already making its presence felt by casting a thin gold thread across the thickly carpeted floor and warming their gently perspiring bodies. She realised she hadn't been able to tell when Darius came, his face had been turned away from hers and he had uttered no sound, nor increased the urgency of his thrusts. Still he withdrew and handed her a couple of soft white tissues from a box next to the bed.

'I'm just going to use the bathroom.'

Hillary watched him climb down from the bed and walk through the thin gold line of sunlight. As he approached a closed door that Hillary hadn't noticed before he glanced back at her over his shoulder.

'I want you to stay here with me Hillary. Think about it and give me your answer when I return.'

She was stunned. Although they'd had a good time in bed she hadn't expected any declarations of commitment, especially not from Darius of all people.

When he re-entered the bedroom ten minutes later, fresh and slickly wet from the shower, she was still in a state of shock. Ignoring her silence and the questioning look in her eyes he began to wander around the room, collecting their discarded clothing and dumping it in a pile on a chair, opening cupbards and drawers, removing clean items of apparel, obviously intending to dress for work.

He glanced at her and smiled. 'It's okay, I was only joking about giving me the answer now. You stay here and get some sleep, I'll be back in a few hours and we'll talk then.' He pulled on a pair of thick green cords and a moss coloured flannel shirt.

'What about Alicia and the others? They might start to worry about me.'

He glanced at his watch. 'No-one will be awake yet. It's too early. I'll ask Fearn to give your sister a note.'

'Okay, thanks.' With a small sigh of langour she lay back against the pillows, content at long last. All of a sudden she felt very drowsy.

Darius crossed the room and kissed her on the cheek, running his hand lightly across her breasts and stomach as he did so. Despite her sleepiness she stirred under

241

his touch. He cupped her pubis. 'I'll deal with you later.' His tone was low and full of promise.

After Darius had gone Hillary fell into a deep sleep and didn't wake for several hours. As soon as she came to she remembered where she was and, with a quiver of uncertainty and excitement, she padded across the bedroom to open the curtains. There was a robe on a nearby chair which she pulled around herself before returning to the window to survey the scene. With a start of surprise she noticed Darius standing in the garden below. Thinking she must have slept for longer than she thought, she watched as Ilona approached him.

They stood talking intently for several minutes, occasionally one or the other would nod their head in agreement. Presently Darius leaned forward, kissed Ilona on the cheek and strode off down the path. She watched as Ilona stared after him for a moment or two, then turned and presumably came back inside the house. A few minutes later there was a knock at the bedroom door.

'It is only I, Ilona.'

Hillary was about to call out to her to enter when the door opened anyway. The older woman's face bore a smile that Hillary had come to recognise as completely false.

'Darius asked me to check that you were alright. Is there anything I can get you?'

Hillary shook her head. 'I'm absolutely fine.' Then, as an act of pure devilment, she added. 'In fact I feel absolutely wonderful.' She stretched luxuriously and smiled at Ilona with a none too small flicker of triumph.

Unconvincingly, Ilona pretended not to notice. 'Has he asked you to stay?'

Her pointed question took Hillary completely by surprise. 'Well, yes. Yes he has, as a matter of fact.'

The older woman sniffed. 'I suppose you're going to accept. You're the type.'

Feeling affronted, Hillary responded with a careless toss of her head. 'I haven't decided yet.'

'Liar!' Ilona's tone was suddenly venomous and her dark eyes glittered dangerously as she leaned forward and whispered harshly, her blood red lips just a fraction from Hillary's face. 'You wanted him the moment you set eyes on him. Don't deny it, I can see all the signs. I used to feel exactly the same as you once upon a time.'

Now they were getting down to basics, Hillary thought. Aloud she said. 'Darius told me you and he had slept together.'

'Oh, we've done far more than that.' Maddeningly, Ilona didn't elaborate.

Deciding to ignore her remark, Hillary crossed the room to the bathroom. 'I'm going to have a shower. Close the door on the way out, please.'

Once inside the safety of the bathroom she leaned against the door, locking it firmly to put even more distance between herself and the hateful Scotswoman. Her heart was thumping in her chest although she wasn't sure exactly why Ilona had angered her so much. Perhaps it was simply her assumption about Hillary's weakness where Darius was concerned? With a sinking feeling, she acknowledged to herself that there was a lot more to her feelings of disquiet than simple rivalry, something about the whole situation just didn't feel right.

Without knowing why, Hillary felt the answer to her question lay outside the bedroom door. Quickly she showered and, still clad only in the bathrobe, she unlocked the bathroom door and tentatively began to explore Darius's suite of rooms. From what she had been able to ascertain the night before, his suite comprised four or five rooms including the bedroom and bathroom. Her route took her through a couple of almost empty rooms and then she found herself in the sitting room where Darius had pinned her against the wall.

With a shiver of recollection Hillary put her fingers to her lips, remembering how bruised and swollen they

243

had felt at the time. She looked around, glancing at herself momentarily in the large ornate mirror. That was strange, she thought absently. As far as she could tell each of the rooms contained an identical mirror, even in the guest quarters.

Suddenly a thought struck her – the mirror downstairs had been a two-way mirror. Darius and his friends had used it to spy on her photographic session the night before. The cold chill of realisation swept over her – perhaps all the mirrors were exactly the same in every respect?

Swiftly she crossed the room and tried to look behind it, to her surprise she found solid wall at the back, although the mirror did not fit flush to it. She tried to see the back. She nodded, satisfied. It was, as she thought, clear glass but to what end if it hung upon a solid wall? There must be something else.

For the first time, she noticed that some wires ran around the room at the top of the wall. She followed their trail with her eyes, perceiving with surprise that they led to the mirror. She peered again into the gap between the mirror and the wall and in the centre she could just see a small black object but couldn't make out what it could possibly be.

Giving up on her examination of the mirror her eyes alighted on a closed door tucked away in the corner of the vast room. Hastily she tried the handle. It was locked. Unwilling to give up her quest Hillary pondered her dilemma, then with a feeling of elation remembered seeing a mahogany bureau in one of the other rooms. Quickly she ran to it, opened all the drawers and rolled up the top. To her dismay, it just seemed to be full of papers. Then, just as she was about to give up her search, she remembered that bureaux of this kind often had a secret compartment. Yes, there it was. To her relief and excitement the compartment sprang open to reveal a solitary key.

Her stomach churning now with the thrill of the chase, Hillary snatched up the key and dashed toward the locked door but just as she reached it the outer door opened and Darius entered the room. Stopping dead in her tracks, Hillary dropped the key into one of the deep pockets of the bathrobe. Darius wandered around, glanced through the doorway into the adjoining room and immediately noticed the open bureau.

'I was looking for some notepaper.' Hillary improvised swiftly. 'I was worried in case you had forgotten to leave a note for Alicia . . .,' her voice trailed off in embarrassment.

Darius's expression softened. He walked to the bureau and closed it carefully. 'I told you I would take care of it and I have. Now, come here.'

Hillary obeyed, breathing a deep sigh of relief which Darius took to be one of passion. 'You can't get enough of it, can you?' he asked, parting the bathrobe to caress her breasts.

'Of you,' she murmured, giving herself up to the delightful torment of his hands exploring her whole body.

Suddenly, Darius stiffened in mid caress. 'What's this?' He felt the outline of the key through her robe. Blushing and stammering with confusion, Hillary explained that she had come across it in the bureau.

'So why do you have it in your pocket?'

'I was curious.' She raised her head and looked him squarely in the eyes, her chin jutting forward in defiance. 'There are too many mysteries in this house.'

'Is that so?' Darius let go of her and walked to the window. For a while he stared out at the garden in silence, then he turned to her. 'I'm going to make love to you and then I will show you something that only Ilona knows exists. I feel I can trust you to keep it a secret.' He smiled dangerously. 'Perhaps you will even find it as stimulating as Ilona and I always have.'

Afterwards, she would ask herself again and again why she hadn't been curious enough to insist on sharing his secret first. Perhaps it was simply that she had been without his caresses for several hours and felt the need for them outweighed everything else? Or perhaps she suspected that she wouldn't like what he had to show her and that that would be the end?

For whatever reason, she allowed him to pick her up in his arms and carry her back to the bedroom, her lips seeking his as they still crossed the threshold. Her stomach clenched tightly as she felt his body move against hers, the opened bathrobe falling away from her shoulders as he lowered her to the bed.

'You are so beautiful, Hillary, I must have you always.'

His words were romantic, yet at the same time frightening in their intensity. She knew then that any relationship with Darius would never be on equal terms. He was not a man who would allow her unlimited freedom. All the same, there was something very tantalising, very exciting about being possessed so totally by another human being.

Pushing all thoughts aside, Hillary gave herself up to the sublimity of his kiss.

A half hour or so earlier, both Darius and Hillary had come. Now, so had the moment of truth. As Darius led the way to the locked room, she felt her heart begin to pound. Nervously she licked her lips and followed him to the other side of the room where they stood for a few seconds, side by side in front of the closed wooden door. For a split second she wanted to tell him not to open it. A huge part of her didn't want to discover what lay behind because, deep down, she knew the knowledge would destroy what little hope they had of a relationship together.

When he flung open the door and revealed the contents of the room Hillary didn't know what to think. Her heart sank, realising that her instincts had been right. She stared at the wall lined with television monitors, then the large black leather chair. With huge eyes, she turned and looked questioningly at Darius. 'What is this?'

246

Apparently oblivious to her confusion, he stepped forward and flicked a switch. Immediately the blank screens sprang to life. Hillary's eyes darted from one to the other in astonishment: there was Ilona talking to Fearn in the grand hallway, there was Torran watching lunchtime TV.

'Oh, my God!' she exclaimed aloud. Several of the screens showed the converted quarters where she'd been staying: the sitting room, the bedrooms – her bedroom! 'How could you? You've been spying on me! On all of us!' She screamed at Darius – furious with him, with his little games and his smug expression.

'I have not been spying as you put it.' His voice was icy, controlled. 'I am a voyeur. I like to watch people, to study their actions.'

'You're a Peeping Tom!' Hillary looked at him with disdain, wondering what she ever saw in him.

'You will not tell anyone about this, Hillary.' His voice was low and menacing.

'I damn well will tell people. I'll tell Alicia and Chloe and Odile for a start and then . . .'

'I think not.' Hillary whirled around at the sound of Ilona's voice. She stood behind them, her eyes full of hatred for the young woman who was her rival. 'You will not tell anyone.' She held up a hand to silence Hillary who had started to protest, 'Because if you do, I will make sure the photographs of you are released to the papers.'

'Ilona!' Darius's tone held a warning but she ignored him too.

'What will the parents of your students think when they see you in such compromising positions?'

Staring at her, open mouthed with astonishment, Hillary had to concede she had a point. Still, she wouldn't give up that easily. 'Please leave us Ilona, I wish to talk to Darius in private.'

Ilona shook her head but Darius nodded.

'Do as she asks.'

Grudgingly, the older woman retreated. 'I'll collect

some clothes from your own room. No doubt you'll be wanting to leave as quickly as possible?'

Hillary sighed deeply. She felt completely shattered by Darius's disclosure, and by Ilona's threat. Darius stepped forward and put his hands on her shoulders.

'She won't do it Hillary, I'll see to that. But please don't tell anyone about my equipment.'

Despite her shock and anger, Hillary almost laughed. She shook herself free of Darius's hands and walked to the sofa where she sat down heavily. 'I need a drink.'

Darius poured them both a glass of brandy. 'I honestly thought you of all people would appreciate the eroticism of such a pastime.'

'Why?' She looked at him. 'Why do you say, me of all people, what does that mean?'

Darius sipped his drink and stared at her, his expression holding its familiar appeal. 'You are one of the least inhibited women I have ever met Hillary. You truly enjoy sex and take pleasure from your own body, and other people's,' he added meaningfully.

Hillary stared at him, feeling herself fall under his spell all over again. 'It's not that I don't understand the thrill of being a voyeur,' she admitted, blushing slightly. 'It's just that I don't like being watched without my consent and nor would the others. Can you appreciate what I'm saying?'

Nodding, Darius put down his glass and stretched his hand out toward her, his eyes glittering dangerously, his lips curving in a seductive smile. 'Now we have sorted out our little misunderstanding, let us continue where we left off this morning.'

'No!' Hillary shook her head vehemently. 'I think I would rather leave now if you don't mind.'

'But I thought we had settled things between us.' Darius looked genuinely confused.

'Perhaps.' Hillary rose to her feet, pulling the robe tightly around her body as she did so. 'But I don't feel like going to bed with you right now. I need time to think.'

'Are you sure?' Darius stepped forward and put his arms around her, caressing her through the thin cotton until she could feel herself weakening beneath his touch.

Just then they were interrupted yet again by a knock at the door. This time it was Fearn carrying an armful of Hillary's clothes.

'Thank you, just put them down.' Darius nodded at the young girl who smiled wanly before fleeing the room obviusly scared half to death by her much older half-brother.

Making the most of this distraction, Hillary disengaged herself from his clutches. 'I have to go Darius.'

'Fine, I won't try to stop you.' He moved toward the door. 'But I expect you to come back to me by this evening, for good.' His words hung ominously between them.

Hillary dressed hurriedly and, pausing only to collect her dress, shoes and stockings from the bedroom, fled to her own quarters.

It seemed strange being back there, as though she'd been gone for much longer than just one night. She was grateful that, for the time being, none of the others were there to greet her. Without wishing to spend another second with her own turbulent thoughts, Hillary lay down wearily on her bed and immediately felt herself falling into a deep, black hole.

Further and further she fell. Looking up she could still see clear blue sky and, peering at her over the edge of the pit, a grinning, evil face; below her lay thick black nothingness. Deeper and deeper she went. Although she felt no fear, she wondered idly who or what would be waiting for her at the bottom – no matter how far she fell she could still see the devilish face just above her. Finally she landed.

With a resounding splash she quickly realised it was not dry land that awaited her. It was water she landed into. Warm, soothing water, as comforting as a bath. The devil face had gone, and now she was left floating in the middle of a calm blue ocean. From the depths of her subconsciousness she understood the prophetic nature of her dream: the choice she had to make was between the devil and the deep blue sea.

Suddenly she awoke. That was it, that was the answer! Without stopping to analyse her actions she began to pack, emptying the drawers and large oak wardrobe in a frenzy, cramming the clothes straight into her cases without bothering to fold them first.

Alicia surprised her by popping her head around the door. 'Going somewhere nice?'

Hillary looked up, her expression serious. 'Yes, Norway,' she paused to consider her automatic reply and amended it, 'or perhaps not.' I don't really know yet.'

'That wasn't the answer I was expecting.' Alicia looked bewildered as she walked across the room and sat on the bed. Characteristically, she made no attempt to offer her sister any help with her packing. 'I thought you'd be preparing to become Lady of the Manor.' She jerked her head in the general direction of the main house.

'No, never in a million years,' Hillary stated firmly. 'Oh, don't worry he did ask me,' she added, noticing Alicia's look of pure confusion. 'At least, he asked me to stay, not to marry him or anything.'

Alicia looked crestfallen. When Hillary hadn't come home the night before she had assumed, or rather hoped, that a grand society wedding might soon be added to her list of engagements. She had been looking forward to being sister of the bride, particularly when the groom was Darius Harwood.

'I suppose you were already planning your wedding outfit,' Hillary stated sarcastically, one look at her sister's face telling her she had scored a hole in one. 'Look,' she said, her tone gentler, 'Darius and I couldn't possibly be happy together, not even for a little while.'

'But you think you could be happy living in Norway with that guy?'

'I don't know the answer to that either.' Hillary glanced down at her crammed suitcases. 'I don't even know if he is still interested in me.'

'Oh, he's interested all right,' Alicia asserted, then added quickly, 'I bumped into him this morning. He was furious that you'd spent the night with Darius.'

'Did you?' Hillary started, but her sister shook her head vehemently.

'No, I didn't tell him. Village gossip travels fast. I think if Darius had been there, Haldane would have torn him apart.'

Hillary shivered at Alicia's words, remembering just how large and strong Haldane's hands were, yet so gentle. 'Whatever happens, I'm going away for the rest of the summer at least, after that I don't know.' She kissed her sister fondly, then picked up her suitcases. 'Would you run me to the quay?'

With a broad smile, Alicia nodded. 'Of course, what are sisters for?'

Hillary smiled back fondly. Her sister was a good person really, although she hadn't offered to help carry her luggage, she realised ruefully.

As they drove up the driveway away from the house, Hillary allowed herself a last glance behind her. Harwood Hall looked every bit as beautiful spread out under the warm summer sun as it had the day she'd arrived, yet so much had happened since then.

Resolutely she turned to face the front, they had almost reached the main road and now there was no going back. She settled back in the seat and smiled happily, her head and her heart filled with the glow of optimism.

No matter what might happen to her from now on she would always look forward to the future – and make the most of the present.

WE NEED YOUR HELP . . .
to plan the future of women's erotic fiction –
– and no stamp required!

THE BLACK LACE QUESTIONNAIRE

SECTION ONE: ABOUT YOU

1.1 Sex (*we presume you are female, but so as not to discriminate*) Are you?

Male ☐
Female ☐

1.2 Age

under 21 ☐ 21–30 ☐
31–40 ☐ 41–50 ☐
51–60 ☐ over 60 ☐

1.3 At what age did you leave full-time education?

still in education ☐ 16 or younger ☐
17–19 ☐ 20 or older ☐

1.4 Occupation _____

1.5 Annual household income

under £10,000 ☐ £10–£20,000 ☐
£20–£30,000 ☐ £30–£40,000 ☐
over £40,000 ☐

1.6 We are perfectly happy for you to remain anonymous; but if you would like to receive information on other publications available, please insert your name and address

_____

_____

_____

SECTION TWO: ABOUT BUYING BLACK LACE BOOKS

2.1 How did you acquire this copy of *Devil and the Deep Blue Sea*?

I bought it myself ☐ My partner bought it ☐
I borrowed/found it ☐ I was given it ☐

2.2 How did you find out about Black Lace books?

I saw them in a shop ☐
I saw them advertised in a magazine ☐
I saw the London Underground posters ☐
I read about them in _____
Other _____

2.3 Please tick the following statements you agree with:
    I would be less embarrassed about buying Black
    Lace books if the cover pictures were less explicit ☐
    I think that in general the pictures on Black
    Lace books are about right ☐
    I think Black Lace cover pictures should be as
    explicit as possible ☐
    I would prefer to buy Black Lace by Mail Order ☐

2.4 Would you read a Black Lace book in a public place – on a train
    for instance?
    Yes ☐   No ☐

SECTION THREE: ABOUT THIS BLACK LACE BOOK

3.1 Do you think the sex content in this book is:
    Too much ☐   About right ☐
    Not enough ☐

3.2 Do you think the writing style in this book is:
    Too unreal/escapist ☐   About right ☐
    Too down to earth ☐

3.3 Do you think the story in this book is:
    Too complicated ☐   About right ☐
    Too boring/simple ☐

3.4 Do you think the cover of this book is:
    Too explicit ☐   About right ☐
    Not explicit enough ☐

SECTION FOUR: ABOUT OTHER BLACK LACE BOOKS

4.1 How many Black Lace books have you read? ☐

4.2 If more than one, which one did you prefer?

4.3 Do you intend to read more?
    Yes ☐   No ☐

SECTION FIVE: ABOUT YOUR IDEAL EROTIC NOVEL

5.1 Using a scale of 1 to 5 (1 = no interest at all, 5 = your ideal),
    please rate the following possible settings for an erotic novel:
    Medieval/barbarian/sword 'n' sorcery ☐
    Renaissance/Elizabethan/Restoration ☐
    Victorian/Edwardian ☐
    1920s & 1930s – the Jazz Age ☐
    Present day ☐
    Future/Science Fiction ☐

5.2 Using the same scale of 1 to 5, please rate the following themes you may find in an erotic novel:

Submissive male/dominant female ☐
Submissive female/dominant male ☐
Lesbianism ☐
Bondage/fetishism ☐
Romantic love ☐
Experimental sex e.g. anal/watersports/sex toys ☐
Gay male sex ☐
Group sex ☐

5.3 Would you prefer your ideal erotic novel to be written from the viewpoint of the main male characters or the main female characters?

Male ☐ Female ☐
Both ☐

5.4 What would your ideal Black Lace heroine be like? Tick as many as you like:

Dominant ☐ Glamorous ☐
Extroverted ☐ Contemporary ☐
Independent ☐ Bisexual ☐
Adventurous ☐ Naive ☐
Intellectual ☐ Introverted ☐
Professional ☐ Kinky ☐
Submissive ☐ Anything else? ☐
Ordinary ☐ _____

5.5 What would your ideal male lead character be like? Again, tick as many as you like:

Rugged ☐ Sexually submissive ☐
Athletic ☐ Caring ☐
Sophisticated ☐ Cruel ☐
Retiring ☐ Debonair ☐
Outdoor-type ☐ Naive ☐
Executive-type ☐ Intellectual ☐
Ordinary ☐ Professional ☐
Kinky ☐ Romantic ☐
Hunky ☐ Anything else? ☐
Sexually dominant ☐ _____

5.6 Is there one particular setting or subject matter that your ideal erotic novel would contain?

_____

Thank you for completing this questionnaire. Now tear it out of the book – carefully! – put it in an envelope and send it to:

**Black Lace
FREEPOST
London
W10 5BR**

No stamp is required if you are resident in the U.K.